LOVE AND DEVOTION

Visit us at www.boldstrokesbooks.com

By the Author

Indelible

Chaps

Split the Aces

Edge of Darkness

Love and Devotion

LOVE AND DEVOTION

by
Jove Belle

2013

LOVE AND DEVOTION
© 2013 BY JOVE BELLE. ALL RIGHTS RESERVED.

ISBN 13: 978-1-60282-965-7

THIS TRADE PAPERBACK ORIGINAL IS PUBLISHED BY
BOLD STROKES BOOKS, INC.
P.O. BOX 249
VALLEY FALLS, NY 12185

FIRST EDITION: JUNE 2013

THIS IS A WORK OF FICTION. NAMES, CHARACTERS, PLACES, AND INCIDENTS ARE THE PRODUCT OF THE AUTHOR'S IMAGINATION OR ARE USED FICTITIOUSLY. ANY RESEMBLANCE TO ACTUAL PERSONS, LIVING OR DEAD, BUSINESS ESTABLISHMENTS, EVENTS, OR LOCALES IS ENTIRELY COINCIDENTAL.

THIS BOOK, OR PARTS THEREOF, MAY NOT BE REPRODUCED IN ANY FORM WITHOUT PERMISSION.

CREDITS
EDITOR: SHELLEY THRASHER
PRODUCTION DESIGN: SUSAN RAMUNDO
COVER DESIGN BY SHERI (GRAPHICARTIST2020@HOTMAIL.COM)

Acknowledgments

I'm pretty damned lucky. I have an amazing partner who, after eighteen years, still loves me like crazy, a fabulously supportive family, a kick-ass publisher, and a diverse circle of friends who challenge me every day to find the lesson life is offering at the moment.

Thank you to Sacchi Green for buying the short story and always encouraging me to write more. You are a pleasure to work with. Andi Marquette, thanks for your relentless support and for picking up the ball when I dropped it. Gill McKnight, who never fails to kick my ass when I screw it up, I truly cherish your friendship. Laydin Michaels, thanks for answering my endless barrage of Texas questions and pointing it out when I got it just plain wrong. Liz McMullen, host of my very first online interview, thank you for your kind, supportive words. Karis Walsh, my new friend and willing reader, I hope you like me because you are officially stuck. And Cathy Rowlands, friend, mentor, and surrogate mom, thank you for everything that you do. My world is a better place because you are in it.

After two years of virtual silence, I wasn't sure if Radclyffe would even remember my name, but she did. And she once again confirmed my belief that Bold Strokes is a place I can call home. Thank you.

Shelley Thrasher, what a joy you are to work with. Here's to a long, long professional future.

Everyone else at Bold Strokes who worked to make this book happen, thank you, thank you, thank you.

Finally, because all things in my world begin and end with one woman, thank you to my partner. Tara, I love you. I'm not sure how I got so lucky or why you agreed to spend your life with me, but I'm so very grateful you did. You are my happily ever after.

Dedication

V. Ilene Milburn
March 9, 1935–January 9, 2011

Chapter One

The crunch-slide of tires on gravel was KC Hall's only warning that she was about to have company. She barely had time to check her teeth for signs of the cold pizza she'd been eating and run her hands through her hair. Lonnie slammed through the door, leaving a string of curse words such as "fucking hell" and "damnation" in her wake.

"Lonnie, what's going on?" KC sounded like she wasn't happy to see Lonnie, which wasn't true. She mostly wasn't happy to see her car—a candy-apple red Mustang—slanted next to her beat-up Accord. No way her neighbors wouldn't recognize it as Lonnie's. There were a few other Mustangs in town, but hers was the only one with a Front Street Baptist Choir bumper sticker on one side and The PTA Gets Things Done on the other.

Lonnie grabbed KC's lapels and kissed her hard. She'd have liked it better if Lonnie had kissed her like she meant it rather than pouring off anger about whatever brought her to KC's door in the first place. KC eased back a tad, teasing the edge of Lonnie's lips with her tongue. This woman was melted-sugar hot, and the taste of her made KC weak. She still didn't know why she'd arrived at KC's door early on Sunday morning for God and all creation to see, but the longer they kissed, the less KC cared.

By the time Lonnie released her, she'd have let Lonnie add a bumper sticker that declared I'm fucking KC Hall.

"I'm going to kill that bastard." Lonnie's eyes were on fire, and not the good kind of fire that said KC'd touched her in just the right way. Nope, this was more of a spitting-mad kind of fire.

KC stepped away. She didn't want to get caught at ground zero if Lonnie decided to give life to that temper of hers. Fortunately, Southern women were simple—a glass of whiskey and a little bit of time was the standard therapy session. She poured four fingers of Jack Daniel's, added some ice, and passed it to Lonnie.

"Thanks, sugar." Lonnie closed her eyes and tipped the glass. The lines of her face softened.

She waited until the first sip passed Lonnie's lips, then asked, "Which bastard?" No doubt Lonnie was talking about her husband. KC liked to pretend he didn't exist, but she asked the question anyway.

Lonnie drained the whiskey and handed her the glass before saying, "Forget about that. We don't have much time." Lonnie zeroed in on KC's lips and kissed her in a way that made her think she was being substituted for the whiskey.

KC pulled away with a gasp and set the empty glass on the counter. Lonnie's chest heaved and she reached for KC, trying to pull her back in.

The flush in Lonnie's cheeks ran down her neck and covered her chest. KC wanted to touch, to ride the wave of Lonnie's labored breathing with her tongue. She moved closer to her, bent her face to Lonnie's neck, and inhaled deeply. The sweet subtle scent of honeysuckle and lavender surrounded her, drawing her in. She exhaled long and soft against Lonnie's skin. "Church starts in an hour."

Lonnie tilted her head to the side, opening the line of her neck to KC. She gripped KC's head, her fingers woven into her hair. "I know. Stop talking."

"Yes."

She traced her fingers over the buttons closing the front of Lonnie's dress and sprinkled tiny kisses across her chest. KC followed the line of her open collar to tease the hint of cleavage. She pressed in tighter, drawing Lonnie to her. She ran one hand down Lonnie's side, over her hips, lower and lower as she inched the fabric of her skirt up with her fingers.

KC loved to undress Lonnie, to unwrap her like a beautiful Christmas gift covered with glittering ribbons and bows, but they didn't have time. If they didn't hurry, they'd be late to the morning service.

Lonnie stiffened slightly and KC circled her with her other arm, spreading her fingers wide against her lower back to hold her firm. She didn't know what had brought Lonnie to her door and she didn't really care. Her time with Lonnie was limited, parceled out like ration tickets to the poor. This was a bonus, an unexpected treat, and she would take full advantage.

"Mmm." KC wanted to comfort Lonnie to a certain degree, but she didn't want to let her dwell on her husband. Focusing Lonnie's attention back to the source of her anger would stop KC from gliding a hand up her stocking-covered thigh. KC reached the lace edge of the stocking and traced the line between skin and nylon, barely touching with the tips of her fingers. She wanted to take her time, to drop to her knees and roll the stockings to the floor. She loved Lonnie's legs, loved to reveal them inch by inch. Today, however, they had even less time than usual.

Lonnie inhaled sharply when KC's fingers completed their journey and ghosted over the fabric of her panties. She teased it to the side and brushed her index finger over the short curls and soft skin.

"God, sugar, right there."

She pushed one finger inside slowly and Lonnie gasped. KC yearned for more foreplay. She'd gladly spend hours kissing every inch of Lonnie's body, deliriously happy to feel her heat as it seeped into her. More often than not, however, this was how they ended up, with them both still dressed and working against a deadline. Regardless, Lonnie was definitely ready. She shifted slightly, opening herself up to KC. Lonnie's arousal, hot and wet, slid down KC's finger and coated her hand.

"So good." Lonnie half-whispered, half-moaned, and KC was proud that she'd distracted Lonnie from whatever Glen had done to piss her off. She was mad enough when she'd arrived to park in front of KC's house, a move that threatened to expose their affair. KC wasn't entirely ready to be catapulted from dirty little secret just to be revealed publicly as a revenge fuck. More than that, she wasn't willing to turn Lonnie away when she was ripe with arousal. KC slid out and pushed back in, quick and hard, two fingers this time, and Lonnie whimpered.

She maneuvered Lonnie back, shuffling with her fingers still inside Lonnie, curling and uncurling, teasing her g-spot as they moved—left foot, curl; right foot, uncurl—until Lonnie's back was against the wall and KC was pressed tight against her. Lonnie's breathing was erratic and hot against her face. She held her lips just out of Lonnie's reach, content to share her air as she pumped into her.

Lonnie's eyes slipped shut and her head fell back against the wall. "This is just what I needed."

KC fucked Lonnie harder, grasping her leg just below the knee and drawing it up to her waist. She used her hips for extra power. She wanted Lonnie to feel her all the way through the church service and on into tomorrow, long after she'd gone home to her husband. She felt Lonnie draw tighter and wanted to be the only person on her mind when she came.

"Next time call on your way over." She spoke against Lonnie's mouth, still not kissing her, but close enough to tease her lips with her tongue. "I'll wear my strap-on."

"Yes." Lonnie gasped and dug her fingers into KC's shoulder. She had long, manicured acrylics, and even through the fabric of her top, KC knew she'd leave a mark.

"I'll bend you over the back of my sofa and fuck you from behind." KC generally avoided vulgarities with Lonnie. She treated her like she was precious china meant to be filled slowly to the point of overflowing. But today they were on a tighter schedule than usual, and KC wanted to take Lonnie in a way that made her forget about her husband and whatever nonsense he'd been up to. She moved her mouth to Lonnie's ear. "That would be so fucking hot. Your panties around your ankles, skirt around your waist, and your ass rocking back to meet my cock."

Lonnie gripped KC's head to her throat and thrashed her hips. She was satin smooth and heaven soft, and KC didn't want it to end. She could feel Lonnie getting closer, her muscles drawing tighter.

Lonnie's legs began to shake and KC smoothed her palm over Lonnie's hip and around to squeeze her ass.

"Oh, my God. Don't stop." Lonnie ground her teeth together, catching KC's shoulder between them. "Don't you dare fucking stop." Lonnie was a loud, appreciative lover. A shouter, a moaner. Today her words were strangled, like she was choking back the moment.

"Let it go, baby." KC added a third finger and Lonnie groaned, her hips thrusting forward. She was tight and KC's fingers cramped together. Any mobility she had to twist and massage was gone. This wasn't about finesse and gentle caress; it was about power and pushing deeper and harder and faster.

One final push and Lonnie collapsed in her arms, tears streaking down her face. Lonnie quivered, that uncontrollable jerking that came from being fucked properly, and her shoulders shook. KC removed her hand as gently as possible and wrapped her arms around Lonnie.

Lonnie clung to her for several moments, then straightened, her clothing falling effortlessly into place. Lonnie possessed a Golden Age movie-star quality. She always looked camera ready, especially when she shouldn't.

"That was perfect." Lonnie smoothed her pinky around the edge of her lips, erasing the smudges and all signs that KC had been there. She patted KC on the cheek and said, "Don't be late for church, sugar."

Lonnie slipped out the back door, much quieter than when she'd entered. Her perfume hung in the air after she left, tormenting KC along with the insistent, aching need low in her belly. She worked to calm her breathing, to settle her racing heart. Lonnie was gone and KC's lingering lust wouldn't bring her back. As always, their one-sided affair left KC unfulfilled and desperate for more.

KC sent a quick text to Emma—her best friend and Sunday morning ride to church—to let her know she was running late. She'd meet Emma there rather than having her wait at her kitchen table. Her house smelled like Lonnie and sex, and the last thing she wanted was for Emma to get a whiff of either. She opened a window and ran to the bedroom to change.

She needed a few more minutes to take care of the throbbing need Lonnie awakened in her. Unfortunately, all she had time to do was pull herself together and head to church. If she was lucky, she wouldn't be late.

❖

KC circled the lot hoping for a miracle. She wasn't asking for a parking space next to the front door. She'd settle for one in the back forty. But so far no opening had presented itself. The good citizens of Fairmont didn't have to search for God on Sunday morning. They knew right where to find him in attendance at Front Street Baptist Church, and half of East Texas had beat KC into the parking lot.

Her mama was going to kill her for being late for church.

KC found Emma's car and parked perpendicular to it. If not for Lonnie's unscheduled visit that morning, KC would be inside with Emma right now. KC's car was short so it barely hung over the lines into the other spaces. The only snag was the car to Emma's left. It belonged to the choir director and his wife. If KC hurried after the service, she'd beat them out of the church and they'd be none the wiser about her tardiness and disrespectful parking job. If by some stroke of demonic luck the choir director's wife made it out before KC…mercy.

Consequences be damned, KC abandoned her car, ran like hell for the side door, and scooted inside just as the choir started up their weekly salutations to God A'mighty. Emma discreetly edged over to make room for her at the end of her pew near the back. As she sat, KC glanced up, hoping to see the back of the choir robes. Every time they watched a Dolly Parton movie, she and Emma would joke about the choir doing some big, fanciful beginning, like turning in one big dramatic sweep of fabric. No such luck. Twin disapproving stares from her mama and her mama's friend and choir mate, Lonnie, greeted her.

The heat in Lonnie's eyes both frightened and excited KC. She looked pissed, but otherwise perfectly put together. After all, Lonnie had an extra twenty years' practice of pulling herself together at the last minute. It took KC just a little bit longer after some decidedly impious attention from Lonnie. Lonnie wasn't nearly as nice as she wanted people to think.

"What kept you?" Emma whispered in KC's ear, and Lonnie's eyes narrowed. She might well be married, but that didn't mean she'd tolerate KC playing around with other women, especially not in the house of the Lord. Never mind trying to convince Lonnie that she and Emma were just friends.

"I got caught up at home." It was the closest to the truth that KC was willing to provide at the moment. She might, at some point, give in and tell Emma all about Lonnie, but today wasn't that day.

"Your mama saw you. And Mrs. Truvall looks ready to skin you alive." Emma held up her hymnal to share with KC. She'd already turned to the appropriate selection. Not that either of them needed it. They'd been singing along to the same hymns forever and joined in right on cue.

They sang about fire in the blood, a recurring theme that their pastor liked to impress upon the congregation. Blood, in all its crimson glory, purified, redeemed, and tasted good when enjoyed with a small wafer cracker. That last bit was KC's own interpretation of communion, formulated when she was too little to partake but old enough to know that her older sister got a snack during church and she didn't.

KC sang along, hoping to appear pious even though her thoughts, and the ache between her legs, were far from that. The only fire in her blood was the leftover rampage from her encounter with Lonnie that morning, an unfulfilled promise with no hope of resolution any time soon.

The choir concluded their song and the pastor took over, continuing the message of redeeming fire that could and would save her from eternal hellfire if only she'd spend her days walking with Jesus. KC suspected their choir director and preacher of coordinating their efforts, but they both swore the Lord spoke to them independently, resulting in the cooperative effect. As yet, the Lord hadn't graced KC with a two-way conversation, but she also hadn't applied herself to His service. She supposed His silence was fair.

"Come with me next weekend." Emma barely whispered the words, her mouth so close her breath tickled KC's ear. Her frustrated libido didn't need this kind of encouragement in the middle of a sermon.

KC wished they were still singing. At least then she'd be able to tip the songbook up in front of her mouth when she responded. "Where?"

"Austin." Emma had designs on moving away from Fairmont to a place where minds were a little more open and gossiping mouths a little more closed. She'd been on the receiving end one too many times to appreciate the local grapevine. Why didn't Emma look toward California, like LA, where anything went, or San Francisco, where gay was practically required? Or maybe the Northwest, like Seattle or Portland, where weird was normal, with its free-flowing stream of marijuana smoke? Or even east to New Orleans, where morality took a backseat to twenty-four-hour, all-day, everyday debauchery. With the exception of her four years devoted to higher education at UNLV, Emma's dreams had never stretched past the Texas border, so Austin was her only real choice.

KC loved Austin, with its burgeoning music scene and influx of liberal idealism. "I'm not sure," she said. She and Lonnie were sort of supposed to have plans. Maybe. If Lonnie could get away. "I'll let you know?"

Emma gazed at her, her face tilted, eyes thoughtful. This wasn't the first time KC had put her off, and Emma was obviously trying to decide if she should call KC on it. KC hoped she decided against it.

The pastor banged his hand against the pulpit, his open palm a gunshot against the lectern. It ricocheted through the church, bouncing off stained glass, brick, and drywall with a force like thunder. KC sat up straight, focusing her eyes front. He had her attention. She leaned forward slightly to see what he intended to do with it.

"Make your commitment to God. Right here, right now, on this Sunday morning." The choir started a low, encouraging hum behind him. "God is patient. He loves you, and He is ready for you to come home to Him."

People stood, arms raised in salutation to the Lord. KC waffled on joining them. Power in the blood she wasn't too sure about, but their preacher was a convincing motivational speaker. And when his gaze briefly landed on her, she gathered herself to stand. Emma's hand on her arm stopped her and the pastor's eyes moved to the next person.

"What are you doing?" Emma said, her voice too loud to be considered a whisper.

And she was right to question KC. All too often, in many different settings, she got wrapped up in the excitement of the moment and forgot herself. The only thing she ever truly worshipped was the glory of a naked woman wrapped around her fingers. Emma was a good friend to remind her.

"Nothing." KC smiled at her mama. Even if she hadn't heard Emma across the church, she always had one eye on each of her children. By KC's math, her mama had at least three eyes, and the count grew as her children started giving her grandchildren. She'd no doubt picked up on the commotion.

"I'm okay now." KC liked that she got swept away, like all true romantics. She just wasn't always sure how to explain her reaction to other people. Emma understood without KC having to break it down.

The preacher concluded his sermon, and the choir resumed their singing. KC and Emma stood to sing along. She was allowed to take to her feet now as the requisite Sunday-morning church service drew to an end with the final song selection. No one would think she was declaring her devotion, so she raised her voice with gusto.

She loved to sing. Her voice did amazing things without her consent or encouragement. Her mama called it a gift. The choir director called it a squandered gift because she refused to join the choir and use it to exalt the glory of God. KC would happily sing any song he wanted so long as he didn't insist on placing her on the risers between her mother and Lonnie. And that's precisely where she'd end up, stacked between two women she wanted desperately to please. No doubt she'd forget herself and, in a moment of rapturous joy, she'd take liberties with Lonnie not meant to be taken in a church or in front of her mama.

No, KC belonged safely in the congregation, next to Emma, where she could sing to her heart's content without risk of town-wide scandal.

With the service concluded, KC ushered Emma out the side door before the pastor could set up sentry at the exits. She needed to move her car pronto and couldn't afford the delay of after-church niceties.

Emma lit a cigarette as soon as she cleared the landscaping. She didn't smoke often—only when stressed or intoxicated. KC hadn't noticed signs of the latter during the service so reckoned church did what church always did to Emma—stressed her out.

Emma was a woman out of time with her circumstances. She looked as though someone had clipped her out of a fashion magazine and dropped her in the middle of Texas. Not that Emma had any clue how devastatingly beautiful she was. If asked, she'd say she was passable. In truth, she made most folks, including KC, forget how to breathe. Her features were so flawless the argument could be made that she'd been carved rather than born and raised like the rest of them. When they were little, KC was a never-ending parade of scratched elbows and bruised knees. Emma made it through all their escapades without a mark. KC was bundled trouble and Emma was flowing elegance. On a good day, KC managed a braid down her back. On a very good day, she'd plan ahead enough to convince someone else to French-braid it for her. Emma, on the other hand, had long blond hair that she swept up into classic styles. KC's hair was brown and reminded her of a chestnut mare her family once had. Emma's hair was spun sunshine—light and beauty. Physically, they were opposites.

"You worry too much." KC paused to give Emma a brief hug. God forbid the day she couldn't spare enough time to comfort her best friend. Without the occasional intervening hug, Emma's smoking would rival a factory smokestack.

"I'm fine, KC." Emma held her cigarette away from KC's body, resulting in an awkward one-armed hug.

KC wanted to maintain contact for a little longer and caught Emma's free hand before she could retract it completely. She held it loosely as they crossed the parking lot. Emma stiffened slightly, but didn't pull away. She did, however, redouble her efforts to cloud the air. KC wasn't at all sure what was bothering Emma, and since Emma wasn't forthcoming, KC guessed.

"You're giving those guys too much credit. They don't know what happens in the afterlife any more than you do. Hell, they don't even know for sure if there is an afterlife." KC leaned against the hood of her car, still holding Emma's hand. She wasn't in such a hurry to move the Accord now, since Emma was allowing physical contact in a potentially public place. The possible scandal of two girls in love in small town Texas, true or not, kept Emma upright and contained. She didn't hold hands and she didn't kiss. Hell, she didn't even allow her glance to linger too long in places the gentry deemed it shouldn't. Emma dated plenty, but did so privately to avoid speculation. KC was being far too bold and forward and she knew it. But this was Emma, her best friend. And if the town folks were still looking for a lesbian scandal from the two of them, then KC couldn't help them. She'd resigned herself to Emma only ever seeing her as a friend, nothing more. The rest of town would eventually pick up on that.

Besides, the parking lot was still empty of human traffic. The other worshipers were no doubt caught up in the bottleneck of farewell wishes at the exit.

"Don't be crazy, KC. I'm not worried about the Eternal Hereafter. I have enough to keep me busy here on the mortal plane." Emma flicked her burned-down Camel menthol onto the blacktop and stomped it out while reaching for her pack. She slipped her hand out of KC's and lit another cigarette.

"If you'd talk to me, maybe you wouldn't need to chain-smoke half a pack in the church parking lot." KC gestured at the fresh cigarette, Emma's lighter poised with the flame a breath away from the tobacco tip.

She glared at KC and touched the flame home while inhaling deeply. "These calm my nerves." She blew a black stream up and away from KC's face. "You should try it some time. Keep you from making an ass out of yourself in the middle of church."

KC laughed. "You worry enough about that for both of us. If you weren't there, I'd declare my devotion for the moment and my mama would praise Jesus that I'd changed my wicked ways." And KC would be okay with that. She didn't mind chasing her impulses wherever they led.

Emma grunted and took another drag.

"Are you coming over for dinner?"

Emma cocked her head to the side, considering KC's question, then countered with one of her own. "Who'll be there besides family?"

KC hesitated. Emma was smart. The less she mentioned Lonnie, the better. Still, best not let Emma catch her leaving stuff out, either. "The Truvalls. You should come."

"I'll meet up with you later." Emma surveyed the parking lot and spotted the choir director's wife at the same time as KC. "Best get going." She turned toward her own car.

"Emma?" KC paused, one leg inside the open driver's side door. "I love you, okay?"

Emma took a breath, one not laden with blue-gray tobacco smoke, held it for a moment, then released it in a whoosh. "Yeah, I know." She climbed inside her car, leaving KC talking to no one.

It was time to get home.

Just like the parking lot at Front Street Baptist, the driveway at her parents' house was full when KC arrived. Now she'd hear from her mama about being late twice in one day. She should have come straight here after church instead of detouring past her own house to change her clothes and collect her thoughts. She hated being rushed as much as her mama hated her being late. It frazzled her nerves.

"Kimberly Carter Hall." KC's mama managed her household and her children with swift and immediate consequences. She had to be losing her touch, however, because KC made it halfway up the driveway before Mama caught her. "What have I told you about being late?"

KC's full name, like that of her sisters, fit a theme. Her oldest sister was Kendall Truman, she was called Kimberly Carter, and the baby of the family was Katrina Kennedy. Using the various presidents' names and the *K*'s in a row made her mama happy, but all they did for anyone who grew up outside of Fairmont was confuse them during introductions. At least her name could be shortened conveniently to KC. And it was an extra blessing that her mama was a Democrat. Otherwise she'd have been named Bush instead of Carter. She'd rather her namesake be a philanthropist than a puppet.

"I'm sorry, Mama. I lost track of time."

When KC had entered college and left Fairmont for Seattle, she'd tried addressing her mother as Mom rather than Mama. She argued that if she was grown enough to live two time zones away, she was grown enough to call her mama Mom. Mama was a term for babies. KC's mama offered to pull her out of hippie-town and back to the bosom of her proper Texas upbringing. KC hadn't argued the point since.

"What am I going to do with you?" She ushered KC into the house. "First you're late for church, now you're late for Sunday dinner. We've been holding it on your account."

That really meant the food had just finished cooking, but KC was last to arrive so she needed to display some proper guilt for her bad manners. She apologized to the group as a whole, because when her family got together, it was one hell of a large, hungry group, and she truly was sorry to be the one standing between them and their food. She scooped up one of the babies from the floor and offered his chubby cheeks slobbery kisses and placating apologies before flying him into the arms of her sister. He giggled during the flight.

Her older sister, Kendall, gave KC a one-armed hug with the baby squished between them. "Thank God you're here. Mama was working up a proper fit. Daddy was fixing to load the tranquilizer gun."

KC knew it was a bad idea when she laughed, but she did it anyway.

"It's no joking matter, young lady." Lonnie sat perched on the arm of the easy chair, her right arm draped around her husband's shoulder. She sipped from a highball glass of whiskey. "It's no small thing to make your mama wait like that." She raised her eyebrow, daring KC to argue otherwise. Lonnie was a true Texas beauty queen, two decades removed from her competing days. Her hair was as blond as early wheat, but not nearly as natural or wild. Her style, along with the color, was the result of a standing weekly appointment at the local hairdresser's. KC's mama, along with several other members of the choir, kept the same schedule.

"Yes, ma'am. I apologize." KC tried her best to look somber, but mostly she was feeling lustful. Lonnie in her Sunday best, sipping Jack Daniel's, was a perfect contradiction—angel and devil. Lonnie didn't see it like that. She was simply living her life, and God and whiskey were the way of things in East Texas. Regardless, KC wanted to taste Lonnie's lips, to lick the residue from her tongue.

It was the right kind of late spring day for dining outside, so her father had set up a long table in the backyard. It was made with a series of sawhorses and thick pieces of plywood, draped with white linen. KC helped carry dishes down the back steps. Since she was little, it'd been her job to set the table. She often wondered what they'd done during the six years she was away at college. Did they all stare longingly at the plates, praying they would miraculously find their way from cupboard to table? More than likely Katrina, the baby of the family, inherited the job.

When they were all seated, no small feat with that many butts to get into chairs, her daddy surveyed the table, pausing at each of his girls. He stopped at KC. "I think, given your questionable timing today, it would be right for you to offer thanks."

"Yes, Daddy." Penance for being late was saying grace before the meal. She bowed her head and tried to come up with suitably pious thoughts that didn't involve worshipping Lonnie's belly button and below.

"Heavenly Father," if nothing else, she knew the proper beginning to a prayer, "thank you for the food we are about to eat. Thank you for giving us a happy, healthy family and allowing us to come together in your name today. Please be with those in need of your grace." KC knew she would be on that list if her mama had anything to say about it. It was time to wrap things up. She went for short and sweet. "In the name of Jesus we pray. Amen."

"Amen." A chorus sounded around the table, followed by a commotion of epic proportions as hands flew out in every direction to nab some food before the opportunity closed.

"That was a lovely prayer, KC." Her mama's smile was the first one she'd been blessed with all day. "Now tell us what was so important this morning that it had you arriving late to church."

"Yes." Lonnie scooped mashed potatoes onto her husband's plate and greens onto her own. "Do tell what kept you." There was that eyebrow again, daring KC to say the wrong thing. Tell the truth and suffer immediate consequences, not the least of which would be banishment from the Promised Land between Lonnie's thighs. Tell a lie and Lonnie would no doubt punish her later for her dishonesty.

"Well," KC focused on buttering her dinner roll, "it's a busy time of year for work." She glanced away from the butter for a moment to see several nodding heads. She purposefully excluded Lonnie from her survey. "I was prepping finals and lost track of time." KC taught literature and English to eighth-grade students through an online home-school program. It granted her a flexible schedule but a heavy workload.

That satisfied her family and she was free to watch Lonnie eat, a rare pleasure she didn't often get to enjoy. Lonnie lived like a Botticelli come to life, a guileless beauty who maintained an air of innocence even while opening herself to debauchery. Simple acts of day-to-day living, like lifting her fork from the plate to her mouth, were graceful art to behold. She didn't acknowledge KC, but Lonnie knew she was being watched. And she was performing for her lover.

Before KC knew it, her family was finishing up and she still sat with a full plate.

"What's a matter, KC? Not hungry?" her older sister, Kendall, asked. Her plate was mostly full as well. She held her baby boy, Winston, on her lap and he was well fed on his grandma's mashed potatoes and gravy.

Kendall was the spy of the family, forever watching closer than she let on. When they were younger, she even had her very own notebook where she wrote down her observations, just like her hero, Harriett the Spy. Kendall scooped another spoonful of potatoes into Winston's mouth, glanced briefly at Lonnie, then back at KC. She smiled. A challenge between sisters.

KC placed her fork carefully on her plate. "I'm sorry, Mama, but Kendall's right. I ate my fill for breakfast." She forced her eyes to remain on her mama and not slide to the right, where Lonnie was no doubt smiling as she ate her salad. "If it's all right with you, I'll just package this and take it home with me. I can heat it up for supper."

Kendall wasn't sitting close enough to kick under the table, and KC had learned long ago not to stick out her tongue at the dinner table. Her mama was mostly bluster, but there were some things she would not tolerate. Tardiness and bad manners at the table were both on the list. KC waited until her mama excused her, then nudged her sister's chair slightly with her hip as she passed on the way to the kitchen with her plate. It was sorry retribution, but the best KC could do at the moment.

She needed to figure out what Kendall knew. Did she see KC staring at Lonnie and assume KC had a schoolgirl crush? Or did she know more? KC was deep in thought when she hit the screen door that separated kitchen from back porch and didn't realize someone else was in the kitchen until she was halfway to the sink.

"Let go." Katrina, the youngest of the Hall sisters, spoke with a low, shaky voice. She was pressed up against the kitchen counter with her hands against her husband's chest.

KC cleared her throat and rattled her fork against her plate. "Hey, Trina, Daddy was asking where you got off to." She set her untouched dinner on the counter. She could box it up later. "I'll let him know you're in here with Jackson and not to worry."

At the sound of KC's voice, Jackson straightened and Trina wrenched her red, splotchy wrist out of his grasp. "I'll come with you." She stepped around her husband and was out the back door before Jackson could speak.

KC caught up with her on the steps. "Everything okay?"

"Yes," Trina said, quick and terse.

"You sure?" KC put her hand on Katrina's arm, just a gentle touch.

Trina flinched and jerked her arm away. "It's fine, KC. Just leave it alone." She took off around the side of the house. KC let her go.

With the kitchen cleared, KC rounded back inside to take care of her plate. Jackson still stood at the counter. He was a big man, six foot three, with broad shoulders and narrow hips. He'd graduated with KC, two years before Trina. He'd been quarterback of the football team, prom king, and Trina had fallen in love with him the second she laid eyes on him in her freshman year of high school. They'd been together ever since, even through the two years when he was away at Oklahoma State and she was here finishing high school. They'd married as soon as she graduated and, at six years into their marriage, were expecting their second baby.

Jackson smiled his prom-king smile. It'd charmed many a cheerleader out of her panties, if locker-room gossip was anything to go by. KC, despite being more interested in the prom queen than king, was still charmed.

"Sorry 'bout that, KC. Trina's been pretty emotional this time around." He pushed a hand through his hair and it fell perfectly over his forehead. "And Buddy still isn't sleeping through the night…" He sighed. "We're both just tired."

"You know I'll watch him any time. He can spend the night tonight if you want." KC hoped Emma wouldn't mind a two-year-old intruder to their evening plans. They spent plenty of time watching movies from her couch anyway; one more night like that instead of going out wouldn't hurt. "Want me to pick him up later? Or I can take him with me when we're all paroled."

Away from Lonnie, KC had decided she was hungry and worked her way through her dinner as she chatted with Jackson. Despite her earlier comment, she was starved. The only thing she'd had to eat that morning was half a slice of pizza before Lonnie descended upon her.

"Would you, KC?" Jackson smiled for real this time. "I have to clear it with Trina, but that'd be great."

"Let me know." KC savored her last bite of chicken-fried steak and gravy. Her stomach was fully satisfied. "I'm happy to do it."

Jackson was on his way out the door when Lonnie entered. "Hello, Mrs. Truvall," he said, and tipped his head slightly to show respect.

"Jackson." Lonnie drew the word out to give the full effect of her hot Southern drawl and kept her eyes on KC as she spoke. "Nice to see you."

The screen slammed shut on the last word. Jackson was long gone and Lonnie didn't notice. She was too busy slinking across the well-worn linoleum, a panther targeting its next meal.

"Lonnie." The name sounded like a prayer, a benediction, even to KC's own ears. "We shouldn't…"

Lonnie covered her lips with her finger and KC closed her eyes, content to breathe the heady scent of Lonnie's signature perfume. She'd been wearing it as long as KC remembered. She couldn't think with Lonnie this close and was content to let Lonnie do that for her.

"Sugar, I need help getting something from upstairs." Lonnie spoke in a quiet, intimate hush and moved closer to KC with each syllable, until she was speaking directly into KC's ear. Her warm breath brushed over the skin of KC's neck. "Can you do that for me?"

KC was dazed, defenseless. Powerless to deny her, she'd have agreed to anything Lonnie suggested. "Of course." She opened her eyes and leaned away a fraction. She needed a little space that wasn't filled with warm heat and summer flowers. "What is it?"

"I'll show you." Lonnie turned and walked toward the living-room stairs. Her hips moved in a slow, hypnotic swing, the generous curve pulling KC's eyes along as she moved. KC was mesmerized. Lonnie looked back over her shoulder and asked, "You coming?" Then she disappeared out of view.

"Absolutely," KC muttered, and tried to collect herself. It was a bad idea, but still she followed like a sixteen-year-old quarterback chasing the irresistible swish of cheerleader skirts.

Chapter Two

When KC was younger, she'd sneak in and out of the house, so she knew exactly how many steps lay between the first and second floor and where the creaking floorboards were. Following Lonnie up the stairs, her eyes fixed firmly on the inviting sway of Lonnie's backside, KC forgot every last one of those places.

Lonnie turned toward her when she reached the top of the stairs. "Come on, lover," she whispered, crooking her finger for KC to follow.

KC climbed faster, and the floorboards kept time. When she reached the landing, she pressed close to Lonnie. They were in full view of whoever might pass below. "Now what?" she whispered back, her voice urgent and hot, to match the thundering in her chest.

"Take me to your room." Lonnie teased the buttons of KC's shirt, her fingers steadily working them free one by one. KC stood rooted to the spot, unable to choose between the warring desires in her body. Lust and logic at odds once again. Lonnie's lips brushed KC's ear. "Please."

Another button succumbed to Lonnie's dexterous fingers. KC's shirt fell open and the decision was made. Lust won this battle, just like all others before, and KC needed to move them away from the landing. She took Lonnie by the hand. "This way."

KC's childhood room remained a shrine to her high-school activities. Cheerleading trophies crowded the top of her overflowing bookshelf, and smiling teen heartthrobs lined the walls. What a difference eight years made. She needed to talk to her mama about giving this room an overhaul. If Lonnie led her up the stairs again, she'd rather not be distracted from their tryst by the poster she won at the county fair her sophomore year, no matter how cute Terri Clark was in that white Stetson.

The door slipped shut behind KC, pushed by one of Lonnie's long, elegant fingers. It latched with a final click that caught in KC's throat. Time alone with Lonnie was a rushed delicacy, and she always tried to savor the moment. The thrill of it, the thought that this beautiful, sexy woman wanted her, overwhelmed KC, left her struggling to find her way back to shore before drowning completely.

Lonnie pushed KC's shirt off her shoulders and paused to enjoy the view as the fabric rustled to the floor. "My God." She traced a finger along the top line of KC's bra. "I can't get over how beautiful you are." She bent her head into KC's cleavage and followed the finger with her tongue, edging it beneath the lace to taste a little deeper.

KC let her head fall back. It hit the door with a soft thunk and she moaned, a combination of concussion and ecstasy. Usually Lonnie lay back and let KC have her wicked way with her, the soft terrain of her body stretched out for KC to explore and pleasure. KC wasn't used to Lonnie taking the lead in the actual touching. The seduction leading up to the lovemaking, sure. But when it came time to follow through on the promise, Lonnie defaulted to pillow queen. Her forward advances made KC light-headed. KC scratched her nails against the door, searching for purchase. Should she right the wagon or let Lonnie tip her over the edge?

Lonnie continued to explore her chest with her mouth, tugging her bra to the side to expose her nipples. When she took one between her teeth, KC stopped debating the merits of top versus bottom and gripped the back of Lonnie's neck to hold her in place. She writhed against the door as Lonnie licked and sucked and bit her way from one nipple to the other. Eventually, after a meteor shower of electric impulse shot from her chest to her cunt and then back again, Lonnie raised her head. When she pressed her lips to KC's she said in a panting gasp, "We need to hurry."

Hurry KC could do. Hurry was what she was used to with Lonnie. Rushed coupling sandwiched between meetings and errands. Frantic groping when Lonnie was sure her family wouldn't miss her. This shifting desperation was the solid ground between her and Lonnie.

KC stopped reveling in Lonnie's touch and set to work revealing Lonnie's body. She loosened the belt that was cinched tight around the middle of Lonnie's flowing Jackie O. style dress. Two undone buttons on the side and she had unfettered access to Lonnie's sexy parts. Well, she would as soon as she got rid of the bra and panties.

"Hurry, sugar, we don't have time for soft and sweet." Lonnie kissed KC hard enough to remind her of her goal: orgasm. Now.

KC pinched Lonnie's nipple through the fabric of her bra, letting her thumb slide over it in a harsh rub of fabric against sensitive skin. Lonnie hadn't dressed for seduction. Her bra and panties were there to provide a matronly barrier between her naughty bits and the rest of life.

Undeterred, KC reached low between Lonnie's legs and slid her panties to the side. Lonnie's breath hitched and KC wanted desperately to hear it again. She kissed the flesh of Lonnie's throat, where she pictured the air trapped between inhale and exhale, suspended in ecstasy. It was a hot, open-mouthed kiss that lacked elegance but held desperate promise. She reversed their positions, spinning until Lonnie's back was flush with the door and she was flush with Lonnie's front.

There, with Lonnie pressed tight against the door, KC explored Lonnie's folds like this was the first time, like her fingers didn't know the delicious slip-slide of Lonnie's passion, like she hadn't memorized the contours enveloping her clit and cunt just hours before. Jesus, she just couldn't get enough.

Lonnie moaned and KC circled her tight nerves to extend the moan, to urge it louder. She wanted Lonnie to sing to heaven about how good KC's fingers felt twisting between her legs.

"KC?" Kendall's voice drifted up the stairs and KC clamped her hand over Lonnie's mouth.

She eased a finger inside Lonnie, long and smooth, not stopping until she was fully sheathed.

"Quiet," she whispered, low and soft in Lonnie's ear. To punctuate the word, she withdrew and pushed in again with two fingers, a little harder and deeper.

Lonnie bit against her hand and curled her fingers into KC's shoulders. The nails pierced KC's skin, a decadent, sharp sting, and KC wished for a hand of her own to muffle her sounds. It took everything in her to not cry out.

Kendall didn't call KC again. She must have moved on.

KC thrust hard but oh so controlled. Sometimes, when they had just a little more time, KC let herself go. During those times, she would thrash and grind and moan along with Lonnie. When they were in a precarious situation, with danger of being caught imminent, she focused everything on making Lonnie break.

She debated sucking the smooth skin of Lonnie's neck, the place where her breath got caught in her throat. She wanted to nibble and bite and leave a bruise of ownership, a mark fitting a teenage romp, not a middle-aged mother. To Lonnie, KC was a tryst. Hickeys and love bites were the products of illicit coupling, the signs of debauchery. But KC loved the smooth perfection of Lonnie's body and wanted to be invited to enjoy the lush wonderland again, no matter how rushed her time.

Instead of an external mark, KC relished the internal. She was sure she was a lot of firsts for Lonnie. Her first affair. Her first woman. Her first multiple orgasm. KC angled her body so she could use the power of her hips and thigh to drive her thrusts a little deeper. Lonnie's body started to shake, the tension radiating out from her belly, and KC kissed a little lower, burying her head in the crook of Lonnie's neck, the soft oasis between neck and shoulder. Lonnie's legs quaked. She was close. Just a little more and KC would have to tighten the seal over her mouth, then release it immediately so Lonnie could breathe. She always pulled in heavy, heaving gulps of air as she recovered.

KC worried the skin above Lonnie's collarbone with her teeth, tested the weight of the muscle with a little more pressure than normal, and Lonnie let out a keening whine into KC's palm. KC thrust harder, bottoming out with her hand slapping hard and fast against Lonnie's clit. Lonnie's body tensed and she held herself stiff and tall, pushing back against the door while simultaneously falling into KC. KC bit down hard enough to leave teeth marks visible the next day, and Lonnie convulsed around her, her voice rising in the cage of KC's hand.

The tension drained from Lonnie's body and she slumped forward. KC held her upright, leveraging her against the door as she whispered sweet words in her ear. She brushed her lips against the impression left behind by her teeth, then breathed kisses into Lonnie's hair. She rocked her fingers gently, then withdrew.

It never took long for Lonnie to recover, but those few soft moments were KC's favorite.

KC wasn't the type of woman who found her satisfaction in the pleasure of others. Lonnie's orgasm didn't leave her feeling well satisfied and complete. The ache left behind from their morning rendezvous had ramped to full-blown need with each step up the stairs. Now, with the scent of Lonnie in the air and the taste of her on her fingers, KC was desperate in her need. Passion flared through her and she tried to tamp it down.

Lonnie was coming down quickly, and their respective families were already starting to miss them. There was no time to worry about KC's neglected libido.

"I'm sorry, sugar." Lonnie caressed KC's breasts, fondling and pinching her nipples. "God, I want you." She nipped at the tense edge of KC's jaw, her fingers teasing but not venturing far enough to follow through. "We need to find more time."

KC blew out a heavy breath and pulled away from Lonnie with a shaky inhale. She took two steps back and grabbed a handful of Kleenex from her dresser to wipe her fingers. She'd rather lick them clean, but their families were close, Kendall the spy was actively searching, and the taste of Lonnie would send KC charging into disaster. No way would she be able to walk away if she indulged even the tiniest bit. She took another deep breath, steadier than the last, and then straightened her bra. As she was buttoning her blouse, she said, "I know, but I don't like it."

From the safe distance of two feet away, she dared to look at Lonnie. Her lips were red and bruised—too much pressure from KC's kisses, followed by her hand. And Lonnie's perfect hair was coming slightly undone. The sight of her made KC's knees weak, and she took another purposeful step away from temptation. She wanted Lonnie *so* badly.

Lonnie reached for her, fingers beckoning, but KC remained steadfast. As much as she wanted, *needed*, Lonnie to touch her, it would be the last time if they got caught. Lonnie made it clear that this was an affair. This fun, mind-blowing sex would stop if Glen got even the slightest whiff of it.

"I'll go first." She raked her fingers through her hair. It was forever a tangle so no one would likely notice it now. On the other hand, the few hairs out of place on Lonnie's head screamed freshly fucked. "You better straighten up."

KC skirted around Lonnie, giving her a wide berth. One touch and all that hard-earned self-control would shatter. She slipped out and left Lonnie to collect herself.

Kendall was waiting on the other side.

"There you are." Kendall leaned against the wall directly across from the door, her arms folded and legs crossed casually in front. She looked settled in for the duration. Alarm bells sounded, and KC hoped her face didn't betray the panic running helter-skelter inside her.

"Here I am." She wiped her hand over her mouth, checking her lipstick. The smell of Lonnie's desire clung to her fingers. She looked guilty.

"Mr. Truvall is ready to leave but he can't find Mrs. Truvall." Kendall raised an eyebrow and gestured toward the closed bedroom door. "Any idea where she might be?"

KC's heart pounded hard and fast. She shook her head. "Kendall…"

Glen rounded the stairs at that exact moment and KC felt the blood drain from her face. She'd never fainted before, but it was a real possibility with only a hollow-core door standing between Glen Truvall and his adulterous wife.

"I found your wife, Mr. Truvall." Kendall straightened, her smile looked friendly and sincere, but it was totally fake. KC recognized it after years of watching Kendall sell Girl Scout cookies. Smile like you have exactly what the other person wants. No one else was ever the wiser, and Kendall became Scout of the Year more than once because of it. KC braced for impact.

"Oh?" Glen returned Kendall's smile reflexively. "Where are you keeping her?"

Kendall laced her arm with KC's. "She wasn't feeling well after she ate. Unsettled stomach." Kendall nodded discreetly, working her audience. "KC helped her find a quiet place to rest."

Lonnie, no doubt listening to events unfold from inside the room, opened the door at Kendall's announcement. KC pictured Lonnie frantically searching for a place to hide, perhaps beneath the bed or in the back of the closet, then sighing with relief when Kendall threw up a smoke screen.

KC's stomach knotted tighter. What was Kendall playing at?

"KC, thank you ever so for your assistance." She kissed KC on the cheek and, with her hand hidden from view, squeezed her ass firmly. The damn woman got off on the duplicity of it all. "I'm feeling a little better."

She gave KC a final little pat on the bottom. Kendall had to have felt the movement. KC came a little closer to vomiting with each second.

"Let's get you home, darling." Glen offered Lonnie his arm. They descended the stairs with him doting on her, promising to take care of her all night.

Kendall released KC's arm and turned to face her. KC didn't mirror her stance. She would fall apart under her big sister's scrutiny. Everything about this situation was wrong and Kendall would judge her harshly. She couldn't deny the truth but didn't want to face it just yet.

Neither of them spoke. KC supposed Kendall was waiting for her, giving her opportunity to say the right thing. KC couldn't find a single word that didn't make her feel like a Jezebel.

"KC." Kendall shook her head. She sounded so sad, so disappointed. "What are you doing?"

"I'm…" KC picked at her cuticle. "I don't know." She swallowed back tears. Her relationship with Lonnie was so simple when they were together. Lonnie swamped her senses, overloaded her until nothing was left but the promise of forbidden pleasure. But when her big sister asked her to define it, to defend it, she came up empty. She didn't have any answers when she stepped out of Lonnie's circle of influence. She took a deep breath and said it one more time. "I don't know."

She walked away and left Kendall standing in the upstairs hall. She could feel her sister's eyes on her as she went.

❖

Emma was already inside the house when KC arrived home. She took a quiet second to collect herself before entering. The last thing she needed was a guilt- and fear-fueled confession to Emma to accompany Kendall's discovery. Damn her sister's need to know everything. The woman was a bloodhound. KC pinched the bridge of her nose between her thumb and forefinger. She'd been told that would release tension, but so far it hadn't worked. Her next step involved a long-neck bottle.

"Hey." KC hung her keys on the hook by the door, dropped her jacket on the nearest chair, and made a beeline for the fridge. "Want a beer?"

Emma held a bottle high above the top edge of the couch. She was facing away from the kitchen toward the television, but it wasn't on. "Got one."

KC twisted the cap off and took a long pull before she joined Emma. She slouched into the cushions and rested her head against Emma's shoulder. This was the safest place she knew. "What are we watching?"

"Is it okay," Emma took a long drink of her beer, "if we don't watch anything? Can we just sit here for a while?"

"Sure." KC laid her hand on top of Emma's. One of her first memories was of her and Emma in their underwear giggling their way through Emma's backyard hand in hand. Since then, Emma's parents had divorced, the house had been sold, and they'd stopped hanging out in their underwear when they got old enough to really appreciate naked girls. Still, their hands belonged together. They fit. That was one of the simple truths in KC's life. "You want to tell me about it?"

Emma turned her hand over so their fingers naturally laced together and laid her head against KC's. "Not yet."

The quiet between them gave KC too much time to think about her relationship with Lonnie. She wanted distraction, not reflection. Still, she gave Emma her time. She was the sort to come around if given room. Pushing her would drive her farther away, not draw her closer.

KC tried to think about lesson plans. Her brain drifted to Lonnie with her hair drawn up in a bun and a twelve-inch wooden ruler in her hand. Hell, KC didn't know she had a hot-for-teacher fantasy, but Lonnie filled the role naturally. KC tried to think about her car and the strange popping noise it made every time she started it. Her thoughts slid to Lonnie bent over the hood of her Mustang, a sexier car than KC's Accord, as KC fucked her from behind.

They hadn't used a strap-on together yet. It would definitely solve KC's problem of being left behind on the orgasm train. She tried to think about the paperwork she needed to complete for finals' week. Paperwork was replaced by images of Lonnie sitting at her desk while KC kneeled before her and brought her to orgasm with her tongue. In each scenario, Lonnie's face slowly morphed into Emma's.

KC blew out a sigh and then sipped her beer. She'd never had such a hard time staying focused before. She prided herself on remaining asexual with Emma. After all, she couldn't act on her fantasies, so why indulge them? But her affair with Lonnie affected KC in many ways, especially her weak control over her libido, and her restraint around Emma seemed to be slipping.

She couldn't take the quiet any longer. "You had a date last night?"

"Mmm." Emma half nodded. If KC didn't know better, she'd think Emma had drifted to sleep. But her body was too tense for that to be the case.

"How was it?" KC pushed for more before her brain continued its sexual exploration of all things naked and Lonnie. She really, really needed to get off.

"It was okay." Emma shrugged. "She was…nice. Just not what I'm looking for."

KC squeezed Emma's hand. "Well, don't give up. You'll find the right girl eventually."

Emma pulled back slightly and rearranged their bodies until she could look KC in the eyes. "What about you? What are you doing to stay warm at night?"

KC laughed, held up her right hand, and wiggled the fingers suggestively. As long as she didn't actually speak, she'd be okay. She couldn't actively lie to Emma. She was her oldest friend and deserved better. But with the lack of reciprocity in her relationship with Lonnie of late, the right hand joke wasn't far from the truth.

Emma laughed with her for a moment, but then her mood turned somber. Her eyes were serious and sad when she asked, "Yeah, but don't you ever want more?"

KC stared into Emma's eyes for a long moment. Hell, yes, she wanted more. But it wasn't on the menu any time soon. She was in the middle of an affair with a married woman. That didn't exactly scream white picket fence. For lack of a better answer, she shrugged.

"Since your fingers aren't getting a workout anywhere else…" Emma slid off the couch, sat on the floor between KC's legs, and gestured at her shoulders. "You can put them to work on me."

KC squeezed the knotted muscles. They were unrelenting. Emma moaned and KC dug in harder. "Damn, you're tight." KC stopped moving, frozen by the double meaning of her words and trying not to lose it.

Emma looked over her shoulder at KC, eyebrows raised. They started laughing at the same time. A misspeak that was only worth a tittering giggle had them both rolling. The tension in Emma's muscles melted as her body went slack against KC's legs. She leaned her head against KC's thigh. "I needed that."

"Me, too." She resumed the massage. Though more relaxed, Emma's neck and shoulders were still a mess. "Why are you so tense?"

Emma let her head hang, exposing the length of her neck to KC. She rubbed her thumbs over the muscle on either side of her spine. Emma groaned when KC hit a spot high on the right, where a knot was tucked into the crevice where skull met spine. She didn't answer KC.

During her undergraduate studies, KC had perfected massage as a form of seduction. If any other woman had been writhing under her touch, KC would have had her naked and moaning for real. She squeezed Emma's shoulders one last time, then collapsed back into the sofa. She needed a little separation. Her world lately was filled with too much skin and not enough touching in the places where she needed to be touched.

Emma left her head down. "I got a job offer."

That sounded like good news to KC. "Why aren't we celebrating?"

"It's in Austin. As a production assistant at KTBC." Emma didn't sound as happy as KC thought she should. This was the job she'd been searching for since college, in the city where she wanted to live.

"Wait, you're going to work for Fox news?" KTBC was the local Fox affiliate.

Emma tilted her head back and rolled her eyes. "It's Texas, KC. All the news programs are conservative."

"It's *Austin*, Emma." Austin was a little oasis of liberal in an otherwise conservative state. That's why Emma wanted to move there in the first place. A job a KTBC was a compromise, an ends-justify-the-means situation. The *ends* for Emma meant living in Austin and the *means* was a job at KTBC.

"It gets me where I want to go." Emma confirmed KC's theory.

"Oh." That wasn't such great news for KC. She would miss her best friend. But it didn't explain Emma's down mood. Austin was her dream. "Well, that's good, right?"

Emma shrugged. "Yeah." She didn't elaborate.

Sometimes talking to Emma was like trying to extract stock advice from a schnauzer. Impossible. KC waited. She could fill the air with chatter, but Emma didn't want that and wouldn't appreciate it.

"I'm going next weekend to look for a place to live." Emma cast a quick glance over her shoulder at KC, then returned her attention forward.

KC nodded even though Emma couldn't see her. "I'll go with you." What other choice did she have? Of course Emma would want her there to vet such an important move.

Emma sighed. That was too many times for one night. Emma carried too much emotional weight. "Good." She moved back up to sit next to KC.

KC clapped her hand against Emma's leg and said, "Come with me to pick up Buddy. He's spending the night."

Emma tilted her head back and looked at the ceiling for several seconds, downed the rest of her beer, and stood. "Why not?" She held out a hand to help KC to her feet. At some point, Emma would stop pretending that everything was okay. KC hoped she would be there to take Emma's hand when it happened.

Chapter Three

KC woke the next morning to the sound of Buddy crying. At Trina and Jackson's insistence, Buddy slept in a portable crib in KC's spare bedroom rather than in the master bedroom with her. She figured he was crying because of waking up in a strange room.

"Em." KC shook Emma gently. As always, sometime during the night, Emma had migrated until she was half sprawled on top of KC. KC had long ignored her body's desire to escalate her physical contact with Emma, but mornings like this tested her resolve. Emma had made it clear years ago that they were friends and nothing more. KC worked hard to respect that boundary.

Emma didn't stir and Buddy cried louder. "Emma." KC shook her none-too-gently. "Buddy's crying."

"Wha…" Emma snuggled in closer and gripped KC tighter around the middle.

KC gave up trying to wake her politely and sat up. Emma flopped to the side and almost bounced off the bed completely.

"What the fuck?" Emma's hair hung in her face, a tangled curtain that blocked her eyes. She shoved it inelegantly behind her ears. Emma was not a morning person.

Buddy let out a lung-bursting cry.

"Oh." Emma flopped back down and buried her head in KC's pillow. "Wake me when it's not the middle of the damn night," she grumbled.

Free from bed, KC faced a battle. Her heart said go to Buddy *right now*. Her bladder said go to the bathroom. She wavered, then decided to go with her brain. If she didn't take care of her morning rituals, she'd have two problems to solve instead of just one: a crying toddler and a pee stain on the rug.

After she ran to the bathroom, she called, "I'm coming, Buddy-boy." If nothing else, she could try for some long-distance comforting. It didn't help. Next she tried singing. She made it through two verses of "Delta Dawn" before she reached his room. He was screaming bloody murder and trying to scale the side of the pack-and-play he slept in. The song didn't help Buddy much, but KC loved any morning that started with singing a Tanya Tucker song.

Buddy was not comforted to see his aunt round the corner instead of his mommy. He cried harder.

KC scooped him up and kissed the side of his head. "Shush shush shush." The universal shushing sound of mothers the world over sounded like a washing machine. Not at all comforting, to her mind. Still, it worked on Buddy. He hiccupped, snuggled his head into her shoulder, then burped long and loud.

At twenty-six, KC's biological clock had started tripping along to an uncertain beat. Most of the time, it was quiet enough to ignore, but when she held one of her sisters' children it clamored too loud to mistake for anything but longing for a family of her own.

She carried him to the kitchen. "Come on, boyo. Let's go fix your Auntie Em some breakfast."

"Don't teach him to call me that!" Emma smacked KC on the ass. Hard. She was headed toward the coffeemaker.

"Here." KC thrust Buddy into Emma's hands, giving her no choice but to take him. She slapped Emma's behind as payback, then reclaimed her nephew.

Emma hopped away and set about making coffee. "No more hitting until I have coffee. At this point I can't tell if it's abuse or foreplay."

"Definitely abuse." KC set Buddy on the counter. He was damn heavy. "What does your mama feed you, boy? You're built like a brick."

Buddy giggled but offered no insight.

"You're too young for coffee." Emma handed Buddy a cup of chocolate milk. "What's for breakfast?"

"Buddy and I are meeting Kendall and Trina at Over Easy, but we're going to fix you some bacon pancakes first." When they were little, KC would spend more nights with Emma than the other way around. Emma was an only child and KC's house was perpetual chaos. Emma never quite took to her mama's cooking lessons, but KC soaked them up. KC made a point to fix Emma's childhood favorites.

"I'm officially in love with you." Emma poured her first cup before the machine finished brewing. Coffee ran over the counter.

KC lifted Buddy off it and set him on the floor, then threw a towel at Emma. "Stop making a mess and hand me the griddle."

Bacon pancakes combined the best of all worlds. Yummy pancake, salty bacon, and sweet maple syrup. Unfortunately, they were a bitch to make. KC started the bacon, then mixed the pancake batter. Emma was well into her second cup of coffee when KC asked, "Did you tell them yes?"

Emma stopped drinking mid-swallow but held the cup to her mouth for a beat longer before she set it on the counter. "I haven't told them anything." She ran a finger over the rim of the mug, studying it with more attention than it deserved. "I wanted to talk to you."

With the bacon cooking, KC set Buddy at the kitchen table with a handful of Cheerios. She didn't want to spoil his appetite, but the boy needed to eat something while he waited for breakfast with his mama. The bacon sizzled and KC pulled it off the griddle. She diced it into small pieces and waited to see if Emma would elaborate. The only sound was Buddy crunching cereal. As she cleaned the grease from the griddle, she said, "And?"

KC ladled pancake batter onto the griddle and dropped the bacon crumble into it. Emma sighed five times but still said nothing.

"Em?" KC slipped her arm around Emma. She gave her a one-arm hug until the pancakes started to bubble.

"You know I want to go. This town is…" Emma sipped her coffee. "I want to go."

KC flipped the pancakes and pulled the syrup from the cupboard. "And?" Emma had been unemployed for so long that KC's brain tripped over itself trying to picture her any other way. God knew it wasn't for lack of trying, but her degree was very specific. There weren't many opportunities in a narrow job market like television production, especially during a down economy. All the reports said new jobs were available every day, but it didn't take a journalism degree to ask folks, "Would you like fries with that?" A legitimate job offer in her field was a dream come true for Emma, so why was she holding back? "Talk, Em."

Emma moved from the counter to the table. She lifted Buddy out of his chair and claimed the seat with him in her lap. Then she bit her bottom lip, a nervous habit since early childhood.

"You aren't getting these until you spill it." KC flipped pancakes onto a plate, added butter, and poured on too much syrup. Emma liked a little pancake with her syrup. She held the dish just out of Emma's reach.

"Okay." Emma played with Buddy's hair as she fumbled for words. "I want to move to Austin, but I don't want to leave you." She let out a huge sigh.

KC put the plate down, then sat in the empty chair. "I don't want you to leave me either, Emma." KC's life was in Fairmont. Her family. Lonnie. She'd always known Emma would leave. She just assumed she'd make lots of trips. She couldn't think of the day-to-day details beyond that. The Emma-sized hole in her life squeezed at her heart. "But it's not like we're breaking up. We'll visit plenty."

Before Emma could respond, KC's phone sang out "The Yellow Rose of Texas." It was Lonnie's ringtone.

Where the hell was her phone? KC carried Buddy on her hip and followed the sound. She found it on the counter beneath her unread Sunday paper from the previous morning. "Just let me," KC held up the phone, "get this. I'll be quick."

Emma nodded then tucked into her pancakes. She didn't look up as KC left the room to take the call.

"Hello?" KC felt breathless and rushed, and only part of it was from the phone search and hefting Buddy around. The thought of

Lonnie left her breathless regularly. Apparently that had spread to include the sound of her ringtone as well.

"Good morning, sugar." Lonnie's voice was languid and sexy, like a summer breeze across a lake. "I've been thinking about you."

KC pictured Lonnie stretched out in her bed wearing a silk nightie and sliding over satin sheets. KC'd never actually seen Lonnie's bedroom, but the fantasy made her wet. "Yeah?" KC grinned like an idiot. Buddy poked her in the nose and giggled. She felt decidedly less sexy as she jerked her head around to keep him from sticking his finger into her left nostril.

"Yes, I feel positively terrible about leaving you stranded yesterday."

"Twice." KC's neglected girlie parts were still yelling at her for attention.

"Twice. That's why I'm calling. I thought maybe I could talk you through it this morning."

KC heard Emma rinsing her plate in the kitchen. Buddy struggled in her arms until she set him on the floor. "Lon, now is *really* not a good time."

"I'm sure we can be quick, sugar." Lonnie's pout registered all the way through the phone. "I need you."

Need is a curious thing, and typically Lonnie's needs overrode KC's. With her nephew climbing up her dresser, Lonnie's needs over the phone didn't seem all that pressing. KC was flat-out irritated. What was she supposed to do? Lock Buddy in the closet until Lonnie was done with her?

"I'm sorry, Lonnie, really I am, but Buddy's here…" If Lonnie kept talking in that sweet-as-molasses voice, if she said just the right things, KC might be persuaded. Emma could watch Buddy for a few minutes. But how would she explain herself? *Give me just a minute, Emma. I'm just going to get Lonnie off over the phone, then I'll be right back out.* No, that just wouldn't do. "What are you doing later?"

Buddy made it to the second drawer and the dresser wobbled. KC dropped her phone as she dove for him. He giggled and said, "Wow."

KC stared at him. Trina didn't mention that he was talking yet. "Say it again, Buddy. Say *wow*." She picked her phone up with her free hand but didn't put Buddy down again. She was pretty sure Trina wouldn't want him back after her dresser flattened him. "Sorry. Buddy almost fell." She sandwiched the phone between her ear and her shoulder and flew Buddy around the room like Superman. "So…later?"

"I'll be at my office this afternoon." A few years ago, while KC was away at college, Lonnie took up selling real estate. She kept an office in town for meetings and such. "Come by?" Lonnie still sounded put out, but resigned.

"Absolutely. Three-ish?"

KC ended the call feeling conflicted. She hated disappointing Lonnie for any reason, but she couldn't help but wonder if their relationship would ever balance out to the point where Lonnie thought about KC's needs.

She let Buddy walk when she left the bedroom. He ran down the hall, laughing all the way.

Emma leaned against the counter, her purse and keys in her hands. "Dishes are done. I best be going."

"Were we done talking?"

Emma nodded and pulled her cigarettes from her purse. She tapped a cigarette out of the pack. "I think we are, KC."

KC didn't have an answer to the defeat in Emma's tone. Until her friend was ready to share what was going on inside of her, KC couldn't do a thing.

"You want to wait until we get ready?"

"I think I'm just going to go." Emma slipped the cigarette between her lips, gave KC a sad wave, then stepped out the kitchen door. She lit the cigarette as the door swung shut behind her.

"Huh." KC picked Buddy up. "Just you and me, boyo. Let's get you dressed."

❖

Over Easy was over-full when KC finally arrived, fifteen minutes late and without her makeup. Maybe Trina wasn't totally exaggerating when she complained about how much time Buddy took up. To be fair, though, Lonnie's phone call and Emma's departure had distracted her.

"About damn time." Kendall thrust a menu into KC's hand before she could even sit down. She dropped the menu onto her plate to keep from dropping Buddy on the floor. Kendall expected KC to be able to juggle children and the rest of life with the same proficiency of Lady Madonna. After all, Kendall balanced a marriage, three kids, and a law practice without breaking a sweat. The least KC could do was show up to breakfast on time prepared to order. "You look like shit."

KC settled Buddy in his high chair and gave Trina, then Kendall a kiss on the cheek. "If this is how you're going to treat me, I'm going to start inviting Mama. Then you won't be able to get away with swearing at me in public."

"Are you saying you wouldn't look like shit if Mama were here?" Kendall was a litigator. KC had yet to win an argument with her.

A glass of water and orange juice waited in KC's place at the table. She drank half the water in one go. "I love whoever ordered this."

Kendall smirked.

"Did you order my breakfast, too?"

"No. And here comes Roxy, so stop talking and start deciding."

"Hey, girls. You ready?" Roxy held her order pad like a weapon, ready to discharge at a moment's notice.

"I'll just have toast. And an egg for Buddy. Scrambled." Trina handed the menu to Roxy without opening it.

"Jesus, Trina, you're supposed to be eating for two," Kendall said.

Trina glared.

"Rox, give me the ranch breakfast. Eggs over hard, bacon, and can you put some gravy over the hash browns?"

"Toast or pancake?"

"Pancake." KC had a craving left over from Emma's breakfast.

Roxy nodded and turned toward Kendall.

"Sheesh, KC, you picking up the slack for Trina?" Kendall sipped her coffee. "Can I get the fruit platter?"

KC and Trina regarded one another, then turned toward Kendall.

"What? My suit was a little tight this morning. Too many Sunday dinners with Mama."

The sisters nodded and Buddy banged his spoon against the table.

KC segued. "Speaking of...I won't be there this coming Sunday. Don't let me forget to tell Mama and Daddy." Not that KC planned to see either of her sisters again before then.

"Why not?" Trina took the spoon from Buddy and gave him a package of saltines.

"He had some Cheerios this morning," KC said.

Buddy chewed on the cellophane wrapper until Trina took the crackers away and gave him the spoon again. He blew bubble kisses against the back of it.

"I swear," Trina wiped his face with a napkin, "he's like a tiny little spit factory."

"What about words? His mouth produced any of those yet?" Kendall asked.

"No. And Jackson is getting impatient." Trina's shoulders stiffened, and she took the spoon and set it just beyond Buddy's reach. "He wants me to take him to a specialist."

"That's ridiculous." Kendall spoke in her lawyer voice. Good luck to Jackson if he ever mentioned that plan in front of the family protector. "He's only two."

"Besides, he said a word this morning." KC hadn't intended to bring it up. Trina wasn't likely to be impressed when she heard about her son's near-death experience involving KC's bedroom furniture.

Trina stared at KC, her mouth open slightly. "What? What did he say?"

"He said *wow*," KC answered, still not sure she should be volunteering the information.

"When was that?" Trina didn't look convinced.

KC smoothed Buddy's hair. "Oh, you know," she gestured vaguely, "this morning."

"I don't know why Jackson is worried about it." Kendall took up the conversation. As the oldest sister, she also had the most experience raising children. "Melissa started talking before she turned two, but Emily had barely started when Winston was born." Emily was three when her baby brother was born. The family joked that she started talking specifically so she could welcome Winston to the family.

"I told Jackson that, but he isn't satisfied." Trina paused, her brows drawn together in a thoughtful frown. "And I'm sorry, KC, but one word uttered out of earshot won't help. If Jackson didn't hear it, it didn't happen."

Kendall shook her head. "That man is a fool."

Trina didn't respond to Kendall's disparaging remark. Instead she asked, "Why won't you be there Sunday?" It was an impressive redirect of topic.

"I'm going to Austin with Emma. She's taking a job there."

"Well, give her my congratulations next time you see her. I'll have my assistant drop a card in the mail," Kendall said.

"Doing what?" Trina had dark circles under her eyes, and KC wondered if Kendall had told her she looked like shit, too. Trina had managed makeup, so Kendall probably gave her a pass.

"What's up with the full face, Trina?" KC made a sweeping circular motion in front of her own face.

"Oh." Trina touched her fingers to her cheekbone and winced. "I haven't been sleeping well. Foundation and cover-up are required before I venture into public."

Kendall stared at Trina a beat longer than normally considered polite, her head tilted to the side in contemplation. Finally she sipped her coffee and turned toward KC. "What was the job offer?"

"I'm not entirely sure. Something at an affiliate news channel." Emma had studied journalism in college. She had designs on production. The details were more than KC could keep up with, but that was true of any career outside of teaching.

"Fabulous news." Trina didn't sound excited, just tired.

"You know, I can keep Buddy for the day. He and I get along just fine." Lonnie would absolutely kill her if she canceled this afternoon, especially after turning her down this morning. But what kind of sister would she be if she didn't at least offer to help?

"If you're feeling lonely, little sister, you can take my three any time you want. Mel gets out of school at two forty-five, and you can pick up the other two from daycare right now if you'd like."

Roxy delivered their food. She'd been waiting tables at Over Easy since her parents opened the restaurant when she was twelve and knew how to do her job without being intrusive.

"Thanks, KC, but Buddy has a doctor's appointment this afternoon. He can't miss it." Trina set the egg in front of Buddy and helped him grip the spoon the right way.

"I can pick him up afterward." KC stirred the gravy into her hash browns. If she was going to say to hell with her waistline this early in the morning, she wanted to be able to taste her extravagance in every bite.

"He's getting his two-year-old vaccinations. You won't want him."

Kendall snagged a piece of bacon from KC's plate. "It'll be good for her. Let her take him."

"Your fruit's not going to help if you eat your fill off my plate." KC buttered her pancake and then spread blackberry jam over the top.

"Just you wait." Kendall speared a chunk of melon and jabbed it in KC's direction. "Eventually you're going to have a baby or turn thirty. Then we'll see how much you're laughing."

"Fat chance she's going to have a baby." Trina nibbled her toast.

"And why is that?" KC bordered on scandalized. Trina avoided all talk of KC's sex life like it was a plague of flying locusts. "Being a lesbian doesn't render me incapable of reproducing."

Trina shook her head and kept eating her toast. She didn't comment further.

Kendall took up the challenge. "Biology 101. Makin' babies requires sperm."

Trina nodded. Kendall smirked. Buddy threw a fistful of eggs. KC rolled her eyes. "They sell that stuff. Hell, I can order it off the Internet and have it delivered straight to my door."

"Really?" Trina's eyebrows just about climbed off her head.

"Pssshh." Kendall was not impressed. "You can get it delivered straight to your vagina for free if you do it the old-fashioned way."

"Yuck." KC set her fork down. "You're going to ruin my appetite."

"I call dibs on your bacon." Kendall stole the remaining piece.

"You want babies, KC?" Trina asked quietly.

"Of course." KC hadn't really thought about it. At some point she'd have a family of her own. It was just the order of things. "Why wouldn't I?"

Trina shrugged and gave her half-eaten piece of toast to Buddy.

"Really?" Kendall looked like she wanted to say more. KC prayed she wouldn't.

"Really." KC tucked into her hash browns before Kendall could target them next. Silence was her best option with the direction the conversation had turned, and keeping her mouth otherwise occupied was the best way to stay quiet.

She tried to picture her future with Lonnie. If she focused on imaginative sex, Lonnie worked fine. The second her musing switched to anything that spoke of longevity in a relationship, Lonnie disappeared from the scenario. Emma hovered in her mind, but she wouldn't fool herself into thinking her relationship with Emma equaled anything more than friendship. They had no future together. KC put away her uncertainty and focused on the day ahead. She might not know her path to contentment, but she didn't expect to find it over breakfast either. She sighed and took another bite of her breakfast.

Chapter Four

KC's stomach clenched with that giddy happy feeling that came along with getting to see Lonnie. She had taken extra care as she dressed for their meeting. She'd even shaved her legs, a chore she detested, but Lonnie was always very vocal with her appreciation of it.

After breakfast with her sisters, KC ran a few errands, recorded two lectures and uploaded them, graded a virtual stack of essays, and thought ceaselessly about what she wanted from her meeting with Lonnie. First on the list: orgasm. Preferably followed by more orgasms. To that end, she'd decided to try something a little different.

"Hello, darlin'. How can I help you?" Lonnie obviously didn't recognize KC.

KC wanted to draw the charade out, to play the part of the man she'd dressed to be. She'd braided her hair and tucked it up under a fedora and wore tailored men's slacks with a crisp white button-down shirt. Hell, she even sported a tie to complete the look.

She took a couple of steps deeper into the reception area, her right hand resting high on her thigh in her best imitation of the gangsta stride. If she had a real cock, her thumb would have brushed against it with every step. When her student-teacher rotation took her through a Seattle high school, she'd laughed at the male students who walked that way. Now it gave her a perfect form to imitate.

"I'm sure you can think of something." KC pitched her voice deeper and gave her not-so-manly parts a squeeze.

"Now listen here, young man." Lonnie changed from solicitous realtor to scolding mama instantly. KC loved Lonnie's feistiness. If she'd tried this with a lover in Seattle, she would have ended up with a face full of pepper spray and being hauled away in handcuffs. Lonnie had no reason to think she was in danger, because in Fairmont she wasn't. Any unruly young man could be put easily back in line with a fiery lecture accompanied by the right amount of finger wagging. "You may talk to folks like that wherever it is you come from, but 'round here we do things different—"

KC grabbed Lonnie around the waist and pulled her close. She was tired of listening to Lonnie rant. She had an agenda for their meeting, and being scolded like a child was nowhere on the list. Lonnie made her heart beat like a wild horse. And she wanted to let the horses run for a while.

Lonnie struggled fiercely and KC squeezed her tight to keep her from escaping. This was getting out of hand. As soon as she touched Lonnie, Lonnie lost control of the situation. That was never KC's intention. She wanted to play, not give her lover a heart attack. Before Lonnie could scream bloody murder, she pressed her lips to Lonnie's ear. "Baby, it's me," she cooed, the words low and soothing. She needed to calm Lonnie down before things got any worse.

"KC?" Lonnie jerked out of KC's grasp. Her chest heaved and her eyes were open wide with fear. She slapped KC across the face. "You scared the shit out of me."

KC rubbed her palm against her cheek, the flesh hot to the touch. Tomorrow, KC knew, she'd need extra makeup to cover the handprint. "Lonnie…" She didn't know what to say.

Lonnie kept her from having to figure it out. She launched herself at KC lips first. "Goddamn, you look sexy." She breathed the words into KC's mouth between sloppy open-mouth kisses.

KC gripped Lonnie's hands at the wrist and pulled them away from her face. She held them down by her side and said, "There's a window right there." She jerked her head toward the large plateglass window, its view one of the reasons Lonnie had selected this office space.

"Oh, hell. You made me forget myself." Lonnie straightened and removed her hands from KC's grip. KC wanted to hold on a little longer, a little tighter, to see what kind of reaction she'd get, but she let go and Lonnie retreated to her office. "Come on, sugar. I've already closed the blinds in here. Hurry."

KC forgot all about her practiced man-strut as she rushed to reach Lonnie. On her list of priorities, getting Lonnie naked, and hopefully on her knees, ranked above posturing. As soon as she cleared the threshold, she closed the door and twisted the lock.

"I don't know what's gotten into you, but I like it." Lonnie spread her hands over KC's shoulders, smoothing the fabric.

"I want you." KC led Lonnie's hand down her front to the juncture between her legs. When she'd slipped into the harness earlier, she wasn't sure how Lonnie would respond. Now she couldn't wait to pull out the silicone cock and make Lonnie beg for it.

Lonnie gripped the width and gasped. "What's this?" She wrapped her fingers around it and squeezed. "God."

Lonnie was a Texas lady. That meant she wore makeup like she was appearing on TV, with her hair high and wavy, and always, *always*, left home wearing a dress. KC dropped to her knees and pressed her open mouth to Lonnie's stomach through the fabric. She eased her hands slowly up Lonnie's thighs, appreciating the feel of real silk stockings and garters. She didn't stop her upward movement until she reached Lonnie's panties. "I want these off." She jerked them down, none too gently, and left them around Lonnie's knees. Far enough down for Lonnie to spread her legs some, but not far enough for her to step out.

KC stood abruptly but left her hands resting on Lonnie's hips inside her skirt. She held her face close enough to feel Lonnie's breath on her lips but didn't kiss her. Lonnie's low, deep moan vibrated down KC's spine.

"Open my pants." KC barely managed a whisper. So much for debonair and commanding.

Lonnie's hands shook as she worked the button loose, then lowered the zipper. She started to push them down KC's hips and KC stopped her.

"Leave them." KC kissed Lonnie, sweet and tender. She poured every ounce of emotion she could find into the meeting of their lips. If she had her way, everything that followed would be anything but gentle. She wanted to remind Lonnie that she cared for her even if Lonnie wouldn't allow her to say the words.

KC left their lips pressed together after the kiss ended. She held Lonnie quietly. With her eyes closed, she savored their connection.

"What do you want?" Lonnie whispered.

KC took a deep breath. "Take it out." She moved her hands to Lonnie's shoulders, squeezed firmly, and pressed down. Lonnie hadn't spent any time on her knees with KC, but that didn't mean she didn't understand what was being asked of her.

Lonnie kneeled with a good deal more grace than KC had managed. She eased her hands into the open fly of KC's trousers and tugged on the cock. It popped out inelegantly and came close to poking Lonnie in the eye. KC wrapped one hand around the base and held it firm. It jutted out proudly and Lonnie took a deep breath. "Oh, my."

KC adjusted her stance. Her pants threatened to fall to her ankles, which would shatter the illusion. They'd officially crossed a line, and the promise wrapped a constricting band around her chest and left her light-headed. She cupped Lonnie's cheek with her free hand and dug her fingers into the wispy hairs at the base of Lonnie's neck. Again, she encouraged Lonnie into motion. Her thumb trailed over her cheek, back and forth, as she coaxed Lonnie forward. God, she wanted to see this woman's mouth wrapped around her cock.

"Suck." Her voice was firmer this time, the command clear.

"Yes." Lonnie's response was barely audible. She licked her lips, then closed the gap between her mouth and KC's cock.

Lonnie's lipstick smeared a red trail over the length, and KC moaned at the sight. Lonnie on her knees, messing up her perfect face to please KC…It was so very debauched, and KC fought the need to thrust. She wanted, she *needed* to be farther inside Lonnie. Lonnie sucked almost a third of the dildo. When it hit the back of Lonnie's throat, KC felt the resistance deep in her cunt. Lonnie gagged slightly and tried to pull back, but KC held her firm by her neck. When Lonnie stopped struggling, KC withdrew, using the motion of her hips.

Lonnie stared up at KC, her mouth open wide with barely the tip nestled inside. KC pushed her hips forward slowly and watched the cock disappear. Her knees buckled when she felt it reach the end again. She wanted to push farther, to breach the barrier and slide her cock down Lonnie's throat until Lonnie could taste the leather of her harness with her lips. She held perfectly still for as long as her trembling legs would allow, then withdrew again.

"God, Lonnie." She pushed in again, a little faster this time. She just needed to fuck. "You look so sexy right now."

Lonnie moaned when KC hit the back of her throat. She hummed around KC and didn't gag.

"Good girl." KC released her cock and framed Lonnie's face with her hands. She held Lonnie steady with both hands. "God, I just want to fuck you so hard." She pressed a little deeper and Lonnie's eyes widened. She gagged slightly, then took a breath through her nose and started to hum again. "So fucking sexy."

KC didn't press hard enough to slide down her throat. She needed Lonnie to still be able to talk when this was over. She knew if she went any farther, she wouldn't be able to control herself for long. She wanted to fuck Lonnie, not destroy her vocal chords by slamming into her like an overly enthusiastic boy. She withdrew and Lonnie whined.

It felt so good, the push-pull of thrusting into Lonnie's mouth. She pushed in again, a little faster, a little harder, but no deeper. She stopped when she felt resistance, keeping a firm grip on Lonnie's head and swirling her hips. The cock slid deeper, an inch, then two. KC groaned. Pleasure radiated from her cunt through her body. She was seriously close to losing her shit, and she hadn't even really started. She pushed just a little deeper and held it. She closed her eyes and tipped her head back. She needed a moment to collect herself, to both revel in the decadence of the moment and to calm her body. She didn't trust herself to move without coming inside Lonnie. Fake cock or not, it was bad form to come in a woman's throat, even if the woman was moaning for more.

Especially if that woman hadn't had an orgasm herself yet. KC was not a selfish lover.

When she felt her impending orgasm recede enough to move, she withdrew completely.

"Up." She tugged on Lonnie's head hard enough to make Lonnie yelp. She was sorry for that, but not sorry enough to stop. She needed back inside Lonnie now.

Lonnie rose hastily and struggled to keep her balance. She was breathing hard, the rise and fall of her chest hypnotic. KC hesitated for half a moment to appreciate the sight. Lonnie's hair was falling down, her makeup smeared, her dress akimbo; KC had never seen Lonnie so undone. She was heady with the power.

She grasped Lonnie by the hips and forced her to turn in a circle. When Lonnie's back was to her front, she guided Lonnie forward until she bumped into the edge of her desk. She kept up the forward momentum until Lonnie folded over the desk facedown, ass jutting out.

Lonnie wiggled her ass and taunted KC over her shoulder. "What are you going to do now, sugar?"

KC didn't have a plan. She was making it up as she went along, doing what felt right in the moment. And right then she wanted to take back the control that Lonnie's teasing had stripped from her. She smacked Lonnie on the ass, once, swift and firm. The popping noise echoed through the office.

Lonnie cried out and turned to say something else. Before the words could leave her mouth, KC spanked her again, harder and in the same spot. "Quiet."

Lonnie whimpered and gripped the edge of the desk. They'd never talked about taking their relationship in this direction. It was uncharted territory and KC was uncertain, but committed. She'd chosen her path and wouldn't turn back unless Lonnie asked her to. Still, she didn't want to genuinely hurt Lonnie. There was no fun in that kind of pain.

With both hands firm on Lonnie's ass, she inched the fabric of her dress up until it bunched around her waist. She smoothed her hands over the firm flesh. The right side was hot and angry red from

KC's palm. She gently rubbed the skin, her fingers barely touching it. Goose bumps rose in a wake behind her touch. She knelt behind Lonnie and pressed her cheek against the outline of her palm, then turned her face to kiss it gently. Lonnie squirmed.

KC gripped Lonnie's cheeks and spread them apart, exposing her fully. Her cunt glistened with excitement. KC could lose herself in worshipping Lonnie's folds, to bringing her pleasure. She extended her tongue and licked along the line of Lonnie's labia. Lonnie's legs tensed to the point of vibrating. When KC licked her the second time, she dedicated extra attention to Lonnie's clit, wiggling her tongue into the folds until she found the hard bundle of nerves. She circled it gently, then flicked over it hard and quick. Lonnie's knees buckled.

KC pushed against her ass to hold her up. She wanted Lonnie spread out over the desk and open to her for a while longer. If need be, she could tie her hands to the front desk legs to keep her in place, but she wasn't sure how Lonnie would respond to that. That was the universal theme for this entire encounter, and so far Lonnie's only response had been to grow increasingly wet.

"God, Lonnie, the things I want to do to you." KC moaned into Lonnie's cunt, her tongue buried as deep as she could get it. She withdrew and pushed it in again. It felt woefully inadequate. KC wanted to fill Lonnie to the point of breaking, to push into her and demand that she open herself. More than that, she wanted Lonnie to beg her for it. She replaced her tongue with her fingers. Soon, she would use the cock dangling impatiently between her legs, but not yet.

"Tell me." Lonnie shifted, her ass pushing back against KC's hands with the desire to thrust. "God, please, KC, tell me."

"First," KC licked around her fingers as she thrust in and out, "I'm going to tease you." She wished she could reach Lonnie's clit with her tongue from that position. Unfortunately, no matter how many yoga classes she took, she'd never reached that level of body-bending flexibility. She removed her fingers and spread Lonnie open. Her cunt was a beautiful pink and dripping. Rather than dip her tongue inside, KC remembered her original target. She teased

Lonnie's clit, moving her tongue in tight, fast circles. She pressed hard and firm. Lonnie clenched and shook, and KC pressed harder, circled faster.

She would give Lonnie this orgasm, and then she would take hers. When Lonnie was close enough to fall, KC pressed her finger against Lonnie's anus. She didn't go inside, just held it against the rim and vibrated. Lonnie keened, then collapsed against the desk, her body limp.

"Oh, my." Lonnie mumbled facedown into the desk. Aftershocks vibrated through her legs and ass. KC gave her clit a gentle kiss then stood.

"Then I'm going to fuck you." KC positioned the cock at Lonnie's opening and pushed inside without waiting for Lonnie to fully recover. As slow and careful as she possibly could, she moved inside at a fraction of the speed her body craved. She let herself settle deep inside Lonnie and waited for Lonnie to adjust to the size. Lonnie's body tensed and she pushed back against KC.

She positioned her hands on Lonnie's hips and held her firm against the desk. She didn't want Lonnie's help. She wanted her to remain still so she could fuck her with all the pent-up energy that had been building since the morning before. She wanted to pound her frustration into Lonnie until it burst. And she wanted Lonnie to let it happen.

"Don't move." KC slapped Lonnie's ass again to emphasize her point, and Lonnie instantly stilled. KC rewarded her by gently smoothing her palm over the red flesh of Lonnie's ass. "Good girl."

KC withdrew just as slowly, forcing herself to be restrained. She paused when she was fully out, not even the tip inside, and waited. Lonnie didn't disappoint. She whimpered, "Please, sugar."

As KC was about to push in, Lonnie's cell phone rang. It sat on the desk just a few inches from Lonnie's face, playing the theme song to *Bonanza*. Glen's picture filled the screen. KC hesitated. She wouldn't stop Lonnie from answering, but she wouldn't stop fucking her either. This was her time with Lonnie, dammit. She had an appointment. Lonnie didn't move and the phone stopped ringing.

KC pressed forward again, then back out without hesitating. She was done teasing, done going slow. The phone beeped to signal that Lonnie had a voice mail and KC let go. She set a hard, fast rhythm that had Lonnie gasping for breath. Once she stopped restraining herself, KC moved quickly to orgasm, the energy in her cunt radiating out until even her fingers felt the increasing need ready to explode.

When she finally came after days of building, KC didn't stop. She paused to shudder inside Lonnie, then continued thrusting. She had more inside of her and wanted to release it all. She gripped Lonnie by the hair and pulled her back until she was flush against KC's front. "Kiss me."

She thrust short and hard, barely moving inside of Lonnie, but pushing ever forward. Their kiss was sloppy and hot and wet. She kept one hand bunched tight in Lonnie's hair, pulling her head back to meet her, and wrapped the other arm around Lonnie's body. She pinched her nipples through the fabric of her dress, a frantic grabbing and twisting that made Lonnie arch and scream into her mouth. She thrust harder and worked her hand lower, her fingers spread wide and pressing hard against Lonnie's abdomen.

"I want you to come, dammit." KC tugged Lonnie's hair, jerking her body taut, then bit the column of her neck. Lonnie was trembling, on the verge of falling apart. KC licked her neck, then pressed her lips to Lonnie's ear. Her thrusts were erratic and poorly controlled. "Come on, Lonnie. Do it."

Lonnie squeezed her body tight and thrust against KC, and KC couldn't hold her still. She thrust and rode KC, despite their reversed positions, until she tensed and shook uncontrollably. "Oh, my God."

"Good, let it go." KC nipped at Lonnie's ear, punctuating each word with her teeth. "So I can push you down and do it all over again."

Lonnie came with a scream and KC released her hair. Lonnie fell over the desk, limp and languid, for the second time that afternoon. KC pounded into Lonnie with renewed energy. She dug her fingers into the meaty flesh of Lonnie's ass and thighs as she held her in place. She fucked until her legs shook and her body heaved. Her lungs begged for a break. And then she fucked harder, driving her cock as deep into Lonnie as it would go, only to pull back and fuck her deeper and harder.

Lonnie's body rose quickly toward release the third time, tension building from her cunt and radiating out until KC could see the muscles of her jaw straining. KC reached around to find Lonnie's clit. She was close, so close to coming, and she wanted to take Lonnie with her. Her movements were abrupt, sloppy and hard. She couldn't make circles with her fingers. She grabbed at it, tweaking it like she had Lonnie's nipples. What she lacked in finesse, she made up in driving power from her hips and a burning desire to please.

Finally, blessedly, when her legs were on the verge of muscle failure, KC came inside Lonnie. She came hard and it overwhelmed her. She collapsed against Lonnie in a shuddering mess.

She needed to move, to pull out and get off Lonnie, but her muscles were spent. She took a moment to breathe and then straightened. She paused, her thighs twitching. Movement was not her friend.

"Sorry. Give me a second." Slowly, very slowly, she retracted her hips until the dildo fell clear of Lonnie. Lonnie groaned.

Lonnie lay prone against the desk and said, "Damn." She clenched her legs.

While Lonnie was recovering, KC got herself in order. She loosened the *O* ring on the harness and removed the dildo. It needed to be washed thoroughly before she could leave Lonnie's office. "I'll be back."

KC collapsed against the inside wall of the washroom. She needed time to think, to process what they'd done. What *she'd* done. None of that, save the orgasm, had been planned. She hadn't even known that sex like that would turn her on, let alone give her a giant, body-quaking orgasm. She didn't have words to describe how it affected her. Nor could she explain the feeling of dread building in the pit of her stomach.

She washed up, careful to clean under her fingernails. She wished she had a toothbrush, but she hadn't thought that far ahead when she left her house. KC stared at her reflection, her hair braided tight and pinned up. Her face hidden beneath the brim of the hat, she barely recognized the angles of it. Beneath the shadow of the brim of the hat, its contours looked carved deep, defined and edgy, instead of the soft curves she was used to. She removed the fedora and let down her hair. It was closer to normal, but still not right. She loosed the braids and finger-combed through the waves. Short hair had always appealed to her, but now she wasn't so sure.

Like the toothbrush, KC hadn't thought to bring a change of clothes. She removed the tie, wound it around the dildo, and tucked the makeshift package into the deep pockets of her slacks. As long as she walked with one hand in her pocket, it wouldn't poke its way out the top. She loosened the top two buttons of the shirt and rolled up the sleeves. This was as good as she was going to get without a personal makeover in Lonnie's office bathroom.

When she made it back to Lonnie's private office, order had been restored. Lonnie looked refreshed, no signs of being recently well fucked. Her hair was pinned up properly, her dress straightened, and her makeup perfect. KC felt a throb between her legs and wanted to mess it all up again. Lonnie shouldn't be able to recover so quickly, so completely, when KC was still falling apart.

"There you are, KC." She smiled politely, like friends meeting at church. "Glen is coming to take me to dinner. He'll be here shortly."

KC's stomach dropped. "When?"

Lonnie glanced at the clock on the wall. "In a few minutes."

"Why didn't you—"

"Lonnie, darlin', you ready to go?" Glen's booming voice sounded in the reception area.

How long had Lonnie known of his visit? Had she planned the close timing? What if they hadn't finished when they did? Questions pinballed through KC's mind. What if they'd gotten caught?

"Oh, hello, KC." Glen tipped his hat to her, ever the proper Texas gentleman. "I wasn't expecting to see you here."

"Hi, Mr. Truvall." KC swayed, pinpoint black circles edged her vision. "I didn't expect to see you either. What a surprise."

"Darling, KC just came by to check on me." Lonnie stretched on her tiptoes to kiss Glen's cheek. "She was worried about me since I was feeling so under the weather yesterday. Isn't that sweet?"

KC kept her right hand in her pocket, protecting her detachable manhood. She prayed Mr. Truvall wouldn't offer to shake her hand. He sometimes did that. The whole lesbian thing threw him off kilter and he wasn't sure which manners to employ. To KC's mind, he couldn't decide if being gay meant she'd spontaneously sprouted a penis and was no longer a girl.

If only he knew.

"Why, thank you, KC," Glen said. "It's very kind of you to check in on Lonnie like that."

"Yes sir, it was no trouble at all." KC scooted toward the door. She needed to get outside so she could breathe again. "I best be going now."

She didn't wait for a response. She walked out the door and straight to her car without stopping. When she was safely inside, with the doors closed and locked, she took a deep breath.

Then she dropped her head against the steering wheel and cried.

Chapter Five

KC tucked the dildo-tie combination into her glove box and watched as Lonnie and Glen exited the building together. Glen wrapped his arm around Lonnie's waist, guiding her. Protecting her. And Lonnie leaned into his embrace. There was no outward sign of what she'd been up to with KC, no evidence that she had a lover outside of her marriage. Lonnie laughed, slapped Glen good-naturedly on the stomach, then turned in the circle of his arms until they were embracing. There they stood, in broad day light, kissing on a public sidewalk for God and all of creation to see. KC's stomach heaved.

She sat in her car long after she stopped crying, unmoving and undecided. She couldn't go home. She was too brain-fucked to be alone in a house that used to belong to her grandmother. Not to mention that Emma tended to pop over unannounced. She couldn't see her right now. Not yet.

She started her car and pulled away from the curb. She'd fallen into an affair with a married woman who had no intention of ever being unmarried. Lonnie loved Glen. As sure as KC knew her own name, she knew that Lonnie would never leave him. Moreover, KC didn't want her to. When did her bit of fun get so complicated?

"What the fuck am I doing?"

KC drove through town with no clear destination. She needed to think. She needed to decide on a place to go and get there. Her head wasn't clear enough for her to be behind the wheel. It wasn't clear enough for her to think. She drove slowly, well below the speed limit, with no idea where she was headed.

She pulled over to the curb and killed the engine. Without intending to, she'd driven to her sister's neighborhood. Across the street, and three houses down, her sister Kendall sat on her front porch sipping an iced tea. KC was parched.

A brick in the pit of her stomach, hard and flat and unsettling, had replaced the flurry of excitement KC felt when she entered Lonnie's office. Kendall would know how to fix this. She left her car and walked to Kendall's house.

She plodded up the walk, head forward, eyes trained on Kendall. She was ready to cry again, but as long as she had a focal point, she could hold back. She stopped at the base of the stairs. The four that would take her up to the main porch level loomed large in her mind.

"What's up, little sister?" Kendall remained seated, feet resting on a wicker ottoman. She wore reading glasses low on her nose and had an open manila file folder in her lap and a pen clipped to her collar. Even when she relaxed on the front porch, she never truly rested.

What was up? What could KC say that Kendall hadn't already figured out on her own? Still, her sister would listen to her as she worked through her maelstrom of emotions, then point her in the right direction. Kendall was thoughtful and methodical. She would choose a path KC's feet could travel without stumbling.

KC tried to smile. It didn't work, so she shrugged instead. "Can we go inside?" She'd already had one crying fit in the middle of the street today. She didn't want to tempt the fates and go for a second.

"Sure thing." Kendall closed the file and rose. She waited at the top of the stairs for KC. "You're in luck. Owen took the kids to the park a few minutes ago. My house is quiet enough to hear one another without shouting."

"Thanks," KC said.

"Head to my office." Kendall's voice was gentle, which made KC want to cry more than ever. Kendall was never nice to her. Sisterly torment was the crux of their relationship.

KC sank into the deep leather armchair and immediately regretted her choice. It had belonged to her grandfather before he died, as had most of the furniture in this office. How was she supposed to talk about her wild and wicked ways while sitting in her grandfather's wingback? He was a pious man. She most decidedly was not.

Rather than taking the seat opposite, the one behind her desk, Kendall sat beside KC in the matching black chair. She took a sip of her tea and waited.

KC had no idea what to say. Every jumping-off point she thought of sounded sordid in her mind. She could only imagine how bad it would sound if she let the words out into the light of day. Finally, because she couldn't bear the scrutiny of Kendall staring at her any longer, she said, "Owen and the kids doing well?"

"They are." Kendall took another sip. "Get to the point, KC."

KC shook her head. So much for a conversation starter. She opened her mouth to speak, but no words came out. She tried again. Still nothing.

"Lonnie Truvall, huh?" Kendall cut straight to the heart of the matter. Three words laid it all on the table.

KC nodded, mute and unable to change her condition for the moment.

"How long?" Kendall asked.

KC shrugged, then realized that actually words were required for this question. "About a year."

"Oh, honey." Kendall set her glass on the desk and squeezed KC's hand. KC in turn gripped the arm of the chair like life itself hung in the balance. If she let go, all would be lost.

The tears started again, completely without KC's consent. She thought she'd got it all out at Lonnie's office, but acknowledging their affair to Kendall brought her raw emotions to the surface again. She was not a neat crier. She wasn't one of those women who could cry silently for a few minutes, wipe her eyes, then look as though nothing was wrong a few moments later. No, when she cried, she committed to the act. Her shoulders shook, snot mixed with the tears, and she sniffled hard to hold it all back. She couldn't talk beyond a monosyllabic repeat of sound. "I...I...I...I...I." Crying for KC was undignified and messy.

Kendall handed her a box of tissue and waited. KC blew her nose enough times for the pile of used tissue on the side table to grow larger than the unused portion left in the box. She cried until nothing was left in her. Then she sucked in a deep breath and hiccupped.

"Done with that now?" Kendall's voice wasn't nearly so soft as before.

KC nodded. "I think so."

She expected Kendall to have questions, but so far she seemed content to sit and listen. That made KC feel like an even bigger fuck-up.

After several minutes had passed without a word from Kendall, KC said, "I love her." That wasn't entirely accurate, but telling Kendall that she wanted her and wasn't willing to not have her when the opportunity came up sounded far too jaded. The truth embarrassed KC.

"Pshh." Kendall didn't hesitate to respond. "Then you're a fool."

KC dropped her head in her hands. She couldn't argue the point.

Kendall sighed. "Tell me how it started."

KC hesitated. How did it begin? Did it even matter? "I've always had a crush on her, starting in high school." She remembered staring at Lonnie during Sunday dinners when she was fourteen and too young to do anything except yearn and be confused by it all.

"You know what? I don't care how it happened. First of all, stop calling her Lonnie. She's Mama's friend. Call her Mrs. Truvall."

"Okay." Kendall was right. The difference between Lonnie and Mrs. Truvall was clear in KC's mind. One was her lover, the other her mama's good friend. The line blurred from time to time, like when Lonnie lured her upstairs in her mama's house, but she never lost sight of it. Still, she couldn't remember if she'd begun calling her Lonnie before or after they began their affair.

"Now, let's talk about what a stupid, selfish girl you're being."

KC was offended. Instead of ready to cry, she was ready to fight. "Way to be supportive, Kendall."

"I'm not supportive of this. Dammit, KC! You're fucking with our whole family here. Am I supposed to say 'Nice job'? or 'Better luck next time'? What's the appropriate response when a person finds out her baby sister's sleeping with her mama's friend? I sure as hell haven't seen a Hallmark card for this one."

"Stop being so dramatic. It has nothing to do with you." KC knew that wasn't true, but the words still flew out of her mouth.

"Really? When you show up on my front porch looking a mess and wanting sympathy for your broken heart, how is it not my business? Do you realize how much this would hurt Mama if she found out? Do you even care?"

"Of course I care." The words sounded hollow and false. If KC didn't believe it, no chance she would convince Kendall.

"Well, you have to end it. Mama doesn't know anything yet. I'm sure of that. She always tells me when Lonnie's out cattin' around. How she kept word of this from Mama, I'll never know."

The floor dropped from beneath KC. "What do you mean she tells you?" KC whispered.

"Glen is a saint. For all Lonnie's running around, he stays with her." Kendall continued her rant without answering. "God knows he has enough worries right now with Leann, without adding you to the mix. Not that he's completely innocent, mind you. They have the most functional dysfunctional relationship I've ever seen."

"What do you mean she tells you?" KC asked again, her voice stronger this time.

Kendall stopped and looked hard at her. "Oh, God, KC. You don't think you're the only one, do you?"

She didn't think it. She knew it. Lonnie had told her she was special, that she meant something. She was worth the risk. KC swallowed and gave a weak nod. "I am."

"I'm sorry, honey, but you're not. Think! She's obviously willing to cheat on her husband, with her good friend's daughter, no less. What makes you think she has any scruples at all?" Kendall delivered her message with deadly precision. She sliced away what little faith KC had in her relationship.

It didn't change anything. KC shrugged. "I still want her."

"How can you? She's a cheat and a liar and she seduced my baby sister and I could kill her." Kendall glanced at her gun cabinet, another heirloom inherited from their grandfather.

"It's not that simple." KC couldn't let Kendall put all the blame on Lonnie, but she had no idea what to say to redirect her.

"Then break it down for me, KC, because from where I'm sitting, it *is* that simple." Kendall spoke quieter, but with no less vehemence. She was angry, and KC hadn't expected that at all.

KC thought back. She'd wanted Lonnie for so long it was hard to remember the exact moment it changed from just wanting to both wanting and having. "I don't know. We flirted and then it just went further, but that doesn't make it Lo—Mrs. Truvall's fault." KC had been overwhelmed when Lonnie returned her attentions. Their first kiss had escalated quickly, and if KC let the memory run, she could almost feel the sensation of sliding her fingers inside Lonnie for the first time and hear her gasp, then plead for more. It had been exhilarating, intoxicating.

"And it's been happening for a year?"

KC nodded.

"Does Mr. Truvall know?"

KC's stomach dropped with the question. Thinking about Lonnie as married, thinking about the hurt she'd cause if Glen ever found out she was carrying on with his wife, it all made KC clench to the point of pain. "I don't know. I don't think so."

"What if he finds out? This isn't fair to him. He's a good man. He doesn't deserve to have his wife running around with a tart half his age. Not only is she having an affair, but this time it's with another woman. She's straight, KC!"

KC flinched at the word *tart*. Kendall wasn't attacking her full bore, but her words hit the target with unerring accuracy. She made KC feel cheap and dirty. She was miserable. She couldn't even argue Kendall's last point about Lonnie being straight. It sure didn't feel that way, but did it even matter?

Kendall dropped into the chair and took KC's hand. "You have to end it."

"I don't know how," KC whispered.

"Do you want to?"

"I don't know."

"KC…" Kendall let her name sit there, like a quiet accusation all on its own.

"I know, I know. But you say it like it should be easy. How would you feel if I told you that you had to leave Owen? Would you be able to do it?"

Kendall shook her head. "It's not the same thing."

"How is it not the same?"

"Because he's not some harlot on the verge of tearing apart my family!" Kendall yelled loud enough to be heard three towns over.

"I'm sorry." KC held out her palms in supplication. "I don't want it to be like this." She didn't want to feel like she was drowning every time she was alone with Lonnie. She didn't want to feel bereft when she couldn't see her. She didn't want to be jealous just knowing Lonnie's husband had more right to touch her than KC did, that he was the one holding her at night. She didn't want to feel used, like she was a toy for Lonnie to play with, but that's how she felt nearly all the time. And she certainly didn't want to feel like a cheap trick, sneaking around, afraid of being caught.

"You really don't understand how bad this is, do you? If news gets out, it'll shake up the whole town. Lonnie and Glen will get divorced. There's no way for him to look the other way on this one. Think about their kids, KC. The boys are away in the Middle East, but Leann's still here. She's in high school. Imagine how much crap she'd get over something like this. Mama and Daddy will be heartbroken. Mama will have to start hating a friend she's had since high school. She's known her a hell of a lot longer than you've been alive, but her baby will come before her friendship. Not that you deserve it. The way you're acting. I swear."

Kendall shook her head, took a breath, and kept going. "What would happen at church? Lonnie and Mama have been in that choir together forever. What happens when they're suddenly standing on opposite ends of the risers? Or, better yet, one of them quits. You know how this town is. Remember when you came out? This will be a hundred times worse. Are you ready for all the stares, the whispers when you walk by? Are you ready to put Mama and Daddy through that? Trina? Me? Our kids? Think about someone other than yourself for ten seconds."

Everything Kendall said was true, and that hurt. She'd always known the things Kendall said, but having her lay it out like a bad prophecy made the possibilities real. For the first time, the damage she could do was more important than the excitement of being with Lonnie. She gave up. "I don't know what to do, Kendall."

"Baby, I'm telling you, you have to end it. This only leads to disaster."

"I know." The road had run its course. She was square in the middle of misery.

"KC, you tell her. Or I will." Kendall squared her shoulders. Big-time lawyer or not, offering to take on a woman who used to spank her bottom when she misbehaved was no small thing. KC was flattered. "This needs to end."

"No. I'll do it." KC wiped her hands over her eyes. "I made this mess. I need to clean it up." She still had no idea what that meant, but it wasn't Kendall's to fix. She'd gotten what she needed from her big sister—sideways moral support and a dose of tough love.

"If you change your mind…" KC knew her sister's words were more than empty platitude. Kendall was a fierce defender of those she loved. She had KC's back.

KC's smile felt stretched and unnatural. She hoped it didn't look as bad. She needed to stop wallowing and let her sister get back to her family. Before she went, though, she couldn't resist teasing to help set the air right between them. She didn't want Kendall to remember her as a crying Jezebel. "You know, you're slipping." She nudged the stack of sixty-page college-rule spiral notebooks on Kendall's desk that Kendall had used to keep track of her thoughts since they were kids. Recording the history of their childhood she'd noticed details no one else ever saw.

"I don't know how I missed it." Kendall returned her smile and placed her hand on top of the journals. The message was clear: tease all you want, but don't touch. "Hell, the whole family thought you were involved with Emma and just waiting to tell us."

KC looked up, bewildered. "Why would I do that?"

"I don't know." Kendall threw up her hands. "Why would you fuck your mama's friend?" Kendall swore with the best of them, but she was rarely vulgar.

KC recoiled at the force of Kendall's statement. The tension that had drained from her returned. She swallowed it down. "That's a fair statement, I suppose."

Kendall pushed both hands through her hair. She had a fabulous mane that looked hairdresser-fresh no matter what she did to it. She blew out a heavy sigh and her shoulders sagged. "No, it wasn't. I'm just surprised by all this. I'm never surprised, KC. Ever. I always see things coming before they hit me. And you've been sleeping with Mrs. Truvall for a year. A *year!*"

"Well, I'm sorry to disappoint," KC said, then turned the conversation away from Lonnie. "Emma and I are just friends." She thought of Emma—sweet, supportive, neurotic Emma. Had Mama and Lonnie been as close as she and Em when they were kids? It would shatter Mama if the truth came out. KC felt like an asshole for putting her in that position. Why hadn't she thought of it that way before?

KC stood. The conversation needed to conclude. "I think I'm okay to drive, so I'm going to head out."

"Wait, there's one more thing." When they had talked about KC and Lonnie, Kendall had looked incredulous. Murderous, but caught off guard. The danger was in her eyes again, but now she seemed calculating. It was her turn to drop the serious bomb. "We need to discuss Trina."

KC sat back down. "Have you talked to her?"

"I don't want to scare her." Kendall hummed thoughtfully. "What do you know?"

"Nothing." KC wanted to be clear. If she *knew* anything, she would have already acted. She wasn't so distracted by her own life that she wouldn't help her family. "But I suspect plenty."

"Like?" The air in Kendall's office got thicker. Yes, the business with Lonnie was serious, but KC wasn't in physical danger.

"Like she has a lot of bruises and she never smiles. And she walks like a woman who has something to be afraid of." There was more, but those were the key points.

"Well, you can move all that from the *suspect* category into the *know* category." Kendall looked sadder than KC had ever seen her. She was the self-appointed protector of KC and Trina. Clearly she felt she'd failed in her role as guardian.

KC didn't take time to indulge her. "What are we going to do about it?" She remained seated through force of will. In her mind, her body had moved from her grandfather's chair to the gun cabinet in the corner. She could feel the slide of the shotgun shells as she fed them into the chamber.

Kendall scolded her. "First thing we're not going to do is rush over there guns ablazing." KC's desires were more transparent than she realized.

She was surprised Kendall was being so levelheaded. Ten minutes ago she was ready to take her rifle after Lonnie. Now she was telling KC not to be rash. As far as KC could tell, a little rashness was in order.

"Don't tell me I can't kick the bastard's ass. It's my right as a Texan." KC should have asked Kendall for details, asked for proof, but Kendall's word was enough. She didn't want the graphic images of her sister's suffering in her head. She'd never be able to shake it.

Kendall's mouth quirked upward. "Absolutely. But first let's worry about Trina."

When KC left Kendall's house, she felt much better. Her troubles with Lonnie paled compared to what her sister faced. She could help her and sort out her own mess later.

❖

Emma entered the side door without knocking. "Are you going to cook or should I order pizza?" KC had a lot of work to do to get her small house in order before Trina could move in. Emma was there to help.

"I'm not the only one who knows how to cook, ya know." KC set the pile of books she was carrying on the couch.

"Come to my house, I'll cook for you. Your house, you cook."

"Did you come here just to give me shit? Or are you here to help?" KC smiled her first real smile since leaving Lonnie's office earlier that day. Emma had been there for thirty seconds and already she felt better. Emma settled her heart.

"It's kind of a package deal." Emma rifled through the menus in KC's kitchen drawer. "Julian's?"

"Mmm, no pepperoni this time." KC made it halfway down the hall toward the bedrooms and thought better of it. She returned to the kitchen and gave Emma a brief hug. "Thanks for being here."

Emma looked bewildered. "Of course." They smiled at each other stupidly for a moment, and then Emma visibly regrouped. "So what exactly is the plan? Why are we clearing your office?"

"Kendall has decided for us to go tomorrow while Jackson's at work and collect Trina and Buddy. Kendall's house is too full, and she doesn't think Trina would want to go back to Mama and Daddy's right now. I agree. That leaves here." KC made a sweeping gesture. She'd inherited the house and thought Trina would find it a comfort and draw strength from being surrounded by memories of their maternal grandmother. She'd been the family matriarch and the strongest woman they all knew. Kendall especially strived to be just like her—strong, capable and trustworthy. KC and Trina were still a work in progress.

While they waited for the pizza to arrive, KC and Emma set about rearranging the furnishings in KC's house. The guest bedroom was already good to go. It held a bed, a dresser, and not much else. It would do for Trina. The spare room, KC's office, was another story. It was full of KC's work. An heirloom oak desk sat in the middle and was home to her oversized iMac. She loved the computer because the screen was big enough for her to not go blind trying to read online essays. It wasn't easy to move, however. She also had three large filing cabinets: one stuffed full with records, the second well on its way, and the third waiting its turn. The online school she worked for required each teacher to maintain records for several years. They were too heavy to move on their own, but Emma had brought her daddy's hand truck.

She hated to pack up her office and move it to a corner of the living room, but it seemed the only way. Hell, Trina might not even want the room for Buddy. She might prefer to keep him close, put his crib in her new room. But it couldn't stay like that for long. Trina was pregnant and Buddy would have to make the sacrifice of big brothers the world over and give up his bed to the new baby. Besides, if the room was empty and ready, maybe Trina would feel like less of a burden. She doubted it, but she had to try.

The doorbell rang as she was hauling her teachers' manuals from office to living room. She added them to the stack on her couch and cursed. "Em, pizza's here."

KC smoothed her hair and hoped she looked halfway presentable. Odds were against it with as much dust and sweat she'd been mired in for the past hour. God, it'd been a long day. KC glanced at the wall clock. It was barely seven thirty. She still had a long evening of work in front of her.

Glen Truvall stood on the porch. The light of day dimmed behind him, and the porch light flickered on before KC could convince her mouth to work. What in the holy hounds of hell brought this man to her home, unannounced, at night? She felt faint.

"Mr. Truvall." KC unlatched the screen door and pushed it open. "What a surprise to see you."

KC cast a look behind her. Emma had disappeared. She didn't know if she should be thankful or disappointed. The last thing she wanted was for Glen to tear her ass up in front of Emma, but Emma's support was a balm. She could make it through anything, even this conversation, with Emma there to guide her.

Glen stepped into the kitchen, his shoulders square and his back straight. He looked like a man with marching orders. "Well, KC, I was hoping we could talk."

Panic flooded her and she felt the blood drain from her face. A voice in her head screamed, *Run! Run you damn fool!* Her feet were nailed to the floor. "About..." The word barely scratched out and she swallowed hard. She craved a tall glass of water. Or a short glass of Jack Daniel's. Either would do. She tried again, "About what, sir?"

Glen twirled his hat in his hands and looked around the room. "I haven't been here since your grandma passed. Looks good."

KC could barely breathe for trying to figure out what Glen wanted She was in no condition to give him a tour of the house that doubled as a stroll down memory lane. "Thank you, sir." The anticipation was damn near killing her.

"This is harder than I thought it would be." His shoulders slumped a bit, but he continued to twirl his Stetson like it was a damn baton. KC wanted to yank it out of his hands. Maybe that would help him speak.

"Mr. Truvall, would you like to come in and have a seat?" If he was here to kill her, so be it. It was his right to seek retribution. That didn't give her the right to be impolite, even though she would have preferred to keep him on the porch where Emma couldn't overhear.

Glen moved inside and selected a chair at the kitchen table. KC poured them both a glass of iced tea and sat opposite. She liked having the distance of the table between them.

Glen took a long pull, drinking half the glass. "KC, I don't quite know where to start."

She waited, sure that Glen was here to call her out about Lonnie. She was also sure she deserved whatever he sent her way. That didn't mean she wanted to rush him through the process. Besides, her lungs were seizing up with fear and guilt. Toxic combination, those two. She could barely suck in a breath. Black spots circled her vision, and the threat of passing out grew stronger with each moment.

"It's about Leann." Leann was Lonnie and Glen's youngest child. At seventeen, she was quite the handful. Still, KC couldn't imagine what she could do that would have anything to do with Glen avenging Lonnie's honor in her kitchen. She tried to take a deep breath, but her lungs refused to cooperate. Her body was in full-on panic mode.

"When I mentioned to your daddy what's going on, he suggested that I talk to you. He said you'd help," Glen said.

It didn't seem as though he was here to kill her, but she couldn't be sure just yet. She relaxed incrementally and tried to breathe again. It worked well enough for her to ask, "What am I helping you with, sir?"

"Oh, that's right. I need to tell you." At this point, Glen was speaking more to himself than to KC. She'd never seen him so upside down. "Well, you see, she's a lesbian."

It was an odd thing for Glen to blurt out. And even odder that he thought KC should help her with it. Odder still that Lonnie had never mentioned it. If it troubled Glen enough to seek her out at home, why hadn't Lonnie said something to her?

"That's very nice, sir." KC wasn't sure what else to say. Perhaps a thank you was in order, since he clearly didn't have homicide on his mind. She would live another day, and that deserved a little gratitude.

"Yes, I imagine it is." Glen half smiled. "But we're worried about her, Lonnie and I. She's been withdrawn…sad. And she just won't talk to us."

"I'm sorry." KC remembered being seventeen and trying to sort out her sexuality in this small Texas town. She'd been fortunate enough to have a supportive family. She could have just as easily found herself exiled. "I'm sure she'll come around. She's lucky to have you."

"I hope so, but it breaks my heart to think she's going through this alone."

"Sir, can I ask, how do you know she's gay if she won't talk to you?" It was a legitimate question. They could be making a completely inaccurate assumption. Hell, Leann could be sad about not getting a new pony for Christmas.

"She told her mama flat out about a month ago. We've been trying to get her to talk to us ever since. But she keeps herself locked in her room most days. Won't even come down for dinner."

Lonnie had been worried about Leann for a month and KC knew nothing about it. Why was Glen the one sitting at her kitchen table? She'd seen Lonnie a half-dozen times in the past few weeks, plenty of opportunity to talk.

"How does Mrs. Truvall feel about all this? Does she know you're here?" KC tried to focus on the conversation, but her brain kept jumping back to Lonnie. She cared for Lonnie enough to put her life on hold just for the chance to spend a few stolen minutes together, yet Lonnie cared so little she never mentioned a real problem in her life. What did this mean for them? And why did KC even care? Their relationship was as good as over. It was just going to take her some time to work up to good-bye.

"Lonnie doesn't know what to do. She's beside herself with worry. Leann is her baby, you know. She doesn't have any idea I'm here. Frankly, I'm not sure she'd approve. But we have to do something."

"And what is it you want me to do?" KC circled back to her earlier question. She still couldn't see what this had to do with her.

Glen looked at her like perhaps he was seeing her for the first time. "You're a lesbian, aren't you?"

KC thought about saying no just to see how he'd react. He looked ready to apologize for calling her a dirty name. But given the circumstances, she couldn't. "Yes, I am."

"Can't you talk to her? Give her someone older to discuss things with? So she can ask questions." Glen reached across the table, his palm outstretched. "I'm worried about her, KC. A father doesn't like to see his little girl suffer. I may not like all this, but she's still my baby and she's hurtin'."

"Are you sure that's a good idea, sir?" If Leann wanted to talk with her, she'd have already done it. They'd been eating Sunday dinner together since Leann was born. It's not like she had no idea how to get ahold of KC. Not to mention she didn't feel like a very good example of what good, honest lesbian living looked like. Talk about awkward. What should she say? *Hey, kiddo, I know times are rough, but since I'm your mama's secret lover I thought I'd check in and see if you need a friend.*

"She needs someone. She used to have friends over all the time. Now? No one."

KC sighed. He was right. Maybe she could convince Emma to go along with her. She was better at reading people than KC. If someone didn't speak plain, she'd miss it. But Emma was more like Kendall, fluent in nuance and subtlety. "All right. I'll do it."

Glen stood, his mission completed. "Thank you, KC, really. This means a lot."

"Happy to do it, sir." KC nodded, not at all pleased with what she'd gotten herself into. Having her lover's husband confront her out of the blue, then feeling so much relief that he hadn't found her out had clouded her judgment and impeded her speech filter. Her heart and head were spinning. She was mad as hell at Lonnie for keeping such an important secret, worried about Leann, and certain the whole deceptive cluster fuck would crash in on her at any minute.

KC shook his hand and bid him good night just in time for the pizza to arrive. Emma materialized at her side with a twenty-dollar bill and a smile for the driver.

Chapter Six

KC stretched, working the sleep out of her system. Emma's body was hot and tousled next to her. After the day she'd had, last night KC had needed to recharge. She needed Emma's comforting presence. They'd always slept in the same bed, starting when they were little. It never occurred to KC that should change, even when she was old enough to own a house with a spare bedroom. Emma belonged beside her.

She couldn't imagine it any other way, but apparently her sister could. And that caught KC off guard. She evaluated Emma as she slept. Did Emma realize that other folks thought they were a couple? What would she think about it? The notion had seemed ludicrous to KC the day before, but was it really such a bad idea?

KC smoothed Emma's hair away from her face. She was a classic beauty, with flawless skin, honey-blond hair, and a smile that brought out the sun. But she hadn't been smiling much lately and still hadn't told KC why. Emma shifted and rolled closer. She dropped her arm over KC's waist and KC returned the embrace, her body heating at the touch. In the half-awake moments of early morning, she had to work harder than usual to control her physical reaction to Emma.

They'd slaved clearing out KC's office, and she felt guilty disturbing Emma's rest. But they'd slept as long as they dared. Any longer and they'd be late.

"Wake up, Em. I'm taking you to breakfast." KC spoke gently in Emma's ear, then kissed her cheek. All perfectly normal. The flare of heat in her cheeks was not.

"Dun wanna." Emma mumbled and held KC tighter. She never woke up easy.

"We're meeting Kendall, remember?" KC shook Emma lightly. "Come on, hon. We've got a long day ahead of us."

Emma whined. "KC. Quit moving."

She walked her fingers down Emma's side and Emma squirmed. When she reached the narrow part of Emma's waist, Emma jumped out of bed with a glare. "Dammit, I'm up." She stomped to the bathroom mumbling about *tickling* and *not fair.*

They arrived at Over Easy a few minutes before Kendall, and KC gloated when she rushed in to find them already seated and holding menus.

"Sorry," Kendall said as she slid into her seat. "Kids." That was enough of an explanation for KC. Kendall's brood were well behaved for the most part, but it still took effort get them all pointed in the same direction.

"Hey, girls. Two days in a row." Roxy poured coffee for Kendall and Emma, and set a juice in front of KC. "What did I do to deserve this?"

KC winked. "Just lucky, I guess."

Kendall smacked her. "No flirting with the straight girls." For good measure she kicked KC's shin beneath the table. Her gaze darted to Emma and back to KC.

"All right, damn, I'm sorry." KC rubbed her leg.

Roxy laughed and walked away. "I'll be back to get your order."

Emma nudged her. "Look, Leann's over there. Didn't you want to talk to her?"

KC turned in her seat. In the back left corner of the restaurant, Leann sat in a corner booth. With Lonnie.

"Now isn't the best time." KC had too much to sort out before she could approach Lonnie. Just because her head knew what she had to do didn't mean her heart and mouth were on board with the decision. And her body clearly had other ideas.

"Shouldn't Leann be in school now?" Emma asked.

"Yes. What do you need to talk to her about?" Kendall unrolled her silverware and set the napkin in her lap. She looked deliberately casual, which frightened KC.

"Nothing urgent." At least KC hoped it wasn't urgent. She glanced behind her at Leann again. She looked sullen, but fine. Unfortunately, she couldn't see inside the girl's mind. She could be two steps from throwing herself off a building, and KC wouldn't know it. "Mr. Truvall stopped by last night and asked me to speak to her. Seems he and Mrs. Truvall are worried about her." KC was careful with her use of Lonnie's surname.

KC studied Leann a while longer but saw no signs of impending mental breakdown. She darted a glance at Lonnie and was met with a hard glare. Only Lonnie wasn't focused on her. She was looking directly at Emma. And Emma was glaring back just as hard.

"Everything okay, Em?" KC asked.

"What?" Emma turned her attention away from Lonnie. "Yeah. Fine."

Roxy returned to take their order. This time Kendall asked for pancakes and bacon instead of a fruit plate. She shrugged. "It's going to be a rough day. I'm storing up."

Emma ordered French toast with strawberries, and KC requested oatmeal. Her stomach was in knots, and she didn't imagine them easing at all as the day progressed.

"What does Mr. Truvall want you to talk to Leann about?" Kendall asked.

"How to be a lesbian in twelve easy steps," Emma stated between sips of coffee.

Kendall raised an eyebrow. "What? Does he want you to give her lessons or something? If that isn't just a fuck-all mess, I don't know what is."

"No. Jesus, Kendall." KC almost spit her juice all over the table. "She's depressed, and he thinks talking to me might help."

"You're the Dalai Lama for lesbians now? Christ."

"Now you're just being absurd. I'm a teacher. I've been trained to relate to young people. And me and Emma are probably the only lesbians Mr. Truvall even knows."

"Yeah, if you don't count his wife." Kendall mumbled the words into her coffee mug and KC's ears burned. She hoped like hell Emma hadn't heard. She wasn't ready to explain that remark to her. Kendall lowered her cup. "Now's your chance. Looks like Mrs. Truvall's headed to the bathroom."

Normally, the invitation from Lonnie would be implicit. If she left the room, KC found an excuse to follow. This time, sitting between Kendall and Emma, she couldn't think of a reason good enough to excuse herself to the little-girls' room behind Lonnie. And she wasn't at all sure she wanted to. Despite the promise of sex, the risk was too great. For the first time, she wasn't willing to take the chance.

"I'm not going to ambush the girl during breakfast." KC didn't want to talk to her at all, let alone between bites of oatmeal.

"I'm not saying you should treat her to a therapy session." Kendall rolled her eyes. "Go talk to her. Ask if you can get together later."

"She'll think I'm hitting on her."

"Not if you don't look at her like she's an appetizer. Seriously, KC, do lesbians not know the difference between having coffee with friends and inviting them to have sex?"

Emma and KC looked at each other, then turned toward Kendall at the same time. "Aren't they the same thing?" Emma asked.

"Lord," Kendall said. "I swear, you two. Just ask if you can get together to talk sometime. Tell her Mr. Truvall is worried about her. That doesn't sound like a come-on, does it?"

"Give it a rest. I'll talk to her when I see her on Sunday." KC felt superior. No way Kendall could argue with that. There was no point in approaching Leann in public today when she could wait a couple of days and speak to her in private.

Kendall wasn't deterred. "You won't be here Sunday, remember?"

"It's true. We're going to Austin." Emma wasn't helping by throwing in her dose of reality.

"Kendall, I don't want to. Tell me why she can't talk to Mrs. Truvall. Why me?" KC bordered on whiney and was irritating even herself. Still, she didn't want to go, dammit.

"Maybe he thinks you can teach her something about being a lesbian that you haven't taught Mrs. Truvall." Kendall smirked.

"Seriously? What the hell is that even supposed to mean?" KC couldn't believe Kendall would go there. Emma was sitting *right here*. Short of smacking Kendall in the head and saying *shut the fuck up*, she couldn't think of a way to effectively communicate that she hadn't told Emma about the affair.

For her part, Emma stared at her plate, then took another bite. No reaction to Kendall's big reveal at all.

"It means that if you have a heart at all, you need to try to help her. Yes, it's awkward. But think, for just a second, about how you felt at seventeen. Go talk to the girl."

"Okay." KC pushed back her chair. This was such a bad idea, but she'd promised Glen. Kendall and Emma stared at her like she needed to do something. She had no choice but to cross the dining room and slide into the booth Lonnie had just vacated opposite Leann.

"Hey." Smooth opening. If Leann didn't confide in her after that, she never would.

"What do you want?" Leann looked at KC levelly, not even the hint of a smile. This wasn't the girl who sat at the same table with her every Sunday.

"Just to say hi." Now that she was here, she had no clue what to say, and so far she was fucking it up. "How are you?"

"Seriously? Our entire relationship can be condensed to a series of polite greetings, and suddenly you show up looking to be friends? I don't think so." She folded her arms.

KC evaluated Leann. Whatever was going on with her, KC couldn't help unless she could convince her to talk. "I just thought you might want to talk." KC shrugged.

"Christ. Did she tell you?" Leann was on the verge of yelling. "I'm *fine*."

"Actually, your daddy came to see me last night. He's worried. I imagine your mama is, too." KC left out the part where she hadn't talked to Lonnie about her. She was still trying to figure out why that was, and she didn't want to explore the details with Leann.

Leann tossed her napkin onto her plate and crossed her arms. KC remembered doing the same moves in high school. She was trying to look bored and nonchalant, but came across as angry and pouting. "There's nothing to worry about."

"Okay, that's probably true. But they still are. Parents do that." She needed to find middle ground. She couldn't recall Leann ever being so defiant in the past. "Mine did it, too, when I was seventeen."

"Did they send someone around to harass you about it?"

"Harass? Leann, that's not what this is. I just want to help if I can."

"I don't want *your* help." Leann put way too much emphasis on *your*, and KC was starting to take it personally.

"Okay, this is going nowhere. I promised your daddy I'd talk to you." KC tried to sort her thoughts. Leann's attitude was making her angry and she needed to step back. "I'm headed out of town this weekend. I'll check with you some time next week."

"No. I don't want to talk. Even if I did, I wouldn't talk to you."

"Why not?" KC was done with Leann's attitude. She needed to get over it, and soon.

"Because," Leann spoke through gritted teeth and leaned close to the KC, "you're fucking my mother."

"Oh." KC reeled. She had no answer for that, but so many questions. So much for discretion. She could feel the fabric of her life unraveling.

"KC, how nice to see you." Lonnie had returned from the bathroom and waited at the edge of the table for KC to relinquish her seat.

"Perfect." Leann made a disgusted noise and slid out of the booth. "I'll wait in the car."

"Leann, wait." KC called after her, but Leann didn't slow.

"Let her go, sugar." Lonnie touched her shoulder and her hand threatened to melt right through her skin. Lonnie squeezed, then shifted to the seat Leann had vacated. She smiled, predatory and wanting. "I'd hoped you would follow me." She left the statement open like a question.

"Leann knows." With that knowledge fresh in her mind, KC couldn't flirt.

"Knows what?" Lonnie pitched her voice low and smooth. The subject of conversation had shifted, but Lonnie's thoughts were single-track.

"About us." KC worked to keep her face neutral. She felt exposed and dirty. "She knows about us."

"I'm aware of that." Lonnie sat posture-perfect, her hands folded in her lap. Her voice no longer oozed seduction. "I told her."

"What?" KC was incredulous. Lonnie had made her promise, over and over, to tell no one. Their future depended upon discretion. She shook her head and asked again, "What?"

"Glen came to your house last night, right?" Lonnie asked.

KC nodded. She wasn't able to connect her question to Lonnie's. It answered nothing.

"She's confused and scared and angry. I thought knowing that I understand what she feels like—"

"Are you fucking kidding me, Lonnie?" How could learning her mother was having an affair help a fucked-up kid cope? Even as self-absorbed as KC had been recently, she was sure that wasn't the answer.

"I was desperate." Lonnie shrugged like it was no big deal.

"And you didn't think to tell me?" KC was numb. This was a disaster.

"Relax. I'm not in the habit of talking to you about my family problems."

"Your family problems?" KC shook her head, speechless. "I gotta go." She didn't try to keep the anger out of her tone. She was flat-out pissed off, and Lonnie seemed clueless as to why. Or she just didn't care.

"Wait, sugar, I want to see you later." Lonnie was back on point toward seduction.

"I already have plans." KC shook her head and walked away. Lonnie wasn't the woman KC believed her to be.

Breakfast had been delivered while she was gone. Kendall and Emma were halfway through their pancakes and French toast respectively. Emma smiled, sad and sweet, and kept eating.

"Everything okay?" Kendall asked.

"Yeah. Thanks." KC hands shook when she unfurled her napkin. "Tell me about our plan."

"It's not very complicated. We wait until nine thirty, then head over and hijack Trina."

"She really doesn't know we're coming?" KC didn't agree with this part of Kendall's plan. Trina was a grown woman. She deserved a say in her fate.

Kendall shook her head. "She'd tell us not to."

"What about Mama and Daddy?" KC picked at her oatmeal, her appetite gone.

"Daddy'd shoot him," Kendall said.

To KC's mind, that wasn't a bad thing. Except she'd like to torture him first, draw it out a little before letting Daddy do him in. "Let him."

"I agree." Kendall finished eating and dropped her napkin on her plate. Nerves always made her eat faster than normal. "But let's get Trina out of the blast zone first."

"Makes sense," Emma said.

Life was a mess. KC supposed she should be thankful things hadn't blown up completely. She'd had a year to enjoy Lonnie. She'd always known the relationship was destined to end, but she wasn't sure she was ready to let go. As much as she needed to sort it all out, the troubles with Trina were much more immediate. Her own problems could wait.

Kendall looked at her watch and dropped a couple of bills on the table. "Nine twenty. Time to go."

All hell was about to break loose. KC focused on her family, resolved not to give Lonnie another thought.

Chapter Seven

"Emma's here." Trina let the curtain drop back into place over the kitchen window. Since Trina had moved in, she'd been hypersensitive to any unusual sounds. A car pulling into the driveway sent her on high alert.

KC unlocked the side door. They'd added deadbolts to both entrances. KC had debated an alarm system as well, but Trina resisted. Trina worried about the cost. KC worried about Trina.

"You sure you'll be okay alone this weekend?" KC was torn. When she'd agreed to go with Emma, she'd had no idea that Trina and Buddy would be moving in. "Emma would understand."

Trina deftly answered around the question. "I know. But this is a big deal for her. You should go."

"I'd feel better if we had an alarm system." They still had time to call the sales guy. He'd promised it could be in and operational by end of business Friday. Today was Friday and she would make him keep that promise. All she had to do was convince Trina.

"KC, stop. It's been three days. If Jackson was going to do anything, he would have already done it." Trina made a good point, but rationalizing the actions of another human was never the safest bet.

Emma entered carrying a large shotgun and a small puppy. "Hey, y'all." She kissed KC on the cheek, then Trina. "Here." She handed off the shotgun to KC and the puppy to Trina, then fished a box of shells from her pocket.

"What's this?" Trina spoke more to the squirming pit bull than to Emma.

"This," Emma pointed at the shotgun, "is for this weekend. And he's to keep you company."

Trina ignored the gun and cuddled the puppy. "What's his name?"

"That's up to you." Emma shrugged. "I signed him up for obedience training. If you don't have time to take him, I can at least get him started before I move."

"I'll take him. It'll give me something to do." Trina smiled wistfully. "I'm going to go introduce Buddy to his new pal."

Buddy was playing in his bedroom, formerly KC's office. Clearing it out had proved to be time well spent.

Emma watched Trina walk down the hall, a concerned frown on her face. "How's she settling in?"

"Fine, I guess." KC wished she knew the answer. "How are women in her situation supposed to act?"

"Good point." Emma reclaimed the 12-gauge. "Let's get this onto your gun rack."

The formal gun rack for hunting rifles and the large gun safe in KC's living room were left over from her grandfather, who'd preceded her grandmother in death by twenty years. KC barely remembered the man, but he'd left a mark on her life nonetheless.

"I'd rather put it in the safe." KC knew how to use a shotgun, just like any other good Texas woman, but she just preferred not to—a quirk left over from time spent in the liberal, tree-hugging Northwest.

"I'd rather Trina not have to fiddle with a safe when she should be feeding in shells." Emma bypassed the safe and set the shotgun on the empty rack. It hung high enough on the wall that Buddy wouldn't be able to touch it.

"You honestly think Trina would be able to use it on Jackson?" KC doubted it. Of the three sisters, Trina was the hunter. She was far more comfortable and accurate than KC. "It's not like Jackson doesn't have a whole slew of handguns and rifles at their place. If she wanted to shoot him, she'd have done it by now."

"I don't know, KC, but better safe than sorry." Emma set the shells on the ammo shelf. "I'd hate for her to need it and it not be here. Besides, the shells are filled with rock salt. My daddy loaded them for her. She can't kill him, but she'll sure as hell get his attention."

"Well, let's hope she won't need them."

When they'd gone to Trina's house Tuesday, it had been a surprising non-event. Trina didn't argue. She just packed her clothes, the things she needed for Buddy, and climbed into Kendall's car without comment. KC and Emma followed in Trina's car. The entire time KC waited for something to happen, for the big explosion, but it never came. None of the neighbors interfered. Jackson hadn't arrived home in a rush and demanded an explanation. Hell, Buddy hadn't even fussed about being taken away from *Sesame Street*. It all felt artificially calm, and KC still expected the floor to drop out at any moment.

"If you want to stay…" Emma slipped her hand into KC's.

"She doesn't want me to." KC wanted to protect her baby sister, but she wasn't willing to treat Trina like she was incapable of making her own decisions. She'd been mistreated enough. She needed to be trusted to think for herself.

Emma led the way to the bedroom. She was there to help KC finish packing, and then they were heading out.

"Sorry to spring the puppy on you without asking. It just seemed like the right thing to do."

"Let's hope she has him potty trained before I get back Sunday night." KC wasn't hopeful.

Her open suitcase lay on the bed. She'd managed to get one pair of jeans and her socks packed before Emma arrived.

"Is this all you plan to wear?" Emma nudged the jeans with her finger.

"Depends. You haven't told me what our plans are." That was partially why KC hadn't finished packing. She had no idea what would be appropriate.

"Well, we have to go dancing at least once." Emma held up a tiny black dress that was barely decent. "You want to wear this or jeans?"

"Jeans." No contest for KC. She wasn't looking for a date, and her ass looked great in jeans without anyone being able to see up it. "That way I can wear my Ropers."

Emma looked disappointed when she returned the dress to the closet. "And I have a meeting with my new boss. You're free to roam the city for the thirty minutes I'll be tied up."

"Duly noted."

"I need to find an apartment, too. Can't move there without a place to live." Emma sat on the bed and gave up the pretense of helping.

KC sat next to her and pulled her into a side-arm hug. "I can't believe you're really doing it."

"Me either." Emma leaned into KC's embrace for a moment, then straightened. "That suitcase isn't going to pack itself." She patted KC on the knee, the signal for her to get moving again.

KC finished in short order. A few shirts, a few pairs of jeans, panties, bras, and toiletries. She was set.

"Let me just check in with Trina before we take off." KC zipped the suitcase and lifted it off the bed. She'd inherited the hard-side Samsonite with the house, solid and indestructible. KC rolled it into the kitchen and found Kendall sitting at the table talking to Trina.

"I didn't hear you come in." KC gave Kendall a quick hug. "How long have you been here?"

"Just a few minutes. I decided to escape my husband and children and have a girls' weekend with Trina. Owen's taking Buddy to Mama's and that leaves just the two of us."

KC'd never been happier to see Kendall. Apparently she wasn't the only one having a hard time leaving Trina alone so soon.

Trina sat with the puppy in her lap. "I'm going to give her a makeover."

"There's a bottle of Absolut in the freezer. The Jack and Jose are in the cupboard over the stove." KC was all in favor of a makeover, accompanied by some serious drinking. That was enough to solve any problem under the sun. KC gave the dog a pat on the head. "Pick a name yet?"

"Berty," Trina said. She snuggled the puppy for a moment then set him back in her lap.

"Where'd you get that from?" Emma asked.

"Liberty. I know it's cheesy, but it felt right." Trina shrugged.

"Perfect," KC said.

Emma took KC's suitcase and headed toward the door. "I'll wait in the car. Bye y'all." She waved at the sisters and exited.

"Kendall." KC paused. Her heart was full of so many things she wanted to say, but it all boiled down to one word. "Thanks."

"Of course." Kendall smiled. "I want to be here." Kendall felt bad about not being able to take Trina in at her place. She'd said it to the point of annoyance over the past few days. This gave her the opportunity to assuage her guilt and get away from her kids for a brief sanity break. Total win-win. "Besides, Owen is going fishing next weekend. He owes me."

"Trina, if you need anything, you have my number. Kendall, don't drink all my vodka." KC was halfway out the door when she remembered the other half of Emma's presents earlier. "And there's a shotgun on the gun rack. Shells are on the shelf below."

KC waved good-bye and headed out the door.

❖

Emma looked more relaxed than she had in weeks. She had the top down, her sunglasses on, and her hair held back in a long braid. A few long strands worked their way free in the wind, and she tucked them behind her ear. When she'd graduated from UNLV, her dad had given her a Mini Cooper that he'd picked up used at a police auction. Emma jokingly referred to it as her blood-money car since he'd given it as an *I'm sorry for leaving you and your mama with no money and no way for her to support you.* Emma had taken the car, but KC didn't think she'd ever truly forgive him for the way he'd gone.

"Thanks for letting me come with you." KC spoke with a formality that was typically missing in their casual relationship, but she wanted to make sure Emma knew she loved her. She appreciated her friendship. She laced their fingers together and held Emma's hand. The smooth press of Emma's palm comforted and calmed her. The past week had been filled with stress. Emma was her oasis.

"I'm sorry you had to leave Trina."

KC shrugged. "She's with Kendall. God knows she's more capable than I am." If Jackson knew what was good for him, he'd stay clear of Kendall.

"Good point." They rolled past CVS, the only drugstore in town. "Do you need anything last-minute?"

"I'm good."

Just past the CVS was Truvall Furniture and Appliance. KC waved to Glen, who looked to be leaving work for the evening. Shannon Lewis walked beside him and both returned the wave. Shannon, who worked for Glen, was a couple of years behind Trina in school and at twenty-two was earning a decent living selling TVs to aging men who liked to watch football on high-definition sets sold by a hot young blonde. KC agreed that all things looked better when a beautiful blonde was involved. Glen helped Shannon into the passenger seat of his Explorer.

"We should have left a little earlier. We're going to hit afternoon traffic," Emma observed.

She was right. It seemed every business in town released their employees onto the streets at once. Rush hour was a thing KC had very little personal experience with, one of the many benefits of telecommuting. She spotted Jackson's Jeep as it pulled into the line of traffic a couple of blocks up, and her daddy passed her going the other way.

KC loved this town. She loved her life and the connection she shared with every other person in it, the way they were all woven together. Her affair with Lonnie threatened to unravel it all. She felt a rush of sadness. She'd been blinded by lust and very foolish with her lack of thought for others. Her friends and family deserved better.

"Why do you want to leave?" KC'd never asked Emma to explain her need to move away from Fairmont. She'd just accepted it.

"I don't belong here." Emma's smile was sad and reflective. "Not since high school. I'm amazed you haven't left."

High school had been miserable for both of them. KC'd gone from high-school royalty to loser overnight when she came out. Sophomore year, Emma had stopped talking to her for months when she'd found KC panting beneath the bleachers with Traci Newman. She'd been half naked and well on her way to losing her virginity. Emma's silence had been far worse than her fall from grace in the hierarchy of high-school popularity. She'd been exhausted. The work that went into creating a false image of herself—perfect boyfriend, perfect friends, perfect grades, perfect looks—was just too much. When her boyfriend accused her of being a frigid lesbian, she'd cracked and screamed the truth at him. The next day it was all over the school.

Thank God she'd reconciled with Emma, or she would have been alone through all of it. Emma had saved her from despair. It was a time in her life that KC worked hard to forget. She'd felt so lost, so out of control. She never wanted to feel that way again. When they got back from Austin, KC would try to talk to Leann again. No one deserved to go through that alone.

"There was a time when I couldn't wait to get out of this town." That was a large part of the reason she'd picked the University of Washington in Seattle. It was a good school and far away from Fairmont in every sense. Physically she couldn't have gone much farther and still been in the continental United States. The big difference, however, was the social atmosphere. It was okay to be a young woman who loved other women. Seattle was where she found herself. "But I missed my family. I missed you. Fairmont is my home."

"I wish I'd been a better friend back then." Emma regretted running away from KC. She'd told her more than once. The pressure to fit in, to do the right thing, in their small Texas town, could be overwhelming. At the time KC hadn't understood, but later, when Emma herself came out at UNLV, it made sense. She hadn't wanted people to think she was gay by association, especially when they would have been right.

"I don't think Leann will ever talk to me." It was a hard truth for KC. She hated the thought that the girl was suffering alone and even more that her selfish actions had made it impossible for KC to offer the help Leann needed.

"Probably not."

"Can you try?" It wasn't exactly what Glen had asked of KC, but it was a better solution all around. Even without the extra layer of complication, Emma was a better listener than KC.

"I will." Emma looked at her briefly. "But I don't know that she'll want to talk to me any more than you. I'm your best friend after all."

KC nodded. There was nothing else to say. At least this way she could say that, between the two of them, they'd tried.

Traffic eased as they passed the city-limits sign. Plenty of folks traveled into town from their farm for work, but they knew the roads and drove them fast in their quest to get home.

"Em, I love you, okay?" KC squeezed back tears. This trip, the impending loss of her friend, was making her sentimental.

Emma swallowed. "I love you, too."

They both waved at the picture of the mayor on the billboard thanking them for visiting Fairmont. Emma dropped her hand back into KC's, and they drove southwest toward Austin.

Chapter Eight

It was almost ten when they rolled through Round Rock on highway 79. A little farther and they'd be able to call it a night. They'd been driving the back roads for almost five hours, minus a stop to use the restroom, and KC was feeling claustrophobic. Emma's car was cute as hell, but not particularly comfortable for a long drive. Austin had never looked so good.

KC reclined the seat back as far as it would go and stretched her arms and legs. "Next time we're taking my car."

"First of all, no way your Accord would make it this far. It's a piece of shit. Second, it wouldn't have been any more comfortable. And third, stop bitching." Emma was tired of driving, which made her more charming than usual.

"It's time to upgrade. I'm going to buy a Camaro." KC had been officially out of school and working for two years. She was overdue for a new vehicle. And the longer she sat in the Mini, the more she wanted a car with some room and an engine that wasn't powered by a complicated network of rubber bands and small rodents.

"Next road trip, we're taking yours," Emma agreed.

KC threw a stale french fry at Emma. "Did you make a reservation?"

"No." The look Emma gave KC said *Don't be stupid*.

They'd gone on countless road trips and never once made a reservation. It was part of the adventure. They drove, then found a place to sleep when they arrived. The tradition had been born out of necessity when they were seventeen. They were too young to have a credit card to make reservations and didn't always tell their parents *exactly* where they planned to sleep for the weekend.

KC's first gay-bar experience involved an unauthorized road trip to Austin, a fake ID, and a night in a pay-by-the-hour hotel that took cash and didn't care about a deposit. The experience had been eye opening. But KC was no longer a teenager sneaking out of her parents' house. She was twenty-six and had plenty of plastic in her wallet to guarantee a reservation. She was tired enough to think it was time to start a new tradition on their next trip.

"I'm beat," she said.

Emma yawned. "Me, too. This trip never used to make me so tired."

"Face it. We're getting old." KC was only half teasing

"Just for that, I'm making you take me dancing tonight."

"God, no, Em. Please, can't we just get a room and sleep? We can snuggle and watch bad porn on pay-per-view." After the week she'd had, KC was pretty sure she'd never fully catch up on her rest.

Emma looked at KC for a brief moment then shifted in her seat, and the air in the car changed from comfortable to awkward. Finally she said, "No, we're definitely going dancing."

KC didn't argue. She never won when Emma was like this.

A few miles past the Austin city-limits sign, she turned into a La Quinta. The lot was nearly empty and she parked directly across from the lobby. KC was thankful to get out of the car.

"You get the room." Emma lit a cigarette while she was still seated. Her strict no-smoking-in-the-car rule was apparently on hiatus.

KC paid for the room for two nights and asked for two electronic keys instead of just one. Normally she'd be with Emma the whole time, so one would be enough. This time she wasn't sure where the day would take them. Emma had appointments and she had papers to grade. They really were getting old.

When she got back to the car, Emma was leaning against the trunk and starting on her second cigarette. KC handed her a room key and tucked the other in her back pocket.

"Pop the trunk, I'll grab the bags." She figured Emma could follow along when she finished, providing she didn't plan to smoke the whole pack.

"I'll finish this and clean out the car, then I'll be up." Emma patted the trunk. "Get your dancing shoes on while you're waiting."

KC had her belongings unpacked and tucked into drawers before Emma joined her. She used to leave her stuff in her suitcase and pull it out as she needed it, but wrinkles were less appealing to her now than ironing. Properly unpacking was the midpoint solution between the two. She heard Emma activate her key card and couldn't remember if she'd told her it was a non-smoking room.

Emma opened the door and stopped abruptly halfway in. Thankfully, she was cigarette free. She stared at the king-sized bed for a long moment, then finally stepped fully inside and closed the door.

"There's only one bed." Emma sounded nervous.

"Yeah, sorry. I didn't realize it until I got up here." KC didn't see the problem. They slept together all the time. Why should this be any different? Still, Emma looked on the verge of hyperventilating. "Do you want me to see if they can change it?"

"No, let's just get ready. It's already past ten. Rusty's will be packed by now."

The dim lights inside Rusty's made it hard for KC to see Emma's face. That was a problem since Emma had worn a red dress that drove KC to distraction. It swished around her thighs with every step and was cut low in the bodice and showed far too much cleavage. It was the type of dress KC would chase all night long if it wasn't hanging off Emma, so KC worked hard to keep her eyes focused above Emma's neck.

"Do you like my dress?" She twirled and the skirt flared up.

KC snorted beer through her nose. "Jesus." Someone pounded her on the back and offered a stack of bar napkins.

"Even if she doesn't, I sure do," the woman said. She had a deep, rich Spanish accent.

Emma squealed. "Maria!" She hugged the woman while KC continued to sputter.

Emma ended the hug and automatically moved her hand to KC's back, massaging a circular path over KC's low back that comforted and reassured. KC found it very disconcerting but didn't know why.

"How you doing?" Maria kissed Emma's cheek. Maria had olive skin and short black hair. She was trim, well muscled, and had dark, intense eyes. She was exactly the kind of girl KC had fucked in college. Then again, that could be said for most women she encountered during her undergrad years.

KC swelled with inexplicable possessiveness. Granted, she and Emma were just friends, but this Maria chick had no clue. She stood far too close to Emma, moving in despite the clear message that Emma wasn't alone. Emma dropped her hand away as soon as KC stopped choking on her beer.

"God, I'm good. It's been forever. It didn't even click that you'd be back in Austin." Emma smiled in a way that KC thought was reserved for her alone. Apparently not.

"I finished up two years ago and moved home." Maria shrugged, her smile a little too big for her face.

KC wrapped her arm around Emma and squeezed her waist. She was tired of being excluded. "Who's this?"

"Oh, KC, sorry." Emma blushed slightly. "This is Maria Gutierrez. We went to college together. Maria, this is KC."

"KC, huh?" Maria stuck out her hand and shook KC's gamely. "I've heard lots about you."

Funny. KC hadn't heard word one about Maria. "So, you're an old friend from Las Vegas?" KC had no idea why she emphasized the word *friend* so heavily, but it seemed an important distinction to make.

Emma hedged. "We were a little more than friends."

"A little? Remember that one weekend? We barely came up for air." Maria laughed. The look in her eyes said she'd be happy for a repeat performance, and KC angled herself between Emma and Maria. The thought of the two of them in bed together made her skin crawl.

Emma smiled awkwardly. "We had some fun."

"That we did." Maria smirked, then tilted her head toward the dance floor. "A dance? For old time's sake?"

Emma hesitated, then asked KC, "You okay? You choked pretty hard a second ago."

"I'll survive." KC forced herself to smile and reluctantly said, "Go ahead and dance. Have fun." She silently urged Emma to stay.

"If you're sure…" Emma eased past KC, their bodies touching lightly.

KC gripped Emma around her waist to hold her in place for a moment. Her thumbs played with the soft fabric over Emma's tummy. "Have fun," KC whispered in Emma's ear. She released her hold and watched as Emma walked to the dance floor with her ex-girlfriend.

Something about Maria was off. On the surface, KC admitted she looked fine. Better than fine. She couldn't put her finger on what was bothering her, but she fought hard against the urge to interrupt their dance, to protect Emma. Of course, Emma would likely belt her one. She didn't need protection from tall, dark, and handsome, especially when she'd already been with Maria.

KC frowned and headed toward the bar. She kept one eye on Emma as she ordered a fresh drink. She was done drinking beer.

"Can I get a whiskey sour?" She had to yell to be heard over the crowd.

The bartender had long auburn hair tucked beneath a white Stetson. She wore a western-cut shirt with pearl snaps, low-cut Wranglers, and a sexy smile. She nodded and mixed the drink.

KC divided her attention. It was never a good idea to take your eyes off your drink in a crowded bar, even when it was still in the hands of the bartender. Yet she couldn't look away from Emma. She had her arms looped around Maria's neck and looked far too cozy. They swayed to an old Patsy Cline song. This was the first time in KC's life she'd wanted Patsy to stop singing.

The bartender finished mixing the drink but didn't set it on the bar in front of KC. She winked and gestured for KC to follow her to the other end of the bar. KC followed. She wanted that drink, and it looked like she'd have a better view of Emma from there anyway.

"How much do I owe you?" The noise dimmed considerably the farther they got from the center of the bar so KC could speak normally.

The bartender ran a long, slender finger over the side of the glass, scooping up drops of condensation as she went. "On the house." Rather than set the drink down, she held it out for KC to take from her.

When KC tried to, she held it for a few extra seconds and said, "I'm Deena."

"Hey." KC glanced at Deena long enough to get her to release the drink, then returned her gaze to the dance floor just in time to see Maria pull Emma closer.

"It's time for my break." Deena spoke lowly and KC could feel her move closer. "You want to join me?" She motioned toward a door marked EMPLOYEES ONLY.

KC focused her full attention on Deena. She'd been so fixated on Emma, she'd missed the fact that this shit-hot woman was hitting on her. She smiled and tried to figure out how to say *no* gently. Obviously her relationship with Lonnie wasn't exclusive; Lonnie's husband made sure of that, but KC didn't feel right about random hookups. Not to mention she needed to make sure that Emma made it back to the hotel safely. It was her personal mission to wipe the smug smile off Maria's face when Emma left with KC at the end of the night instead of her.

"What do you say?" Deena's mouth curved into a slow, confident smile.

"That's really sweet." KC took a shuffling half step away from Deena. "And I'm flattered. But I'm spoken for."

Deena looked pointedly at the dance floor and KC followed her gaze. They landed on Emma as Maria slid her hands down to Emma's ass and squeezed.

"Looks like your girlfriend has other plans." Deena moved into the space KC had just backed out of and spoke into KC's ear. "And I'm not trying to be sweet."

The words traveled down KC's neck and spine on a shiver. Deena offered a distraction from her drama with Lonnie, from Emma's inviting red dress, and from Maria fucking Gutierrez's presumptuous hands. KC was tempted.

She studied Deena, her tight jeans, the open snaps that created a delicious *V* to guide KC into her cleavage, and her easy, inviting smile. Her gaze retuned to Emma as Emma pulled Maria's hands from her backside and stepped out of her arms. Their dance was over.

"Thanks. Really." KC raised her drink in a minor salute. "But I'm still going to pass." She took a sip of her drink and turned her full attention back to Emma.

Emma stood on the dance floor, unmoving in a sea of motion. She stared at KC, her eyes narrowed with a frown creasing her brow. She raised one eyebrow in a perfect question and looked pointedly at Deena.

KC shook her head and took a step toward Emma. Over her shoulder she said, "Thanks for the drink."

She met Emma halfway between the bar and the dance floor. Sweat glistened on Emma's forehead. Too many people were dancing, which made for a hot, sweaty time even for a slow dance.

KC slicked her thumb over the damp skin. "Did you have a nice time?"

Emma shrugged. "It was okay."

She wrapped her hand around KC's whiskey sour, covering KC's fingers. Cool glass pressed against her palm in contradiction to the heat of Emma's skin. KC felt faint.

"How's your drink?" Emma lifted the glass, and KC's hand, to her mouth and took a long sip. She held KC's gaze as she swallowed, then licked her lips. "Mmm, good."

Maria joined them and Emma released KC's hand.

"It was great seeing you, Emma." Maria kissed Emma's cheek. "Keep in touch, okay?"

Emma nodded in agreement and then Maria was gone. KC breathed easier.

"We should dance." Emma grinned at KC. This was their ritual at Rusty's. Emma insisted until KC eventually gave in and followed Emma onto the floor, at which point KC immediately felt like an uncoordinated oaf with no rhythm, and Emma flowed around her like music was hard-wired into her soul.

"I just got this." KC tipped the glass and took another sip. It would only stall Emma for so long.

"Let me help you with it." Emma downed half the glass, licked her lips, and then smiled Cheshire big and cheesy. "Yum."

KC held firm to her glass the next time Emma reached for it. She took a slow drink herself, then said, "So, you and Maria?"

Emma sighed. "That was a long time ago."

"Looked pretty current to me." KC pictured Maria's hands cupped around Emma's ass and saw a flare of red. Emma was too good to be groped in public.

"What you saw was crossed signals." Emma straightened KC's collar, then smoothed her palms over the fabric of KC's lapels. "She was trying to help."

"I swear to God, Emma…" KC took a calming breath. "If she… did she…did you want her to touch you?" KC was five seconds from finding Maria and punching her in the throat. It wasn't cool to touch a woman, especially Emma, without permission.

Emma kissed KC high on her cheek, then left her lips close to KC's ear. "You're so sweet. My knight in shining denim."

Emma's warm breath caressed KC's neck, bringing her to full attention. She felt vividly alive and yet like she might be dreaming all at once. Her heart pounded hard in her chest and she was sure Emma could feel it beneath her touch. Emma's breath slowed, then hitched as she leaned in closer to KC. She whispered KC's name and it burned across KC's skin like a branding iron.

They stayed like that, immobile yet with their whole lives racing around them, for several moments. They were in a still pocket, protected from the chaos of bar activity. KC pulled Emma to her, tightening their embrace. She paused, reveling in the moment, the beauty of Emma's touch, and the clarity of thought she found only with her.

A rambunctious cowgirl bumped into KC, and KC's drink sloshed over the rim and trickled onto her hand. The cowgirl apologized with a drunken laugh and KC released Emma. She offered the rest of her drink to Emma, who took it and quickly drank the remainder. She regarded KC, her gaze soft with the effects of alcohol. Whiskey dripped from KC's fingertips, and she brought her hand to her mouth and licked off the residue. Emma's gaze followed the movement of KC's tongue.

The energy between them was far too tight, and KC was afraid of what they'd do if it snapped. If it were any other woman, she'd know exactly what was happening. Their actions constituted foreplay, and that thought made KC's head spin even faster. This wasn't just any woman. It was *Emma.*

KC took her by the hand. "How 'bout that dance?"

Emma dropped the empty drink glass on the nearest table and followed. They made their way to the middle of the floor, where Emma pulled KC tight to her in complete contradiction to the fast song the DJ was playing.

KC settled into Emma's embrace and let her set the pace. If Emma wanted a slow dance, that was fine by her. Emma guided her, inviting her into her rhythm, and she surrendered to it.

"So, you and the bartender?" Emma asked the mirror to KC's earlier question, and KC almost laughed. She'd forgotten all about Deena. The woman didn't register even a blip on her landscape of the night.

"She offered. I turned her down." KC said it like it was no big deal. She hoped Emma would drop it.

"Why?"

"She's not my type," KC lied. Deena was everybody's type.

"Oh?" Emma played with the back of KC's collar, her fingers teasing through KC's hair at the same time. "What is?"

KC thought of Lonnie and her patented Texas beauty; then she thought of the way Emma felt in her arms at that moment. Her head spun faster and she realized she had no hope of catching up with her thoughts any time tonight. She laughed and shook her head. "I'm not answering that." She couldn't. Her "type" seemed to be shifting by the second.

Emma teased her. "I'll get it out of you." She pressed a kiss to the side of KC's head. Most of it got lost in KC's hair, but it still tingled against her scalp.

"You probably will." She spoke softly and nuzzled her head into the nook where Emma's neck met her shoulder. Emma wore heels to KC's polished boots. That gave her an inch or two over KC.

KC inhaled Emma's hair and let the sweet smell of apple blossoms infuse her, seeping in at a cellular level. It left her heady and confused. Emma was clearly in reach, ripe for seduction. The lines between best friend and lover blurred, and KC couldn't focus on which side she was meant to land on.

Emma moved her hands until they rested low on KC's back. She splayed her fingers wide and played with the top edge of KC's belt. A shiver worked its way up her spine, and KC pulled back to put a small amount of space between them. She needed room to remember Lonnie, to remember her fractured commitment. If her relationship with Emma was going to shift, KC wouldn't let it happen like this. They both needed to be clear-headed and sober. And unquestionably single.

"You okay?" Emma asked sweetly, and brought one hand around to touch KC's face. She held her fingers there for a moment, rubbing her thumb gently over the apple of KC's cheek.

KC took a steadying breath. "Yeah, I think so."

Emma's mouth curved into a smile and she played with the loose tendrils of KC's hair. "Remember when we were kids and you cut your hair short to match your dad's?"

KC laughed. Emma read her so well. The memory gave KC the emotional reprieve she needed.

"My mama was so mad." Right after her tenth birthday, KC took the scissors to her long hair, tired of the morning ritual that involved her mama yanking her head around just to get her hair settled into two braids. Her mama had been fit to be tied when she found KC in front of the bathroom mirror with a pair of scissors in her hand and all her hair in the sink. They had a family portrait scheduled a few weeks later. That year's Christmas card featured KC with a stylish pixie cut provided by her mama's hairdresser. She'd barely been able to salvage the mess KC'd made. KC loved that haircut, but her mama had refused to let her do it again. As she got older, she just got used to having long hair.

"That haircut gave me my first girl crush." Emma pulled KC closer, closing the gap between them. Her fingers flowed in a slow, torturous path through KC's hair, trailing through the ends, then starting over again. The rhythmic pull filled her scalp with electric energy.

"Yeah?" KC hated Emma's new ability to render her dumbfounded and speechless. She was accustomed to being charming. Monosyllabic grunts, à la *yeah*, weren't charming in the least.

"Yeah." Emma threaded her hand into the hair at the base of KC's skull and firmly cupped the back of KC's head. "I was really bummed when you let it grow out."

"I can cut it again," KC offered. Surely she could find an all-night barber in Austin. She'd go right now.

"If you want." Emma shrugged and her fingers pulled tighter on KC's hair. "I like it like this, too."

KC subconsciously leaned closer to Emma, her lips parted and eyes half closed. She looked desperate and needy and she didn't care. Emma's hand slipped into the gap between the bottom hem of her shirt and the waist of her jeans. She spread her fingers wide and held KC tight as they swayed slowly on the dance floor. Her touch melted into KC's skin, whose resistance to Emma faded to a dull buzz, barely audible in the back of her mind.

KC groaned. "Emma."

"Yes." Emma moved even closer, their lips almost touching. When she spoke, the word entered KC's mouth on an inhale.

KC searched Emma's eyes. They were clouded with so much desire. They also held fear and uncertainty. KC pressed her lips gently to Emma's, not more than a barely there brush of skin, then pulled away completely. She stepped out of the haven of Emma's arms and into the confusion of reality. "I love you."

KC had said those words to Emma more times than she could count during the course of their friendship, and they'd never seemed so important. Emma deserved so much more than KC could give her in this moment, and that bothered her. She'd never spent much time evaluating herself, her motivations. Usually if it felt good, she went with it and didn't think much about what it all meant.

Emma was sure and steady. She had a plan, weighed the impact of her decisions, and made sacrifices for those she loved. Emma loved completely and generously. Somewhere along the line, while KC was being selfish, Emma had grown up beautifully. KC was ashamed that she fell so short of the mark set by Emma. She wanted to be worthy of love and to be able to return it in kind.

Chapter Nine

It was well past last call when they finally left Rusty's. By the time they made it back to the La Quinta, the alcohol had worked its way clear of KC's system, but her head still felt heavy and full. She suspected her buzz had more to do with Emma than the residual effects of too many whiskey sours.

Emma locked herself in the bathroom to change, leaving KC alone with her thoughts in a hotel room with a king-sized bed that seemed to grow smaller by the second.

KC pulled on her nightclothes. The oversized T-shirt and boxer briefs weren't very appealing, but they were comfortable. Emma was the only woman she could share a bed with and not worry about dressing right for the occasion. Tonight she wished she'd put more thought into her pajamas.

KC's phone played "The Yellow Rose of Texas." Just as she pressed the button to say hello, she heard a crashing noise in the bathroom coupled with a very loud, "Fuck!"

"You okay?" KC held the phone far enough away from her mouth that she wouldn't be yelling in Lonnie's ear. She might not have been quite ready to play nice with Lonnie again, but that didn't mean she wanted to deafen her either.

"I'm good. Just dropped my makeup case." Emma's reply was muffled through the door, but it still sounded like a lie. A makeup case accidentally dropped on the floor didn't sound like something being thrown at the wall.

KC let it go. "Okay, so long as you're not hurt." She pulled the phone to her ear.

Lonnie was saying her name over and over, trying to get her attention. "KC? KC? Dammit, KC! Listen to me."

"I'm here. Sorry." KC wondered if she'd ever reach a point where her chest didn't flutter at the sound of Lonnie's voice. She tried to separate her visceral reaction to Lonnie from the emotional and mental. Lust did not equal love did not equal logic. Logically this was a very bad idea. Emotionally, when she stripped away the lust, she felt she was being used, and she didn't like that. Close behind that, she felt sadness and regret. As always, though, the lust remained clear and focused and threatened to overpower all else.

"Oh, sugar, there you are. I've been worried about you." Lonnie didn't sound worried. She sounded horny. Dollars to donuts, this was a late-night booty call, not just a friend checking in.

KC hadn't talked to Lonnie since breakfast Tuesday morning. She knew what she had to say, but didn't trust herself to get the words out properly yet. Her relationship with Lonnie had to end, but that didn't mean she was ready to cut ties. Lonnie, for all the wrong in their getting together, made her feel wanted.

"I've just been busy, Lonnie. Nothing to worry about." KC inwardly cursed. She'd tried to sound aloof, but she sounded eager and turned on just like every other time Lonnie called her. She shouldn't have waited to tell Lonnie it was over. Every day that passed since talking to Kendall left her more clouded and confused.

"I miss you, KC. Can't you come over?" Lonnie never invited KC over. She was too afraid that Glen or Leann would come home. She must be feeling desperate.

"Not tonight." She thought about telling Lonnie she was in Austin for the weekend but decided she sounded stronger if she left that part out. Let Lonnie think she was able to resist. "Besides, isn't Glen home by now?"

"He had to work late. Inventory or some such. I swear, that man loves to count his toys."

"Inventory? What about Leann?"

"She's spending the night at her grandma's." Lonnie lowered the pitch of her voice. "It's just me, all alone here, sugar. Can't you please come help me?"

KC shifted and squeezed her thighs together. Lonnie's voice had the most amazing effect on her body. With just a few words, she could shift all the moisture to between her legs and chase all the thoughts clean out of her head. She'd spent the evening feeling guilty and turned on by Emma. Lonnie shifted her attention. Their relationship might not be healthy, but at least it was clearly defined. Until KC said the words *it's over* aloud to Lonnie, Lonnie was her lover. Being excited by Lonnie was comforting in its familiarity.

"God, Lonnie." KC groaned. So much for sounding strong. She took a breath and tried again. "I can't."

"Well, maybe you can help me from there. I can't stop thinking about Monday." Lonnie paused and KC leaned forward, listening carefully to the change in Lonnie's breathing. "About the way you bent me over my desk and took me from behind. You've never been like that before."

"I know." KC still wasn't sure how she felt about that. The sex had set her on fire, but the emotional aftermath had left her shaken. For a moment, she let herself go to the memory. The thought of Lonnie's ass, bared and ready, with her dress pushed around her waist, left her light-headed, and the tactile image had her hands palming the air and her hips moving in rhythm with the memory. She forced herself to stop, to focus on calming her body. She thought of Lonnie in her choir robe, standing next to her mama. It helped a lot. She thought about Lonnie secure in Glen's embrace on the sidewalk after the encounter Lonnie claimed she couldn't stop thinking about. She'd looked the picture of a devoted wife and mother.

It hit KC like a flash. She couldn't trust Lonnie. Lonnie was using her. She'd always known it, in the back of her mind. The knowledge was ever-present but easily dismissed. Even Kendall saying the words aloud less than a week ago hadn't been enough to truly penetrate. Now it was all she could think. *Does Lonnie even like me?* She didn't know the answer.

"Are you sure you can't come over?" Lonnie's voice melted KC from the inside out, but the liquid state hardened in her stomach as she thought of the damage their affair would cause if her family found out. She heard the muffled sound of fabric rustling in the background. "It's just me here alone in this big ol' bed." Lonnie let the image settle for a moment then added, "Naked."

If she let her imagination run, she'd be done for. Even with her newfound understanding of their relationship, she still had years of practice lusting after Lonnie. Lonnie was her bad habit and she needed to find a way to break it.

She'd be okay if she schooled her imagination, reminded herself of the look on Leann's face when she spit the words *my mother's lover.* If she thought only about the core foundation of her family and how much rested on her ability to just say no, to keep it in her pants. If she thought about the sense of unease building in her gut after every encounter with Lonnie. If she did all that, she would be able to get off the phone with only a minor hit to her personal pride. She'd be able to regroup. She might even begin to piece together her battered integrity.

She just needed to trust herself enough to do it. Right now her honorable intentions were winning the battle with her libido, but she worried about what would happen next time she saw Lonnie face to face. It was one thing to say no over the phone, where the temptation seemed far away. It was entirely another to say no to a live flesh-and-blood woman who wanted her.

"Lonnie, I can't do this." KC was proud of herself. Those words were empowering.

"Are you really going to leave me here to take care of myself alone?" KC could hear her pout through the phone.

KC clenched and unclenched her hands. She didn't *want* to leave Lonnie hanging, but she *needed* to. If she gave in now, she'd hate herself. "This isn't going to happen." She left off the *not now, not ever again* from the end of the sentence. That was a conversation she needed to have in person.

The sound of the toilet flushing and the water running in the sink registered peripherally, but it didn't fully click until the door opened and Emma emerged. The light from the bathroom haloed her body and she looked like an angel, like some ethereal being sent from on high to save her from her own lack of willpower.

KC jumped out of bed and dropped the phone. She could hear Lonnie yelling "What the hell" as she scrambled to pick it up.

She stared at Emma and held the phone to her ear. "I gotta go." She fumbled with the END button and realized she'd held the phone upside down. She disconnected the call and sat on the side of the bed.

"You look...different."

Emma wore a gray camisole and matching satin briefs. KC was caught up in Emma's soft femininity. When Emma slept over at KC's, she invariably forgot to bring nightclothes and ended up wearing one of KC's old T-shirts and a pair of sweats. At home, it was easy to forget that Emma was even a girl. Here, wearing that, KC felt like a fool for ever overlooking that fact. KC realized her mouth was still hanging open and she clamped it shut. *Idiot.*

Emma's lips curved into a half smile. "Thanks. I think."

KC's phone rang and Emma stopped smiling. "Are you going to answer that?"

"Huh? What?" KC looked at her phone, looked at Emma, then back at her phone. She pressed the button to send Lonnie to voice mail. Talking to her was a bad idea, made worse by the expression on Emma's face when she heard Lonnie's ring tone. "No, I'm not." She set the phone to silent and laid it on the bedside table.

Emma held KC's gaze, shuffled her feet a couple of times, then turned away. She took her brush from her bag and started in on her long hair. She brushed until it was silky smooth and flowed between her fingers. KC stared the entire time.

"Are you ready?" Emma asked as she put her brush away.

KC swallowed. She wasn't ready at all. "For what?"

"Bed. Or do you want to watch TV or something?"

KC's earlier suggestion to snuggle and watch porn came back to her, and her face flared with heat. Emma, her best friend, made her blush.

Maybe two beds would have been better. It didn't seem like a big deal when she'd first walked into the room, but now she sure as hell felt like it mattered a lot. Maybe she just felt different because the room was rented. Two adults in a hotel for the weekend should be up to a whole lot more than just sleeping. And if she'd danced with any other woman the way she had with Emma earlier, sleep would not be an option.

"Um, whatever. I just need to use the bathroom first." KC rounded the bed. She had to make it past Emma to get to the bathroom, and that had her brain sputtering like crazy. She told her legs to turn, to veer around Emma, but they made a straight path toward her. KC's only choice was to stop or plow right through her. Emma exhaled sharply, and KC was close enough to feel Emma's breath on her skin.

Neither of them spoke. KC stared into Emma's eyes, searching for the answer to all the questions pinging through her brain. She found more questions bouncing back at her. And she found the answer to all of them. *Emma.*

A strand of hair, meticulously combed, yet still rebellious, drifted into Emma's face and clung to her bottom lip. KC, suddenly afraid to touch her, raised her hand halfway, then stopped. She wanted to ask if this was okay—her desire to remove the hair and return it to where it belonged—but she was equally afraid to speak. Emma blew gently in an attempt to dislodge it. The hair danced out and tickled KC's cheek, but otherwise stayed firmly in place.

"Stubborn." KC stared at Emma's lips, soft and moist, and her mouth went dry. She licked her own lips absently. "Let me…"

She raised her hand slowly in order to give Emma plenty of warning about her intentions. She was going to touch Emma—touch her face, her lips—and she wanted Emma to be okay with that before she made contact. Emma didn't move. Her eyes remained trained on KC's until KC's finger brushed her skin. They slipped shut at the touch.

KC held perfectly still, barely touching Emma's cheek. The gentle contact felt like an awakening and it scared the crap out of her. This was Emma. Her best friend. *Emma.*

As slow as she possibly could, she eased her forefinger beneath the strand of hair. Every movement prolonged and amplified the current building between them. She felt herself leaning closer and couldn't stop it from happening. She hooked her finger around the hair and pulled it away from Emma's lip. Emma's tongue chased it, licking along the contour where the hair had been seconds ago. KC tucked it gently behind Emma's ear and combed it into place with her fingers.

She was overstepping. She knew it but didn't stop. She trailed her fingers through the soft locks. She'd touched Emma's hair plenty of times before; this was the first time she'd really felt it. The silky smooth flow teased her fingertips, begging her to delve deeper. KC cupped the side of Emma's face, her fingers still tangled in the hair at the base of Emma's neck. She stretched her thumb and swiped it first over Emma's cheek, the soft curve of her smile, then reached farther. She traced Emma's lip, catching the moisture left behind from Emma's tongue.

Emma leaned into the touch and her eyes fluttered open, dark and heavy.

KC was mesmerized. "Em..."

She moved to close the gap, to touch her mouth to Emma's. She brushed her lips carefully, gently against Emma's. Her body was rioting, demanding more, but she existed inside the eye of the storm, soft and sure.

Emma sighed into her mouth, kissed her once more, her lips quick and fleeting, then pulled away. Her eyes were closed again when KC recovered enough to look at Emma. She rested her forehead against Emma's and breathed her in, the faded sweet scent of the apples and jasmine in her shampoo, blended with the smell of her desire. Emma placed her open palm against KC's chest. KC's heart threatened to pound clean out of her rib cage.

Emma raised her head. When KC tried to follow, she held her in place, her hand hard against the beating of KC's heart. Emma opened her eyes and the desire was still there, but overshadowed with sadness.

"I can't do this." Emma stepped away, her fingertips stretched to maintain contact with KC, and then her hand dropped to her side.

KC didn't understand Emma's words. She heard them, but they just refused to register. She felt colder than she ever knew was possible. She stepped closer to Emma and a tingle of warmth worked over her body. Emma stepped away. KC was bereft.

"I don't understand." KC sounded lost to her own ears.

Emma sighed and pointed to the bedside table. "Your phone is ringing again."

KC looked behind her and saw the screen lit up with a picture of Lonnie's face. She had no intention of answering it. She turned back just as Emma slipped out the door. She'd hastily thrown on a pair of sweats and T-shirt, transforming her back to the Emma that KC was familiar with.

"I'm going to smoke." The door clicked shut behind her.

KC sat on the bed, head in her hands. What the hell was she doing?

❖

When KC woke the next morning, the bed beside her was empty. She listened for signs of movement in the adjoining bathroom but was met with silence. Emma wasn't in the hotel room.

She'd finally fallen asleep after hours of lying awake. She'd never felt so painfully awkward and aware of her body with Emma next to her as she had last night. She just couldn't relax her mind enough to sleep. Emma, for her part, had lain there rigid and unmoving. Normally she flowed with KC, her body languid and following where KC led in the night. If she shifted to the left, Emma moved with her. If she rolled onto her back, Emma would nestle into the crook of her arm. If she moved to her stomach, Emma would drape herself over KC's back.

Emma's breathing had relaxed and KC assumed she was sleeping around two a.m. She'd hoped in sleep Emma would return to normal behavior, but Emma stayed politely on her own side of the bed. The distance was agonizing.

She hadn't imagined the energy between them. She knew that. Things had shifted and Emma had clearly wanted KC to kiss her just as badly as KC wanted to do it. That didn't explain why Emma had bolted as soon as she actually made the move. Emma had been there, fully present and participating. KC had been overwhelmed, but she hadn't imagined Emma's reactions to her touch, the way she leaned in to KC's caress, the way her eyes clouded over with lust. She'd wanted KC.

KC stumbled to the bathroom. Her eyes were heavy and filled with sand. She rinsed her face and dried it on a hand towel. She looked at the mirror to assess the damage and found a note in Emma's loose cursive.

Went to an appointment. Back soon.

Well, that explained why she was alone. Emma had given her her full schedule for the weekend, but she'd forgotten. Too many other thoughts were roaming inside her head. She couldn't think straight enough to remember the itinerary.

She took a long hot shower, letting the water pulsate against her body, against her scalp, and hoping it would wash away a layer of confusion. She stayed until the water ran cold.

As she dressed, her brain worked to align facts, to pull what she knew from the melee of what she felt. A few firm bits emerged.

First and foremost, she and Lonnie were done. Their relationship had been destined to be short-lived and it was time to let it go. Yes, she enjoyed the sex. Still, it was time to call it. As much as she'd worried about how to say the words to Lonnie, about whether she'd be strong enough to say good-bye, she knew it would be all right. With the spray of water sloughing over her, she felt a growth of confidence.

Second, as much as she'd wanted to kiss Emma last night, she was glad it hadn't escalated beyond that. With the distance of a few hours she recognized how truly devastating that would have been to their relationship if she'd pushed for more so quickly. The urge had swept over her, too soon after her conversation with Lonnie.

She wasn't sure she trusted herself to make that kind of decision. Emma was special. If she fucked up, it would cost her so much. Frankly, she wasn't sure it was worth the risk. She needed time to sort that out. For all she knew, when she saw Emma later that day, everything would have shifted back to the way it was. She might look at Emma and feel nothing beyond the usual affectionate love. If that were the case, she'd made a giant ass out of herself the night before. But Emma was her friend and they could laugh it off together.

Third, she had to get the two women separated and sorted, both emotionally and physically. She needed to make sure she wasn't assigning emotions to Emma out of a sense of loss. Emma could not be a surrogate for Lonnie. She was pretty damn certain the two weren't emotionally connected for her, but she didn't want any room for doubt. If her relationship with Emma was going to change, it needed to happen in its own time and space, and not with the shadow of Lonnie hanging over them.

KC toweled dry and dressed in a pair of faded jeans and an old UNLV T-shirt of Emma's.

Clearly, she and Emma needed to talk. But first she needed to call Lonnie and make it clear she wouldn't be answering any more late-night calls.

She thought of a thousand reasons to put off talking to Lonnie. She should get something to eat first. She should call and check on Trina. She should make a voodoo doll of Kendall to get back at her for planting the idea of her and Emma as a couple in the first place. She should…

She picked up her phone and dialed Lonnie's number.

Chapter Ten

"Hey." Emma set her keycard on the table next to KC's laptop and then sat on the bed.

"Welcome back." KC made a notation of the page she was grading so she could pick up where she'd left off. "How'd it go?"

"Good. I got to see my new office—well, cubicle—and meet a few people." Emma picked at a loose thread on the comforter. "My boss seems nice."

"That's good, I guess." KC didn't know what else to say. She hadn't felt this awkward with Emma since high school. She closed her laptop and moved to sit next to Emma.

Emma shifted away for a moment, then back. Her leg pressed against KC, hip to knee, and she laid her head on KC's shoulder. "We need to talk."

She lifted Emma's hand and carefully laced their fingers together. "Yes, I suppose we do."

Neither ventured further and they sat quietly for several minutes. Finally KC asked, "You want to go first?"

Emma took a deep breath. "Not really. But I will." She didn't say anything else and the silence was getting to KC. She was the type to charge in and fill the gaps in a conversation.

"Okay," she said. "First, I'm sorry. I shouldn't have kissed you like that." She had been caught off guard by her reaction to Emma. She'd enjoyed kissing her but knew it shouldn't have happened. The timing was shit.

"Oh, KC." Emma shook her head. "I wanted that…so much." Emma squeezed her fingers. "I want to do it again right now."

"Yeah?" Maybe her impulsive action wasn't complete disaster after all.

"But I'm not going to." Emma sounded defeated.

"Oh."

They shared a few more moments of awkwardness while she gathered her thoughts. Emma held her hand, her grip familiar and strange at once. And the thought of kissing Emma again excited her. It shocked her to learn how much she wanted to repeat their kiss, to draw it out and make it last. As much as she wanted to, she couldn't do it. She loved Emma too much to use her like that. Emma deserved someone with true intentions, and hers were too uncertain. She couldn't make any promises.

"I want to do it again, too," she said. "But I'm not going to either." Her history of following her impulses with Lonnie had come full circle to bite her in the ass. She didn't want to repeat the same mistake with Emma. In this moment, she wanted to kiss Emma. But what about a week from now? A year?

"Right."

Why, when they agreed, did it feel like they were still miles apart?

"Em?" She played with Emma's fingers, tracing their lengths with her fingertips. "Will you tell me why not?"

"Oh, my." Emma sat up straight and pushed her free hand through her hair. "I've wanted to forever. Since before I found you with what's-her-name in high school."

"Traci?" KC asked.

"I *know* her name." Emma's voice was sharp and cutting.

"Sorry." She was stunned. Her head spun with the new information. "I had no idea."

"Yeah, well, I didn't tell you, did I?" Emma said.

"Why didn't you?"

"You're an idiot about women and I didn't want to be a part of that. I don't want to feel like this, KC. I keep hoping it'll go away, but it never has."

"That's a little harsh."

"Is it? You don't *think* when it comes to sex. If your clit twitches just the right way, you chase it and that's that. To hell with everyone else."

KC sat with her mouth open, unable to think of a response.

"I'm sorry. I shouldn't have said that." Emma lost some of her fight. "It's just the way you are. I know that."

"I'm trying to be better," she whispered.

Emma scoffed. "Really? Tell that to Mr. Truvall."

"What does that mean?" KC wasn't sure she wanted to continue this conversation. This was a little too much honesty for a weekend away.

"KC, I'm not stupid. I know about Mrs. Truvall." Emma's tone left no doubt in her mind. Emma might not be stupid, but she sure as hell thought KC was.

"It's over." She felt a pang of regret as she said the words. She *knew* it wasn't possible, but she'd always hoped for more from Lonnie. As illogical as it was given the circumstances of their lives, at the time she'd fooled herself into believing it would all work out in the end. How naïve and selfish.

"Really? That's why she was blowing up your phone last night?" Emma shifted farther away and her hand slipped from KC's grasp.

"I haven't exactly told her yet." She picked at the skin around her fingernails. It took all her will to not reach out for Emma again. Emma kept her from fidgeting.

"Please tell me you're not ending it because we kissed." Emma's eyes slipped shut. The sadness on her face made her want to kiss Emma even more. She could make Emma happy, she knew it. But for how long?

"No, that's not it. But since you asked, only a fool would choose Lonnie over you." She didn't like how clearly she defined herself as a fool with that statement. In her defense, she hadn't known Emma was an option when she started her affair with Lonnie. What would she have done differently a year ago if presented with Emma's feelings then?

"Don't do that." Emma maintained the distance between them but stretched her hand over the divide to touch KC's face. Emma caressed the planes of her cheekbone and the line of her jaw with the backs of her fingers, then reversed her hand to cup KC's cheek. Emma teased the edges of her hair, her palm hot and silky against KC's skin.

She felt ready to burst from the heat of Emma's touch. She cuddled into it, solidifying the contact. "Do what?"

"Act all sweet. I'm mad as hell. At you. At me. I'm not ready to let it go." Emma dropped her hand, ending her caress and leaving her wanting more.

"Tell me what you want." She edged closer to Emma. That was such a bad idea. They needed to be clear-headed and logical for this conversation. But Emma's touch was perfection. Who would willingly give that up? She moved until their legs were once again touching and forced herself to be satisfied with that small comfort. She wanted more but couldn't define what *more* involved. Did she long for Emma's touch because they always touched? Theirs was a very tactile friendship. They held hands. They snuggled. Did she want to protect that closeness? Or did she want to escalate the connection?

"The same thing I've always wanted. You." The yearning in Emma's voice made KC ache.

"Wow." She couldn't breathe. She focused on the rhythm of her lungs. Inhale. Exhale. Despite how plainly Emma had been speaking, it didn't really hit her until that one sentence. This was real, at least for Emma. Emma wanted so much more than just a kiss, just one touch. She was in this for the long haul and willing to wait for her to get her shit together. Emma had been waiting.

"It doesn't matter. You're not ready. Until you are, it's not going to happen." Emma's words were heavy with the weight of finality.

"How do you know I'm not? I could be." She wanted to be.

"You're not." Emma was emphatic. She stood and started pacing. "You're having an affair with your mama's friend."

"I told you, that's over." She knew the words were weak without any action to prove them true, but she couldn't help but say them. She had to offer something in her own defense.

"And the next time Mrs. Truvall calls, what will you do? Or the next time she leads you into the nearest bathroom?" Emma picked up her pack of cigarettes and twirled them methodically between her fingers. "You take ridiculous chances when it comes to sex. Say you follow through and actually end it with Mrs. Truvall, which I seriously doubt. What happens when the next sexy little thing shakes her ass in your direction? You take risks. That's who you are. And that scares the crap out of me. I can't trust you."

KC didn't answer. She'd never thought about herself in those terms, never heard herself defined so succinctly and so unflatteringly. She had no defense.

"You say it's over, but does she know that?" Emma smiled sadly. The cigarettes stopped their circular trip through her hands. They sat poised, waiting for her answer.

"Yes. No. I don't know." She watched Emma. She could feel her disapproval and wanted to undo her past—at least the parts that hurt Emma so deeply. But she couldn't. And she didn't think an apology would help.

Emma started twirling the cigarettes again, her disappointment clear. "You need to know."

"I turned her down the last few times. She knows something's wrong. She just doesn't know what exactly." At the time, when faced with the decision of "talk to Lonnie or let it ride for another day," waiting seemed the best choice. Now it sounded weak and uncertain. Was she holding on to Lonnie because she was convenient and willing? She'd hated how much Lonnie strung her along throughout their relationship but understood because Lonnie was married. KC was poaching, and that made her more patient when plans didn't work out.

"And why haven't you told her?" Emma sounded hopeful yet sad, like she was leaving room for KC to convince her but didn't think it would happen.

"I was waiting until…" Until what? She couldn't tell Emma she wasn't sure if she was strong enough to say no in person. That wouldn't help convince Emma she was ready for a real relationship. She wasn't even sure she wanted the pressure of a bona fide girlfriend, but she hated being dismissed, being judged as unworthy. Even if she did deserve it.

"Until what? You know what? It doesn't matter. The point is, you didn't tell her. You left her hanging. I don't want to be that person with you. It would kill me to feel you slipping through my fingers like that, to know that I love you and you're just using me until you figure out how to end it."

"It's not like that." It wasn't the same. Lonnie didn't love her. Not really. "Lonnie—"

"Forget it. I don't want to talk about Mrs. Truvall any more. This isn't about her. It's about you. And me."

"Em, stop pacing. Come sit with me again." She held out her hand. Emma's pacing was driving her batty. Of all things, she was absolutely certain that Emma belonged with her, beside her. That's how they'd always been, for as long as KC could remember, save a few long, painful months in high school. She didn't want a repeat of that separation.

Emma took her hand and sat again with a sigh. "Tell me what you want."

"I..." This wasn't some chick she was cruising in a club. This was Emma. What she said next mattered. She couldn't kick into seduction mode and chase her newfound desire. That would ruin things between them. More than anything, she needed to tell the truth, even if she was unsure what the truth was. "I don't know."

Emma nodded and began to stand up. KC held her hand tight. She refused to let Emma walk away from her now.

"I don't know what I want because you're right. I'm a fool with women. And I need to fix that. You deserve better. I love you. I wanted to kiss you last night. I want to do it again. But I don't know what it means. And if you don't want me to do it again, you shouldn't wear that camisole around me." She nudged Emma's shoulder, a physical reminder that above all else, they were friends first.

"You liked that?" Emma's mouth curved into a reluctant smile.

"God, yes. I felt like I was seeing you for the first time." The friendly ease between them shifted and swelled with tension, and the weight of their conversation settled squarely on her chest.

"I wore it on purpose." Emma hesitated. "I'm so tired of waiting, KC. I'm afraid you're never going to figure it out."

"So you decided to torture me?" She meant the question teasingly, but it sounded much heavier. For all her uncertainty, this conversation and Emma's admissions were important.

"No. I decided to seduce you." Emma winked and placed her palm on KC's thigh, high enough up to be distracting.

She forced herself to focus. Hand or not, Emma said she didn't intend to allow anything else to happen between them, and KC believed her. "What changed your mind?"

"Your damn phone. I heard you talking to Mrs. Truvall. And she kept calling. With her picture popping up on your screen every five seconds I just couldn't pretend she doesn't exist." Emma shrugged. "I couldn't go through with it." She pulled her hand away from KC's leg.

"I really wish I'd talked to her before we came here." She smiled her very best flirty smile. It usually melted clothes and parted thighs, but Emma had seen it directed at a lot of women over the years. She was probably immune at this point.

"Me, too. But I'm glad you didn't, too."

"I don't understand." If she had a clear end with Lonnie, maybe she would be ready for more. At the very least, she'd be closer to having a grip on her emotions and understanding exactly what the affair meant, and didn't mean, to her. A therapist would have a field day with her engaging in a "committed" relationship with a married woman.

"KC, I don't want to be a replacement for someone else. I don't want to be a rebound, and I don't want to be second choice. I want you. But I'm not willing to sacrifice myself to make it happen."

"I want you, too." She wanted to take the words back before they were fully formed, but she wasn't able to hold them in. Emma had criticized her for letting her libido dictate her motions, yet here she was, willing to do the same thing again.

"I wish you wouldn't say that."

"Why?" KC knew why but was so very bad at tracking Emma's thoughts. KC wanted what she wanted. If the want didn't match up with what she needed, or what was good for her, oh well. Emma suppressed her wants and kept a clear eye on what was good for her. Regardless of what their future held, she recognized the value of Emma's way of thinking. If she'd thought a little more before she fell into bed with Lonnie, she wouldn't be picking up the pieces now.

"Because how do I know it's real? I need to know, when we take that step, that it's a forever kind of thing. I won't be able to go backward. And until you're really ready, I'm not willing to give up my best friend. It's easier for me to ignore my feelings when you're oblivious."

"So where does this leave us?"

"Exactly where we have been." Emma sagged a little with the admission, but it puffed KC up. Nothing between them was broken. Maybe, if she was really lucky and didn't fuck it up completely, they could build from here.

They'd looked at five apartments so far and Emma hated them all. The one they were standing in was by far the worst. Water-stained ceilings, no off-street parking, and the master bedroom seemed to be a converted storage closet. The only thing she liked about the place was the neighborhood. Central East Austin was close to downtown, right off the Interregional highway, and easily within Emma's budget. Best of all, it was close to Rusty's and Lipstick24. Not that proximity to her favorite bars should be the deciding factor, but it sure didn't hurt.

"I wish I could afford to buy." Emma had made that statement at every single stop. She sounded even more regretful this time. But a new job in a new city coupled with the current lending criteria meant she couldn't get financed. Hell, with her employment history, she'd be lucky to qualify for a rental.

"Rent for a year. It won't be that bad." KC peered out the dust-covered window. "Just not here."

"Okay. I'm done for today. You're taking me to dinner." Emma thanked the property manager and they drove back to their hotel.

KC almost suggested room service because they'd had a long, overly emotional day stacked onto a night of no sleep. But suggesting they stay in the room seemed too intimate, given the circumstances. She'd worked hard all day to be normal around Emma, to act naturally. All she'd accomplished was a lot of second-guessing and a general feeling of awkwardness.

"I don't really care where we eat, but I want to go out afterward." Emma held up a dress KC'd never seen before and KC's brain stalled for a moment. It was small and red and dangerous. Jesus, how many little red dresses did Emma own? The one last night had unraveled KC, and that was *before* their talk. This one looked shorter and lower cut and even more like it belonged on the floor of KC's bedroom. If that was her reaction to the *thought* of Emma wearing it, she was in serious trouble if she actually put it on.

"I'll take you anywhere you want to go, but you have to wear something else."

"Why? This is perfect." Emma studied the dress. "Don't you like it?"

"I like it a lot." KC nodded sagely. "But I'm trying like hell to be honorable here. And that dress..."

Emma blushed, her face damn close to the same color red as the dress. "You'll just have to control yourself, because I like it." And with that, Emma claimed the bathroom.

KC gave herself a pep talk while she changed her clothes. She'd managed to make it to twenty-six without treating Emma like a sex bomb. One more night, regardless of what Emma was wearing, was totally doable. Besides, it was time for her to prove, to herself and to Emma, that she was capable of thinking with something other than her sex drive.

"I'm coming out now." Emma gave fair warning, then emerged from the bathroom. She hadn't done her hair or makeup yet, simply changed outfits.

It was just a dress. Beneath the dress was Emma. Her best friend. Telling herself that didn't stop KC's breath from hitching in her throat. "You look beautiful."

She forced herself to stay put, to not cross the room. She naturally gravitated to Emma, and their bodies found one another, even in sleep. It felt unnatural to hold herself back, to deny the urge to move closer, to be near Emma. Finally, after several moments of scuffing her boots over the carpet, she gave in. She stopped when she was close enough to touch.

"Really beautiful." She wound a curl of Emma's hair around her finger. It was soft and light, and she couldn't imagine a world where she wasn't allowed to feel such beauty.

"KC." Emma's voice trembled. "You're doing that thing."

KC leaned closer and added another finger, trailing the fine strands of hair between them. "What thing?" She whispered.

"The thing where you look like you're ready to devour me. I like it too much and I forget why this is a bad idea."

She stared at Emma's lips. They moved gracefully, moist and full, and oh so inviting. She indulged the image. She wanted to move nearer, to bring their mouths together, but she didn't. She held herself close to Emma, content to inhale on Emma's exhale.

Emma mirrored her pose and raised her hand cautiously to touch KC's face. She lightly traced the lines of KC's brow and down the slope of her nose. KC closed her eyes and reveled in the touch. Emma was soft and gentle, and KC couldn't believe she was only now learning this side of her. She felt starved for missed past experiences. Emma trailed her thumb over KC's bottom lip, a barely there caress. KC inhaled sharply and her heart pounded out a new, insistent rhythm. The only thing that existed for her in that moment was Emma. She was surrounded by Emma, swallowed up by new awareness.

She took a step back and Emma's hair slipped from her fingers. If she didn't remove herself now, she never would. Her strength to resist was waning. "I'm sorry."

Emma took a deep breath. "Me, too."

KC stepped back again. Maybe a little distance would help clear her head. Currently her mind was filled with all things Emma. "Is this dress part of the seduce-KC wardrobe?"

Emma looked chagrined, her ears tinged pink. "Yes." This time she stepped closer. "Is it working?"

"God, yes." She sidestepped Emma and made a break for the bathroom. "Which is why we need to finish getting ready."

Emma moved to join her in the bathroom. Her makeup bag was on the counter. KC shut the door between them and locked it. She took a shaky breath and rested with her back against the door.

Self-deprivation sucked. She would much rather be halfway to naked with Emma right about now, but she wouldn't survive if it was a onetime thing. Emma wanted her, thought she was worthy of seduction. Hope blossomed in her chest.

This is what it felt like to tell herself no, and it wasn't nearly as bad as she thought it would be.

Chapter Eleven

By Sunday evening, the tension between them was thick as Texas chili. After dinner and another night of dancing on Saturday, KC had been coiled tight and on the verge of breaking. Every crappy apartment they'd looked at Sunday morning reminded her that Emma was leaving. Emma still hadn't found a suitable apartment, and KC was struggling more and more with the idea of letting her go.

She'd loaded their suitcases into the tiny trunk of the Mini while Emma checked over the room one last time for forgotten items. She was well past ready to return home. They'd traveled nearly the entire five hours without speaking. She held Emma's hand the entire time, moving her thumb restlessly over the arc of skin between Emma's thumb and forefinger.

If she could reverse time to Friday and repeat the weekend without the kiss, would she? Yes. No. Maybe? She'd loved it as it happened, but their relationship went off the skids immediately after that. And it perpetuated the pattern Emma had pointed out. Once again, KC's clit had twitched and she'd jumped on the impulse before thinking. Only this time she'd jumped on Emma.

It was high time she owned up to her reckless behavior with regard to sex. She worked hard and behaved responsibly in every other aspect of her life. She attended family functions, including church every Sunday, regardless of her personal preferences. She'd finished her education and returned to Texas. God knows she'd thought about staying in Seattle, but the need to be near her family won out over Tevas and patchouli incense. She found a job quickly in a challenging market and even more challenging industry. She'd worked hard and turned a part-time, flexible position teaching the occasional online class into a permanent full-time position with benefits. Her grandma had entrusted her home to her, explaining in her Last Will and Testament that she believed KC would do the right thing. God knows she'd tried.

For all the clear-sightedness, KC was a mess with women. When she started the affair with Lonnie, she honored Lonnie's request to keep it a secret. Lonnie was married and intent on staying that way. To KC's way of thinking, it wasn't anyone else's business what she did with Lonnie. So long as they were discreet and kept their encounters private, no one would be the wiser.

Apparently, they weren't as discreet as she thought. The list of people who knew about their relationship was too long to be safe. She hadn't considered the impact on her family, especially her mama. Now with the secret slipping closer and closer to public knowledge, she felt foolish. She'd behaved like a selfish girl and it was up to her to fix herself.

Emma drove past the illuminated signboard that listed all the churches in town. Fairmont was a God-fearing town.

"Emma." KC spoke carefully. She needed to reassure Emma, but her thoughts were a jumbled mess. "I want you to know how sorry I am for everything. I wish I was a better person."

"You're not bad." Emma kept her eyes firmly on the road.

"Maybe. But I've been selfish. And I need to sort that out." She didn't know how to say that she wasn't sure of anything right now. She'd been careless and impulsive with Lonnie, but was she poised for a repeat with Emma? She wanted Emma. God, did she. Her body hadn't stopped clamoring for Emma since the moment she saw her exit the bathroom in those sexy satin pajamas. But was it desire born of exposure and proximity? Last time she'd been alone with Lonnie, she'd been consumed with lust, acting out her baser impulses. What would happen next time she saw Lonnie? Would her feelings for Emma prove true? Or would she be on a repeat of the familiar ride her libido took any time Lonnie came into view?

Emma squeezed her hand, then released it. She held the steering wheel at ten and two, her grip white-knuckle tight. "I understand."

"Do you?" KC played with the frayed inside seam of her jeans. "Do you get that I want you so bad right now I can taste it. I'm used to feeling all turned on by Lonnie. I'm confused as hell because I don't know what my attraction to you means."

"I really, *really* don't want to hear about how much Mrs. Truvall turns you on."

"Sorry."

Emma turned into KC's driveway. Both porch lights were on and Kendall sat on the back porch. She waved when they pulled up. Emma left the engine running.

"Aren't you going to come in?" KC knew the answer before she asked.

"I don't think so." Emma shook her head slowly. "I'm tired."

"It looks like Kendall and Trina are still up." As much as she hated to have her actions dictated by appearances, she wasn't ready for the third degree from Kendall about why Emma drove off without saying hello.

Emma killed the engine. "All right, but just for a minute." She squared her shoulders as she exited the car. Emma faced difficult situations head-on.

KC reached for Emma's hand then pulled back. She didn't *always* have ahold of Emma, so it would be okay if they weren't touching this time. Even with her straight back and clear eyes, Emma looked close to falling apart.

"Hey, you two. Welcome back." Kendall closed the file she was reviewing and rose to greet them. "How was your weekend?"

"Frustrating." Emma climbed the steps and gave Kendall a brief one-arm hug. "I swear I looked at every available apartment in Austin and didn't find a single one that works for me."

Trina slipped out the back door. The puppy followed at her heels. He looked to be completely in love with his new mistress after two days. "Buddy's finally asleep." Trina appeared tired, but a few of the storm clouds had cleared from her eyes. Without makeup, the yellowish outline of a bruise was visible on her cheek. She hugged KC first, then Emma.

"She did get to meet her new boss and see where she'll be working." KC touched Emma's arm with her fingertips, then immediately stepped out of touching distance. "So, that's good," she hastily added.

"How's Berty?" Emma gestured toward the puppy.

Trina stooped and picked up the dog. She scratched behind his ears and KC swore he smiled. Trina definitely did.

"He's good," Trina said. "So smart and sweet. And Buddy loves him."

Did he pee on the carpet? That's what KC wanted to know, but she didn't ask. Really, if he helped Trina feel safe and loved, then he was doing his job. Potty training could be learned.

"How's Buddy like his new room?" The question was code for all the questions KC was afraid to ask yet. Did Buddy realize Daddy wasn't here? Was he happy or sad about it? How was Trina feeling about leaving Jackson now that she'd had a few days to settle into her new surroundings? Did she miss him? Did she cry more now or before she left? Would she be able to stay away? A lot of women couldn't. Love did a tremendous job of fucking people up. Especially when love got twisted into dark-black knots of bruises and secrets.

"He's settling in. He's been coming into my bed about halfway through the night. He's just not sure what's going on." Trina shrugged and focused her attention on Berty. Kendall put her arm around Trina but said nothing.

"He'll get used to it pretty soon. Kids are resilient." KC had taken a handful of early childhood education classes, but none had prepared her for comforting her two-year-old nephew through the separation of his parents. And the one elective she'd taken in general psych was woefully inadequate for helping Trina make it through the stages of grieving. Hell, she wasn't even sure if the stages applied in this situation.

"And pretty soon he'll have a baby brother or sister to distract him." Trina patted her stomach. Despite being almost through the second trimester, she still didn't know the sex of the baby. Jackson hadn't wanted to know, so she'd skipped that part of the ultrasound. Was Trina happy about that?

"We should figure out where we're going to put the crib. Do you want it in the room with you? Or with Buddy?" Kendall continued the conversation, focusing on the details so they could ignore the reason Trina was here instead of home with Jackson.

Trina took a deep breath and said, "I haven't said thank you yet, and I need to." She shook her head. "It's hard to be thankful for having your life upended. Jackson...I love him. I probably always will." Tears threatened to fall from Trina's eyes. "But I want better for Buddy. He watches Jackson, sees the way he is. I don't want my son treating his wife like his father treats me." One tear escaped and traveled the distance of Trina's cheek, followed by another. "And now with the baby...I'm glad you guys came and got me. I am. But God help me, I miss him."

Emma took the puppy from Trina and handed him to KC. Then she enveloped Trina in a long hug. KC'd been on the receiving end of hugs like that, so she knew when she saw Trina's shoulders shake that she felt safe enough to let it out. Emma had chosen a career in television production, but she should have gone into counseling. She had a way of making people feel better.

KC fidgeted with the soft hair on Berty's neck. Trina clung to Emma and cried. Kendall, stalwart and strong, cried with her.

After several long minutes, Trina pulled away and wiped her eyes. "Thanks." She reclaimed the puppy from KC. "So, did y'all do anything fun?"

"We went dancing." KC hadn't considered their night out fun. Torturous was a more apt description. Emma had been on display, a beautiful reminder of everything KC couldn't have, everything she wasn't ready for. After their dance, she'd wanted to leave, but Emma was determined to have fun. She'd danced in turn with every cowgirl in the place while KC pouted her way through drink after drink. By the time they left, KC was an emotional drunk and Emma was happily holding a stack of "call me!" phone numbers. Emma had tucked them into her purse, and KC was still trying to get them from her without looking like a jealous, controlling freak.

"That sounds nice," Kendall said. She, like Trina, had skipped the party phase in college and jumped straight to getting married and playing house. Owen had proved to be a better husband than Jackson, but Kendall still expressed regrets about moving too fast.

"Yeah, it was." Emma's voice was flat and unconvincing. Perhaps the night had been harder on her than she'd displayed at the time.

Trina let the silence settle for a few seconds, then said, "I'm glad I got to see you, Emma, but I'm beat. I'm going to head in." She gave Emma one last hug then took Berty inside.

"I'm with her. Good night." Kendall followed and left KC alone with Emma.

She searched for the right thing to say. Five hours of thinking on the way home from Austin wasn't enough time for her to come up with the magic words to make their relationship all better. How long would be long enough? "I should get my suitcase."

Emma followed her to the car and opened the trunk. KC took her bag and set it at her feet. Emma tapped out a cigarette and lit it. How many times had Emma smoked because KC made her sad? She looked up at the stars. They blanketed the night sky, infinite and bright, but they held no answer.

"I'm going to go." Emma blew out a long stream of smoke.

KC stepped closer but didn't touch. "You could stay."

"Not this time." Emma shook her head, slow and final.

KC nodded and swallowed the lump in her throat. "I'm going to talk to her, Em."

Emma opened her car door and paused, half in, half out. "I hope so."

She nodded earnestly. "I will." Her words wouldn't convince Emma. After so much disappointment, Emma needed to see action.

Emma smiled but didn't respond. Her eyes glistened in the dim light of the dashboard. She closed her door and started the car.

KC watched her drive away. Her heart ached with wanting Emma. It was time to get to work.

Chapter Twelve

KC pulled up in front of Kendall's house but didn't cut the engine. It was rude as hell to not go to the door, but she was a stressed-out wreck and needed a moment to breathe. Besides, Kendall was halfway down the walk before she could do much more than inhale and exhale purposefully. Kendall had been waiting for her.

"Do you want to get breakfast first?" she asked as Kendall arranged herself in the passenger seat and set her travel mug of coffee in the cup holder.

"Are you kidding me?" Kendall looked at her like she might smack her upside the head at any moment.

"No, I just thought you might be hungry."

"You just thought you could put this off." Kendall called her on her delay tactics. "Don't be a coward. It's time to deal with things like a grown-up."

She pulled into traffic. "You make it sound so easy. Tell me, when was the last time you broke up with someone?"

"Don't make it sound like you're going steady. She's married, for God's sake."

"I *know* that." She hated Kendall's incessant need to remind her about Glen. She liked to keep him as far from her thoughts about Lonnie as possible.

"Do you? Because I can't for the life of me figure out why you've been carrying on with a married woman."

"Kendall, can you just…please, don't do this." She was a mess. She hadn't talked to Emma since they arrived back in Fairmont Sunday night and was suffering serious withdrawal. But she couldn't call her until things with Lonnie were resolved, and Lonnie kept putting her off. She said she didn't have time to talk. Strange, considering how willingly she made time to fuck.

"I'm trying really hard here, KC. I just don't understand any of it."

"I can't explain it. It just is." She could talk until she was blue in the face and Kendall would never see her side. Kendall lived in a world of black and white, whereas KC was awash in grays. Thankfully, the hard edges were finally coming into focus. "I was wrong."

"Okay." Kendall nodded thoughtfully. "So what's your plan?"

"She's at her office. I'm going to talk to her."

"And you want me to come with you?"

"No. I have to do this alone. I just want you with me, in the car, for moral support. It'll help." If she had to report back to Kendall immediately, she might stay focused. She wished she was certain enough to know what she would do without Kendall there to keep her honest, but she still wasn't sure. So far she remained intent on ending things, but she hadn't been alone with Lonnie yet.

"I can do that," Kendall said.

They drove through town without talking. Kendall sipped her coffee and KC fiddled with the radio stations, flipping to a new one every few seconds until Kendall placed her hand over hers to get her to stop. Then Kendall turned the music off.

"What's going on with Emma?" Kendall asked the question too casually.

KC turned into a parking space in front of Lonnie's office. "What do you mean?" She tried to sound just as casual.

"I mean she left on Sunday night. Wouldn't she normally sleep over? And Trina said she hasn't been over since."

KC deflected. "She has a life. She's busy with the move and all."

"And that's another thing. Shouldn't you be helping her pack?" Kendall pointed out one of the main staples of friendship. "If your best friend moves, it's your job to help pack."

"I don't want to leave Trina right now." KC hit a ringer with that answer. No way Kendall would encourage her to leave their baby sister to fend for herself.

Kendall challenged her. "Trina said she wants to help her, too. As thanks."

"Then why is Trina talking to you about this instead of me?" KC sounded a little more irritated than she wanted, but goddamn, her family was nosy.

"Don't be stupid. She doesn't know how to bring it up. Trina is the nice one in the family, remember?"

That about summed up the sisters. Kendall said the hard things and asked the unpleasant questions. After KC finished her MA, found a good job, and took over her grandma's house, her mama started calling her willful instead of wild. KC appreciated the nod toward her efforts to get past her teenage reputation. And Trina, the good girl, was polite and sweet and kind.

The more KC thought about it, the more pissed off she got at Jackson. "He's a real bastard, isn't he?"

"Yeah." Kendall nodded. "He really is."

"I wish we'd realized sooner. How long was it like that? Do you know?" Even though she'd been home for the past three days, Trina hadn't mentioned word one about Jackson since Sunday night. KC hadn't been willing to broach the subject. She figured when Trina was ready, she'd talk. But Kendall had a way about her. She and Trina had obviously discussed her situation at length.

"It started shortly after she found out she was pregnant this time." Kendall spoke quietly, then took a deliberate sip of coffee. "Other things happened after Buddy was born, but he just started hitting her a few months ago."

Trina was in her second trimester. They'd announced the pregnancy to the family about two months ago. No telling how long they'd known before that, but no matter the answer, it was too long for her to have suffered Jackson's temper without help.

"She should have let us know." It wasn't Trina's fault, not by a long shot, but KC had failed to protect her. Kendall had been six when Trina was born, and she'd explained what was expected of KC now that she was a big sister. Things were different when you weren't the baby. At two, KC couldn't fully appreciate her wise six-year-old sister's message, but the basics took hold. It was her job, along with Kendall's, to look out for Trina. To make sure no one hurt her.

"She was scared. And embarrassed." Kendall sipped her coffee. "And she loves him." She shrugged.

"How many things are justified in the name of love?" KC couldn't imagine hitting someone she loved. Hell, she couldn't imagine hitting somebody she barely tolerated. Kendall had been a brawler growing up. She'd take all comers and win. KC stood safely behind her and made raspberry faces at whoever had drawn Kendall out. As a result, KC'd never learned to tolerate the feel of her hand striking another. Just the thought made her squirm. As for Kendall, she gave up fistfights in favor of pom-poms by the time she hit her sophomore year of high school.

"You tell me, KC. Seems you've done a bit of justifying yourself." Kendall's voice was frosty and clipped. She was along for the ride to support KC, but KC would be foolish to forget how very much Kendall disapproved of her affair with Lonnie.

"You're right. But when you're in the middle of it, it doesn't feel like that. It just feels like…you're doing what you have to." She shrugged. Not to mention she'd never been in love with Lonnie. Not really.

"I'm sure Trina felt the same way."

"Probably." She turned off the engine. Lonnie's Mustang was parked three spots over. She was here and KC couldn't keep stalling. "I should get in there."

Kendall gave her an awkward hug over the center console. "I'll be here when you're done."

"Thanks." KC had a grip on the door handle when Emma passed by on the sidewalk. Maria Gutierrez walked beside her. "Shit." She slumped into her seat.

"What? Oh, hey, Emma. We should say hi." Kendall started to open her door.

"No." She grabbed Kendall's hand. She wasn't ready to talk to Emma. Not here. Not now.

"Okay." Kendall drew the word out and turned it into a question, but still settled into the seat again. "Who's that with her?"

"Her ex." KC stared hard at Maria. She was too close to Emma, leaning in to listen as Emma spoke. When Maria touched Emma's arm, KC climbed out of the car. "I'll be right back."

"Emma!" She jogged to catch up with them. "Hey." She smiled in a way she hoped said she was happy to see Emma while simultaneously telling Maria to mind her manners. If she wanted to be Emma's friend, KC was all in favor of that, but the next time her hand moved anywhere close to Emma's ass, KC was going to remove it for her.

"Hi, KC." Emma hesitated, then hugged her.

She indulged herself, holding Emma as tight as she could without crossing the line from decent to pornographic on a public sidewalk. She swept her fingers over Emma's back, enveloping Emma as completely as possible.

"I missed you." Emma whispered the words into KC's neck.

"Me, too." She wasn't sure if she spoke or not. Being that close to Emma after their several-day separation overwhelmed her sensibilities. She closed her eyes and sank into their reunion.

Maria cleared her throat next to them. KC closed her eyes and wished for Maria to go away. Maria cleared her throat a second time. Emma released her.

"You remember Maria," Emma said.

"Of course." She kept her voice flat and nodded once. That was all the acknowledgement she was willing to give Maria.

"KC." Maria folded her arms over her chest and rocked back on her heels.

KC kept her arm around Emma as she spoke. "Why are you in town?" She thought she'd left Maria behind when they drove out of Austin. But here she was, like a bad penny stuck to the bottom of Emma's shoe.

Emma, to KC's surprise, didn't shrug off her arm. Rather, she settled beneath it. "She had a few days off and offered to help me pack some stuff."

Fuck. Fuck. Fuckety fuck. That was KC's job, goddammit. She needed to stop floundering and get her shit together. She didn't want Emma to move on before they even had a chance to get started.

"Long drive for that." She prayed Maria wasn't staying over at Emma's but couldn't keep herself from asking.

"She got here last night." Emma's neck and cheeks flushed red.

"Well, that's nice." She bit out the words.

Maria looked smug.

"It is," Emma said softly. "It's good to have a friend's help."

She didn't know if Emma's statement was meant to reassure her that Maria was just a friend or if it was an indictment of her for being a bad friend by not helping. Either way, she wasn't moving her arm from Emma's shoulder until Emma made her.

As she searched for something to say that would delay Emma's departure, Lonnie stepped into view in her office window. Her arms were crossed, her eyes cold and hard. KC waved to Lonnie and increased her hold on Emma. Lonnie didn't wave back.

"Don't do that." Emma stepped away.

"What?"

Emma looked down for a moment, shook her head, then met KC's gaze. "I don't want to be used, KC."

"Used?" She sputtered. "No, it's not like that, Emma."

"Have you told her?" Emma crossed her arm in a mirror pose of Lonnie. In less than ten seconds, she'd managed to piss off both women. God help her.

"Not yet. That's why I'm here now." She sputtered again. It didn't matter what she said, Emma needed to see her follow through, not hear more excuses as to why she hadn't.

"And you thought you'd show instead of tell?" Emma was working her way to angry.

"No, Emma, I swear. I didn't even think." Story of her life. She didn't think.

"You brought Kendall with you." Emma pointed to her car and Kendall waved merrily out the window at them.

"Yeah…" She sensed a trap.

"Why?" Emma asked.

"Why what?"

"Don't be dense. Why did you bring Kendall? Is she supposed to do it for you?" Emma obviously struggled to keep her voice in check. She was doing that scary angry thing where she yelled without raising her voice.

"What? No. Of course not. Kendall's here…" She couldn't tell Emma she'd brought her sister along to keep her from chickening out. "This is hard, Emma. Kendall's here because we all need some help from time to time. You said it yourself. This is one of those times for me."

"You brought along the family pit bull to act as your friend? Who are you kidding, KC?" Emma loved Kendall, but she clearly didn't love her being with KC when KC should be inside ending things with Lonnie.

"Don't be mean, Emma. That's not fair." She stepped closer to Emma and spoke softly. Emma had a right to her anger, but KC didn't. Even if Emma was being unreasonable, she didn't get to react. She had to make Emma feel better. To date she'd done a crappy job of it. She wanted to do better on this day and every other day going forward. Still, she didn't want Emma to take it out on Kendall.

"A lot of things aren't fair." Emma spun around and took off down the sidewalk, leaving KC and Maria behind. Maria looked at her and shrugged, then ran after Emma.

"Shit." She rubbed her face with both hands, then pushed them through her hair. So far it'd been a bang-up day.

Lonnie glared at her through the window, and KC debated getting back into her car and driving away. What was there to say to Lonnie? *Sorry, but I can't be your fuck toy anymore.* A few more missed dates and she'd have that message loud and clear.

"How you doing?" Kendall asked quietly. She'd joined KC on the sidewalk.

"Not great." She turned away from Lonnie to face her sister and found Kendall staring Lonnie down.

"You don't have to look at her like that. This isn't her fault." KC figured she would always feel the need to defend Lonnie. It was an old habit that didn't show signs of breaking any time soon.

"The hell it's not. She crossed a line. She doesn't deserve to get off scot-free." Kendall was righteously angry, which had sharpened her tongue.

"Probably not, but I'm not asking you to punish her. That's not why you're here."

"Doesn't mean I don't want to." Kendall continued to glare at Lonnie.

"Well, the way you're looking at her probably has her scared to the point of running." KC doubted it. Lonnie, just like any other God-fearing Texan, wasn't about to run from anything.

"Good." Kendall loosened her stance and looked at KC for the first time since the conversation began. "Ready to tell me what's going on with Emma?"

"I kissed her." The words slipped out and a rush of relief filled KC. It felt good to let the truth about Emma breathe life in the real world. When she'd told Kendall about Lonnie, she immediately wanted to take the words back, to squash the reality from growing stronger. But with Emma she was left with a strong urge to say it again, to as many people as possible.

"You kiss her all the time." Kendall shrugged. Sometimes she'd act dense to get the other person to 'fess up. This was most likely one of those times.

"This was different. I didn't want to stop."

"Oh." Kendall smiled her *I knew it* smile.

"Yeah, oh. And now I'm confused as hell." She kept saying she was confused because that's what she *should* be feeling. In actuality, she hadn't stopped thinking about Emma, and her thoughts had grown clearer with every passing minute. Emma was her life.

"What's confusing?" Kendall played her part of the good counselor. But it felt to KC like she was being humored.

"Until last Monday, I thought things were great just the way they were. Emma was my best friend and Lon…I mean Mrs. Truvall and I were doing great. Now everything is…different."

"KC, you and Mrs. Truvall were *never* doing great." Kendall shook her head. She looked ready to shake KC's, too.

"I know that now. But I put off talking to her and then things happened with Emma. And now Emma feels like she's a replacement."

"Holy shit. You told Emma about Mrs. Truvall?" Kendall did a double take. "Seriously?"

"I didn't tell her. She already knew." She smiled ruefully. "She's smart like you."

"What a cluster fuck." Kendall succinctly summarized KC's love life.

"Yep." KC agreed whole-heartedly.

"So why haven't you talked to Mrs. Truvall?"

"I've tried. She keeps putting me off." For once, the delay hadn't been on KC's part. She'd sorted out what she needed to say Sunday night after Emma and Kendall had gone home. She'd called every day, starting Saturday before she left Austin. After too many days of hearing *not today, sugar*, she'd given up on seeking permission. She'd called Kendall to come with her as support, and now she just needed to follow through.

"Is she expecting you today?"

"No. I just can't wait anymore," KC said.

"Jesus, KC." Kendall shook her head. "Are lesbians always this dramatic?"

She smacked Kendall in the shoulder. "Don't be a dick."

"Okay, sorry. But seriously, you need to take a deep breath."

"I know." She inhaled for show and then said, "It's time. Wish me luck."

Kendall hugged her and whispered, "I'm right here if you need me."

Kendall returned to the car and KC went inside. Lonnie was sitting behind her desk and didn't rise to greet KC. Per the usual, she'd closed the blinds to her office.

"Sugar, to what do I owe the pleasure?" Lonnie's smile was mechanical.

KC opened the blinds and waved at Kendall, then took the seat opposite Lonnie. "We need to talk." Her heart pounded in her throat like it had her first day of student-teaching. She'd been so nervous she'd thrown up in the bathroom at the school. But once she'd started talking, she'd been okay. She hoped this proved to be a similar experience.

"Do we now?" Lonnie leaned back in her chair and crossed her legs.

KC paused to collect her thoughts. The last time she and Lonnie were alone in this office, she had Lonnie bent over the desk in a very unladylike position. She gave the memory room to wander through her mind, to see if it awoke any impulse to repeat the event. It didn't. For the first time, she was certain she could do this.

KC smiled gently and said, "It's about time, don't you think?"

Lonnie leaned forward, fingers pressed against the polished surface of her desk. "No, I really don't."

"We can't keep doing this." KC kept going despite Lonnie's resistance.

"Why not?" Lonnie asked in an even, measured tone. Her face was strained.

"We've been careless. Too many people know." That wasn't the only reason, but it was a good place to start.

"So we'll be more careful." Lonnie folded her hands in her lap like it was all decided.

"Kendall knows." KC shook her head. "What if she tells my mama?"

"She won't. If she were going to, she would have already done it," Lonnie said defiantly.

"You don't know that. That's taking an awfully big gamble." KC couldn't believe how willingly she'd risked her family's trust. "Don't you even care about what she'd think?"

"Of *course* I care, KC. She's my friend. But I'm not ready to give you up."

KC heard the word *yet* at the end of the sentence even though Lonnie left it unsaid.

"And what happens when you are? Then we can end it? And to hell with what I want in the meantime?"

"Don't be silly." Lonnie waved her hand dismissively.

"What about Glen?"

"You leave him out of this." Lonnie was angry.

"How? Lonnie, you told Leann. It's only a matter of time until he finds out. Until everyone finds out."

"What is this really about? You haven't given two shits what anyone else will think for the better part of a year. Why the sudden streak of conscience?"

"Maybe I'm growing up."

"Is this about Emma? I see the way that girl looks at you. I swear—"

"It's not. It's about me." She was tired of trying to be soft with her message. Lonnie wasn't hearing any of it and KC was done. "It's not about Mama, or Glen, or Leann, or Emma, or any other person we can think to toss in the mix. It's about me. I don't want to do this anymore."

"Well, why the hell not?" Lonnie looked flabbergasted. "We have a good time. What's the problem?"

"Lonnie, I *hate* the way you make me feel. Like I'm a toy for you to play with, but nothing more. I'm supposed to drop everything and come running the second you call, but when I call, you are *never* available. I've been trying to see you for days and all I hear is no, no, no. I'm tired of it, Lonnie. Just plain tired. It's not right."

"KC, sugar, don't be rash. We can work something out."

"What? What can we work out? I'm done." She shook her head and stood. "There's nothing left to say."

"Wait." Lonnie stood but didn't round the desk. "Please don't go."

"Why? You don't love me. Why are you holding on so hard?"

"Don't tell me how I feel. You have no idea." Lonnie looked on the verge of crying.

"You're right. I don't." Talking about Lonnie's emotions was a dangerous place to go. It always led to KC putting herself second to what Lonnie wanted. "But I know how *I* feel. And I don't want this anymore." Their entire relationship had been founded on deceit and secrecy, and the thought of her eager participation made her sick to the stomach.

They had so much more to discuss, but she needed to get out of that office. Lonnie wasn't going to disappear from her life just because she said the words *it's over*. They went to the same church, sat at the same table for Sunday dinner. Their families picnicked together in the summer and sang carols together in the winter. They were intrinsically linked, and nothing KC said today would unbraid that cord. She said none of this Lonnie. They could sort out the details later.

"Good-bye, Lonnie." KC walked away.

Chapter Thirteen

"KC, get off that damned computer and come help Mama," Kendall yelled from the pantry. She'd arrived thirty minutes ago and hadn't stopped issuing commands since.

"Leave your sister alone, she's working." Her mama scolded Kendall, and KC had to give her mama props. She knew how to keep her family in line. Kendall might be preparing to take over the role, but Evelyn Hall wasn't ready to relinquish the title of matriarch just yet.

KC, Trina, and Buddy had been at their family home since early that morning. They'd been commandeered for a day of spring-cleaning. So far they'd shampooed the carpets, polished the family silver and china, cleaned the crystal chandelier in the formal dining room, cleaned the blinds, and dusted the crown molding. Her mama showed no signs of slowing, but KC was exhausted so she'd excused herself when they moved into the kitchen and pantry. It was time to take stock of what needed to be canned and preserved this season, and that couldn't be done without thoroughly washing the empty jars and organizing the existing inventory. Her mama took feeding her family seriously.

By rights, KC should be at her place, rather than at her family home. It was the end of finals week and she was up to her ass in grading essays. But she was going stir-crazy at home trying to keep her mind off Lonnie and Emma. Lonnie because she knew that even though she'd finally done the right thing and ended their relationship, it could all blow up in her face if the wrong person found out. And Emma because the longer she went without seeing her or hearing from her, the more certain she was that she'd blown her chance before she even knew she wanted it. And God did she want it.

Emma haunted her thoughts nonstop. She'd pour herself a cup of coffee and remember that Emma liked hers with cream and a bit of cocoa. A poor man's mocha, she called it. She'd change for bed and picture Emma in a baby-doll nightie and then feel guilty about objectifying her. But instead of banishing the image, her guilt would take a backseat to her lust as she mentally dressed Emma up in the entire Victoria's Secret catalog. She graded an essay about car safety and worried that Emma's Mini wasn't large enough to protect Emma from injury. Her mind was on an all-Emma-all-the-time loop.

Her compromise to satisfy her need to help her mama and still complete her work was to show up early in the morning and work most of the day. Then she brought out her laptop and graded papers. She'd stationed herself at the newly buffed and shining mahogany table, which glowed beneath the sparkling chandelier she'd spent an hour polishing. It took forever to wipe down every facet of every leaded crystal teardrop hanging from the monstrous thing. Thank Jesus her grandma and grandpa hadn't had a formal dining room with requisite gaudy ceiling lighting, or she would be forced to do the job twice each year instead of just once for her mama.

"Seriously, loser, get off your computer and come help." Kendall used language KC hadn't heard from her since high school.

"What is this? 2002?" KC stuck out her tongue without looking up from her computer screen. "Get off my ass. Nobody complained when you skipped out this morning because you had to work."

"KC, language!"

Kendall smirked.

"Sorry, Mama."

KC made it through a good two-thirds of the essays before their next interruption. Her mama, along with Kendall and Trina, joined her in the dining room. Her mama set a plate filled with a sandwich and some chips next to her laptop. Kendall, Trina, and her mama had similar meals.

"Eat." Her mama nudged the plate.

KC saved her work and closed her laptop. "What about Daddy and Buddy?"

"Your daddy took Buddy to get a burger," her mama said.

That was good news. She'd been worried about how Buddy was adjusting without the constant presence of Jackson in his life. Children needed a man to look up to. Her daddy was a good man.

"Great." She took a bite of her sandwich and considered their shifting family dynamics. When she was little, her daddy went to work every day and came home tired. He provided for his family but left the raising of his children to his wife. She couldn't remember him ever taking one of them for a burger alone. "What brought that on?"

"I asked Daddy to spend more time with Buddy." Trina stared at her sandwich as she spoke. "He agreed it was a good idea."

"Owen is going to take him and Winston for some boy bonding once a week as well," Kendall added. Spending time with Kendall's husband and son, his Uncle Owen and cousin Winston, would be time well spent for Buddy.

"Has Jackson asked to see him?" KC felt out of touch despite sharing the house with Trina. They divvied up household chores and KC helped with Buddy whenever she could, but the two of them never really talked.

"I haven't said a word to Jackson."

"He hasn't called or anything?" KC didn't want Jackson coming around, but she still couldn't believe he'd gone more than a week without checking on his wife and child.

"He told Owen he's trying to give Trina her space," Kendall said.

"What does that even mean?" her mama asked. "You young people always need your space. It's foolishness, if you ask me."

"You think I should have stayed?" Trina asked quietly. Their mama's approval was important to all three of them, but more so to Trina as the baby of the family.

"Katrina, honey, I said no such thing." Her mama patted Trina's hand. "I think you girls should have come to us and let your daddy handle this. He would have put a stop to it right quick."

"Or he would have made it worse." Kendall didn't mince words, not even to protect her daddy's ego.

"Yes, I guess that's possible, too. But right now he's feeling like he should have done something. It hurts a man's pride to not be allowed to protect his daughters."

"You raised us to take care of ourselves." Unlike Kendall, KC was reluctant to disagree with her mama. But they were raised to be self-sufficient, to not ask for help when they could do for themselves. She considered it an asset.

"Yes, I guess I did." Her mama looked like she wanted to say more, but held herself back. KC could only imagine the guilt she and her daddy were feeling after finding out how badly things had declined between Trina and Jackson.

"Well, we'll be forced to talk about it soon. Kendall filed a restraining order for me at the courthouse yesterday. Jackson was served this morning."

"At work?" It was a small town. Even though KC wanted to personally torture Jackson in severe and creative ways, she couldn't imagine the humiliation of being handed court papers while surrounded by work colleagues. If that happened, the gossip would come back to land on Trina as well. She was already fragile. She didn't need to be pushed any further toward the edge.

"No. Before."

"Your daddy said Jackson never made it in to work today," her mama said.

Jackson, for his notable flaws, was a hard worker. KC had to give him that. To her knowledge, he'd never missed a day of work save when Buddy was born. "Wow."

"I just don't want to take any chances."

They ate in silence. KC chewed carefully, thankful for once that she didn't have to carry the conversation. She hadn't known what would happen between Trina and Jackson, but had figured she might go back to him at some point. She'd been so wrapped up with Lonnie and Emma she hadn't really considered that Trina and Buddy might be a long-term addition to her home. A restraining order wasn't permanent, but it set some clear boundaries and gave a good indication of where Trina's thoughts were headed.

"We should switch rooms."

"What?" Trina sounded surprised.

"That way you'll have more room for the crib. It's only fair." Logistically it made good sense.

"KC..." Trina swallowed hard and her eyes shone. She was trying hard to keep hold of her emotions. "I've already put you out. I won't take your bedroom, too."

"Don't be silly. You're already cramped in that small bedroom. There's no place for the baby."

"She has a good point." Kendall spoke slowly, like she wanted to convince Trina but knew a full-on charge would only cause her to dig in further.

"It's KC's house," Trina said firmly.

"Bullshit." That was the second time KC had sworn in front of her mama, and she would surely pay for it later, but for now her mama sat quietly and let her girls sort out their disagreement. "We all know Grandma left me the house because she thought I was the only one who'd need it. Kendall was already married and you were well on your way. I needed a stabilizing factor in my life, and her house was it. It's as much yours as mine and you know it."

Technically that wasn't true, at least not on paper. The deed had been signed over to KC in the months prior to her grandma's passing. She'd protested at the time, but the transfer went through in her name only. Her grandma had an agenda, and there was no stopping her even when her health was in decline. Her grandma hadn't stopped loving her when she came out to her years before that; she'd just shifted the way she intended to take care of her. Kendall and Trina had respectable men to do that, but KC never would. Grandma wanted to fill that gap, and KC couldn't convince her that she didn't need a man, or her grandma, to take care of her. She was just fine on her own.

"She's right, Trina. But if you don't feel good about it, you could always move back here with your daddy and me. We have plenty of room." Her mama reached out and grasped KC's and Trina's hands. Trina reflexively grabbed Kendall's. Every day growing up they'd held hands over the table as they offered thanks before meals. She wished Kendall were closer so they'd be able to close the circle. Still, the contact made KC feel whole for the first time in too long.

"Thanks, Mama, but I don't think I could." Trina shook her head. Where to move her had been a point of little discussion. Kendall ruled out her own home due to overcrowding and their parents' home for similar reasons. Yes, there was physical space, but the memories of growing up there would close in on Trina just as quickly as Kendall's noisy children. Moving back to her childhood bedroom, which she left when she got married, would feel too much like a failure. She didn't need to go there when KC had empty rooms at her place.

Trina smiled at KC and swallowed. "Okay. I'll think about it."

"Good." Her mama squeezed KC's hand even tighter and tears streaked her face. "I'm so proud of you girls."

They sat that way long enough for KC's arm to cramp. The angle was awkward, but she wasn't willing to disturb the connection.

Finally, her mama released them and said, "Now that that's settled, tell me what else is going on in your lives."

KC filtered through her current life to find something suitable to share. Mama already knew about work. Finals week was a bitch and KC worked hard to keep up. Her living situation had changed, but it wasn't like her new roommates would be news. KC sure as hell wasn't going to talk to her mama about Lonnie. That left Emma. Was she ready to discuss how their relationship was evolving? Or was it too new to be sure?

Kendall spoke before KC could follow her train of thought to completion. "Owen and I are looking at vacation homes in Marble Falls." What that really meant was that Owen was looking at property and Kendall was looking at writing a check. The two of them had an unconventional relationship by Texas standards. Kendall worked and Owen minded the family and home. Finances also fell under his jurisdiction, and he was a wizard. He managed their money carefully and had a knack for finding the right stock at the right time. If Owen said it was time to buy property, Kendall wouldn't question his decision. KC respected his financial acumen. Starting with her first professional paycheck, she entrusted a percentage of her earnings to her brother-in-law to invest on her behalf.

"Why now?" At twenty-six, KC felt a little too young to be thinking about things like vacation/retirement homes, but was still curious about whether the timing was specific to their stage in life or the real-estate market. She could picture herself with Emma, old and gray, and perfectly content to sit on the front porch holding hands. Would Emma like Marble Falls?

"Owen says we can't put it off any longer. The market is showing signs of recovery, but housing prices and financing are in the right place still." Kendall shrugged. She understood more about real estate than she let on, at least the legal side of it. She might not understand market fluctuations, but she sure as hell knew the contract law that bound it together.

"That's lovely, Kendall." Her mama was a homebody. She'd said on more than one occasion that she didn't understand folks who had two houses. She could barely keep up with the one. But she was still proud Kendall was doing well for herself.

"Has he looked at Austin at all?" The question was out before KC had a chance to reflect on its origins. Emma couldn't qualify for financing, so why bother looking?

"No. Why? Are you?" Kendall raised an eyebrow and smirked. She really was insufferably smug sometimes.

KC laughed. "No. Emma's move just has me thinking, that's all."

"Oh, how is Emma? I've seen her at church but haven't talked to her recently."

The last time KC spoke to Emma, she'd stormed down the sidewalk to get away from her. She hadn't seen or heard from her since. She was sure, however, that Maria fucking Gutierrez had stepped in to fill the gap for her. KC cursed her own lack of certainty, coupled with her ridiculous schedule. She could have and *should* have called

Emma after she spoke with Lonnie on Wednesday, but had a million excuses why she hadn't. Yesterday she'd worked all day until late into the night. Today she'd promised to her family. Not that they'd mind excusing her for a quick phone call. In reality, KC didn't know what to say. It was a toss-up between *Want to go on a date with me?* and *I love you. Let's get married and live happily ever after.* Both made her feel like she was risking something precious, and that made her feel like she wanted to throw up. Silence was her compromise.

"She's good, I think. We haven't really talked since we got back home last weekend." The conversation on the sidewalk didn't count as talking in KC's mind.

"Why not?" Her mama's face displayed more concern than a week of non-communication warranted. She'd witnessed firsthand how miserable KC was when she and Emma weren't on speaking terms.

"We've both been busy." KC shrugged. She hoped that answer would satisfy her.

"That never stood in your way before." Apparently it didn't.

"Yeah, well, I guess it's different this time." How much did KC really want to reveal to her mama? She took a deep breath. "I'm thinking about asking Emma on a date." That sounded innocuous enough, didn't it?

"What?" Her mama looked stunned. "Oh, my."

Evelyn Hall was not shy about sharing her opinion. She felt it would be unfair to deprive others of her great insights when they were trying to make a difficult decision. Her silence worried KC.

"That's it? Oh, my?" KC asked.

"I, for one, think it's brilliant," Trina said with a smile.

"About damn time," Kendall added.

"Yes, of course, but why in the world did you wait until Emma's moving to have this epiphany? You're setting yourself up for heartache, aren't you?" And there was the opinion from her mama that KC had been waiting for. She didn't much like her summation.

"Austin's not that far. We can still see each other." Her feelings were too fragile to risk full examination, but that's exactly what she needed.

"Not only that, but are you sure you're ready to jump into a new relationship?" For all her pushing KC toward Emma, Kendall chose now to question the timing. She couldn't have done it when they weren't sitting at a table with their mama and baby sister?

"I'm fine." KC gritted her teeth and sent mental messages to Kendall to shut the fuck up.

"What are you talking about, Kendall?" Her mama shifted her focus from Kendall to her, then back to Kendall. "Why wouldn't she be ready?"

Kendall looked at KC and hesitated. KC spoke before Kendall could. "Because I've been seeing someone else. But we recently split up."

"Why am I just now hearing about this?"

"It wasn't serious." KC shook her head and cursed Kendall. What the fuck was she playing at?

"How long were you dating?"

KC flinched. The word *dating* didn't even come close to accurately describing her relationship with Lonnie. "A while."

"How long?" Her mama's voice was clear and concise and left no room for hedging.

"About a year." KC almost whispered. She couldn't remember the last time her mama had been legitimately angry with her.

"A year? Kimberly Carter Hall, I do not like being kept in the dark about the important parts of your life."

"It was never serious." KC tried to explain without explaining too much. "More convenient than anything." That statement bordered on flat-out lie. Her relationship with Lonnie had been far from convenient most days.

"Who was it?" Her mama looked like she was inventorying all the known lesbians in town.

KC closed her eyes and took a deep breath. "She's not out, Mama."

Her mama shot back, her patience spent. "So that means she doesn't have a name?"

"It means she doesn't want folks to know and I'm not going to betray her." She looked her mother square in the eye, trying to silently communicate that, even though she loved her, she wasn't budging.

"Okay." Her mama nodded. "But don't think you can block us out of your love life because you're trying to protect your daddy and me. We know who you are and we accept you as you are. We want to be a part of your life. All of it."

KC came damn close to crying at her mama's heartfelt declaration. It was the closest they'd come to actually talking about the fact that she was gay since she came out. And then the only thing her mama had said was, *Are you sure?* When KC said yes, she'd pulled her into a long hug and that was that. End of discussion.

"Thank you." Her voice was rough.

"We just want you to be happy, honey." Her mama held out her hand and KC took it. She squeezed her mama's palm like a scared little girl, which brought her even closer to crying. Before she could cross the line completely, her mama said, "Bring her to dinner Sunday. It's time we got to know her a little better."

Sunday dinner meant Lonnie and Glen. Introducing Emma to the mix with all the changes in relationship dynamics between her and Lonnie and her and Emma meant complete and utter disaster. "Um, I'll try. She might have plans already."

"I won't hear of no, KC. You bring that girl to dinner."

"Yes, ma'am." KC answered as a matter of reflex. When her mama used that tone, no other answer would do.

The sound of the front door opening interrupted their exchange. Her daddy and Buddy were home.

"Looks like our girl time is over," her mama said when Buddy ran into the room and climbed into Trina's lap. "I think we should call it a day. Thank you for your help." Her mama collected their plates and took them to the kitchen. They were dismissed. On Sundays, the job of cleanup fell to Kendall, Trina, and KC, while her mama visited with her friends. The rest of the week, she didn't want other people tracking through her kitchen.

KC took the opportunity to pull Kendall out onto the back porch while Trina was occupied with Buddy and their daddy.

"What the *fuck*, Kendall?" Now that she wasn't scared out of her wits that Kendall would blurt out Lonnie's name to her mama, she was working up some pretty righteous anger.

"I'm sorry. I don't know why I said that." Kendall looked remorseful, though KC didn't believe her.

"Bullshit. You *always* know what you're saying and why you say it. You don't make careless slips like the rest of the goddamned planet."

Kendall pressed her fingers to her temple. "You're right. I was angry. I'm still angry. But I shouldn't have said that."

"Goddamn right you shouldn't have."

"I'm sorry. Really." This time she believed Kendall's apology.

"Why are you mad?" She folded her arms over her chest. This was her mess and she was trying like hell to clean it up. She'd ended things with Lonnie. What else did Kendall want as penance? "Do you think I should tell Mama?"

KC saw that confession as pure disaster, but she'd been weighing it in her mind since her initial conversation with Kendall. Maybe she should just come clean all around and accept the consequences. She deserved them.

"God, no. That wouldn't help anyone."

"You don't think it's the right thing to do? Get it out in the open and stop keeping secrets."

"KC, that kind of revelation would hurt everyone around you. It might make you feel better to not have to hide, but I don't give a damn. You don't get to break Mama's heart just so you can feel better about finally doing the right thing." Kendall put air quotes around the word *right*. "That would be selfish and wrong."

KC threw up her hands in frustration. "Then why the hell did you bring it up in front of her?" She was even more confused.

"Because sometimes I'm selfish, too. I told you I'm pissed off at you. I'm trying to be supportive, but you were so *thoughtless* and what? You just get off with no consequences? That pisses me off even more. You shouldn't be able to just walk away and live happily ever after when you've treated the people around you like shit for a year, even if they don't know about it."

"I know." KC fought back tears. She wasn't the victim. She was the perpetrator and as such didn't deserve to cry on her sister's shoulder and beg for sympathy. She'd done that once and Kendall had been very patient with her, considering. It was time to own up.

She just hoped her past actions with Lonnie wouldn't cost her future relationship with Emma.

Chapter Fourteen

"I'll get the bags." KC spoke quietly so she wouldn't wake up Buddy in the backseat. After she and Trina left their parents' house, they'd stopped at the market and picked up a few items. Between the car seat and the grocery bags, KC's small car was packed. She was seriously overdue for a vehicle upgrade.

"Thanks." Trina slid the diaper bag high onto her shoulder so it wouldn't fall, then eased Buddy out of his car seat. It was a two-door car, so it was an impressive juggling act to get him out without waking him. Trina hummed a low, constant shush, shush, shush in his ear. He squirmed once, then snuggled into her arms and continued sleeping. Next time KC would remember to grab the diaper bag, too. Being a mom wasn't for the weak or uncoordinated, that was certain.

Berty jumped at Trina's legs when she entered the house. He'd been home alone for too long and missed his mistress.

"You need to get that pup into training." KC thought animals should be well behaved. That included not jumping on people.

"It's a process, KC." Trina sounded more annoyed than tired for once. It was a welcome change. "Potty training first. Isn't that what you said?" Trina didn't wait for an answer. She headed down the hall with Berty at her heels.

Thankfully, Trina waited until Buddy was tucked into bed and they were putting groceries away in the kitchen to bring up Emma. Trina transferred produce to the fridge and asked, "So, Emma?"

KC stacked cans of soup and considered her answer. She wasn't sure exactly what Trina was asking. Finally she used the question as the answer. "Emma." What else was there to say?

"Have you told her?" Trina asked.

KC nodded. "She knows."

"And how does she feel?"

"She…" What if KC said aloud that Emma loved her, but wasn't sure that she wanted her? The thought of adding breath to the thought made it hurt even more. "Emma loves me."

"Obviously, but what does that mean?"

KC turned so the counter was to her back and she was facing Trina. If the conversation went on much longer, KC was totally cracking the seal on the full bottle of Absolut in the freezer. "It means…" KC shook her head and sagged against the counter. "I don't know what it means."

Trina continued putting produce away—lettuce, broccoli, and apples into the crisper, tomatoes and bananas into the basket on the table. She didn't push KC for more.

"It's just complicated. She says she loves me, but she's not sure I'm ready. I swear, if I had her self-control, her ability to say no to the things I want, I wouldn't be in this mess."

"She knows about Mrs. Truvall, huh?" Trina spoke far too casually for that big of a bombshell.

"Wait. How do *you* know about Lonnie?" KC was going to *kill* Kendall. First the crack earlier in front of their mama, and to top it off, she told Trina? Fuck.

"KC, I have eyes. You two haven't been very subtle." Trina faced her fully. "I've been distracted, not living in a cave." Trina hesitated on the word *distracted*. She'd been so much more than that with all that happened between her and Jackson.

"How long have you known?"

Trina shrugged. "A few months."

"Why didn't you say something?" She felt queasy. How many other people knew?

"Why didn't you? I figured you'd talk about it when you were ready. Besides, I know who you're sleeping with is hot news in your life, but I had other things on my mind."

Those *other things* were definitely more pressing. KC felt like an ass. She had been turning her love life into a daytime soap, while Trina was trying to avoid getting hurt in her own home. And still Trina had noticed the happenings in KC's life months prior, whereas Jackson's abuse had escalated from yelling to full-on battering, and KC hadn't noticed anything wrong until it was too obvious to miss.

"I'm sorry, you know, for not seeing." KC paused, searching for the right words. "For not helping. For acting like my mini-drama was more important than what you were going through."

"It's okay. I could have told you. Or Kendall. Or Mama. Hell, I could have told Jackson's mama. She would have put a stop to it, too. I worked really hard to hide it from you."

"Why?"

Trina pulled out a kitchen chair and sat down heavily. "I was embarrassed. And I really thought he'd stop. If I tried harder, made things easier for him…"

KC bit her tongue. She had plenty of things to say about Jackson but didn't want Trina to feel judged. Best she kept her opinions to herself and just continued to remind Trina that she now had a safe place to live with people who loved her.

"KC, I *know*, without any doubt, that man *loves* me. As wholly and completely as any man has ever loved a woman. And I love him just as much. I didn't want to admit that we were so broken, that a love like ours could be that fractured and tarnished. We just… cracked and split apart under the pressure."

No amount of pressure justified Jackson raising a hand to Trina. God help him if KC ran into him any time soon. She wasn't confrontational by nature, but she'd stand up for her sister. He needed to see what a woman who was willing to fight back looked like.

"I pushed him. Too hard. And he just couldn't take it." Trina's hands shook and she clasped them together in her lap.

"I don't care, Trina." She chose her words carefully. It would be so easy to rant about what a failure of a man Jackson was. Trina didn't want or need to hear that. She knew better than anyone. "You have to know, no matter what you said to him, you deserved *better*. You shouldn't be afraid in your own home."

"I know." Trina nodded once, firmly. "I know. But I also know that there are two people in a relationship, and we both did our part to break it. He crossed a line, but I had a hand in things, too. You need to believe that."

"Why?" Her stomach rolled. Why was Trina so bent on defending Jackson? Love or not, at some point she needed to be able to lay blame where it belonged in order to move forward. "No matter what you say, I'm never going to believe that you earned a beating from your husband, Trina. Never."

"You weren't there. You don't know everything that happened."

"I don't need to." She was firm. Trina was her baby sister. No matter what, KC was on her side.

"Well, it doesn't matter now. I'm not going back." Trina sounded sadder than KC thought she should. She was thrilled that Trina had left Jackson and would do anything she could to keep her away from him.

"Good." She grabbed the last grocery bag. Just a few more items and they'd be done for the night. She wanted to change the subject, distract Trina from such heavy thoughts, but her mind continuously cycled from Emma and Lonnie, then to Trina and Jackson. She circled around the four of them over and over. "Wait, does Jackson know about Lonnie?" Holy hell, what a mess that would be.

"Probably not. We never talked about it."

"Thank God." The last thing she needed was a jilted and angry Jackson shouting her business all over town. "It's over. Me and Lonnie. I ended it."

"Good." Trina mustered a small smile and stood. "I'm going to check on Buddy."

KC needed to say something, to be reassuring somehow. Every thought in her head sounded disingenuous, like an empty platitude. But she couldn't just leave it. Trina needed to know that she was loved and supported, even if it sounded hokey. "I'm here, Trina. You don't have to do this alone."

"I know." Trina held KC's gaze for half a second, then walked down the hall. She snapped her fingers and Berty trotted along behind.

❖

KC fell asleep at her workstation in the living room. One minute she was grading a never-ending stream of essays, and the next she was being jolted awake by the sound of pounding and a frantic dog barking. It took a few seconds to clear her head before she figured out that Jackson was banging on the back door.

"Trina! Goddammit! Let me in. I have a right to see my son." He punctuated each word with a jamb-shaking fist against the door.

Trina stood in the hall, just out of Jackson's line of sight, shaking and crying. She held Berty in her arms, and the pup was trying hard to do his job. He barked and tried to get down. He knew he was supposed to eat the bad guy. She opened her mouth to respond, but KC stopped her with a shake of her head.

"Go take care of Buddy. I got this." She squeezed Trina's hand, then let her go with a nod. "Call Daddy."

Jackson yelled loud enough to rouse KC's neighborhood, and if he kept it up, Buddy would be awake and wailing right along with his daddy. Poor kid needed his sleep, not an angry man pounding on the door to get to him. KC dialed 911 and tucked the phone between her ear and shoulder. Then she pulled Emma's shotgun from the rack. She was willing to let the authorities handle things, but she refused to wait helplessly for them to arrive. She fed shells in and waited for the dispatcher to pick up.

Mabel Hawkins, an old family friend, came on the line. "Nine one one. What is your emergency?"

"Mrs. Hawkins? This is KC Hall. I need the sheriff at my place as soon as possible." Her stomach became as hard as a rock and a tremor ran through her. She was flat-out afraid. It made her sick to think that Trina had been living in the middle of that kind of fear.

KC heard a window shatter, and Jackson's voice rang through the house without the layer of glass to muffle it.

"Hurry, please." KC dropped the phone without hanging up and stepped into the kitchen.

She waited until she was close enough for Jackson to hear the unmistakable sound of a shotgun being racked, then brought it to her shoulder. She hated shotguns. Last time she'd used one, she damn near blew her own arm off. The recoil was too powerful and she hadn't braced herself properly. In this situation, though, with her adrenaline spiking and her hands shaking, she was thankful Emma had provided this weapon instead of a lightweight .22. If she pulled the trigger, no matter how much fear was running through her system, she would do some real damage. A shotgun had serious stopping power even when the shells were filled with rock salt.

She called out. "Jackson, this is KC. You're not talking to Trina tonight."

"You have no right to keep me from my family!" Jackson reached through the broken pane of glass to unlock the door. He twisted the handle and the door opened. He took two full steps inside before he looked up and saw the shotgun leveled at his chest.

"You just broke into my house. I have every right." KC was impressed with herself. Her voice was steady and the gun barrel didn't waver.

KC was a Texas homeowner. She could shoot Jackson dead on her Linoleum and no jury in the state would find fault with her. And Jackson knew it.

He wobbled on his feet. His eyes were bloodshot, and he smelled an awful lot like a Jack Daniel's distillery.

"Sheriff is on his way, Jackie." KC spoke softly and used his childhood nickname. She forced herself to remember that before he was her brother-in-law, he was her friend. That barely held her anger in check. "Why don't we wait outside for him?"

Jackson deflated. His bluster and anger seemingly drained right out through the soles of his boots. He shuffled through the door and sat on the long bench that lined the side of her house. He dropped his head into his hands and cried, shoulder-shaking, heartbreaking sobs. She sat next to him and shifted the shotgun to the side opposite him. She patted his back with her free hand and fought the rolling wave in her stomach. God help her, she didn't want to throw up on her shoes.

"I miss them so much." His voice was muffled and weak. He was a long way from the proud football hero she remembered.

"I know."

"She ain't ever coming back, is she?"

"I don't think so."

Jackson sobbed harder. KC rubbed circles on his back, comforting him like a child and struggling to reconcile the grieving man before her with the husband who brutalized his wife. She'd seen the bruises and was living in the midst of the fallout. Hell, she'd been faced with his fury not five minutes ago. He'd moved from crazy with rage to total contrition at a dizzying rate. He was pitiful.

"I fucked it all up." Jackson rubbed his eyes and sat up. "But don't think for a minute that I don't love her. KC, I do. I would die for her." His voice rang out solid and true. Alcohol and anger had no part of his claim that he would protect his wife to his last dying breath. KC believed him. But apparently that love ended when his temper was tested.

"Sometimes that's not enough." She patted his back again.

"She filed a restraining order."

"I know." She wanted to be able to say something better, but she had no other words. She was torn between comforting him and telling him to go to hell. She could only imagine the state Trina was in right now.

"Sorry about your window. I'll fix it."

"Jackson, you can't come here again."

"But I have to fix it, KC. I can't just leave it broken like that." Jackson pleaded with her, desperate, she thought, to fix anything just to show that he could.

"I'll send you the repair bill. You can make it right that way." She offered the compromise. He'd never be able to mend his relationship by writing a check, but sometimes a person had to learn the hard lessons and do what he could, not what he wanted.

He nodded and dropped his head back into his hands. "I want to be a father to my son."

"So be one."

"Do you think she'll let me see him?"

KC shrugged. "I don't know. It's not up to her. That's what the courts are for." She sure as hell hoped not, if this was how Jackson normally behaved. "But Trina's always been reasonable. You know that."

They sat quietly for a moment. KC heard a car pull into the driveway. No sirens, so it could have been her daddy or the sheriff pulling in silent.

"You have to do better, Jackson. You can't be like this in front of Buddy. It's not right."

This time he was the one to say, "I know."

KC's daddy rounded the corner and stepped onto the back porch, his .45 holstered on his hip. He looked from KC to Jackson to the broken glass, then back to KC.

"I see you have things in hand here." He nodded at her.

"Hi, Daddy." She felt a rush of relief. She imagined she'd always appreciate having him come to the rescue, no matter how old she got. She stood and kissed his cheek.

"Hello, sir." Jackson stood. He was slightly more stable than when he'd arrived, but not by much. How much had he drunk before heading over?

"Sit back down, son." Chester's voice was firm, but fair and soothing. He was hurting over this as well.

Jackson reclaimed his seat and KC took that as her cue to leave. She said, "Sheriff's on his way. I'll go check on Trina."

She left her father to watch over Jackson and went back inside. She stood in the kitchen for a moment and willed her body to calm. No luck. The adrenaline she'd been suppressing in order to hold the shotgun without accidentally shooting a hole in her wall rushed through her body and landed square in the pit of her stomach with a heavy thunk. She dropped to her knees and vomited in the trashcan.

When she was done, she wiped her mouth, drank some water, and decided against emptying the trash while Jackson was still out there. It could wait until later. Instead, she ejected the shells and returned the shotgun to the rack, then went to check on Trina.

Trina sat on the floor next to Buddy's crib. She ran her fingers through his hair, petting his head. "He slept through it all." Trina was no longer shaking. Berty was in her lap.

"That's good."

"I'm sorry," Trina said, her voice small and so very tired.

"About what?"

"All of it." She gestured vaguely toward the front of the house. "Jackson, the window, taking over your house. Everything."

"Oh, Trina, honey, you don't need to apologize. None of this is your fault. I'm glad you're here." *Where I know you're safe.*

"My head knows that, but my heart can't help but feel like I could have done more to make my marriage work."

She settled on the floor next to Trina and held her hand. They stayed that way until their daddy came to tell them that the sheriff had taken Jackson home. He'd file a report and let Jackson sleep it off in his own bed. Trina had excused Jackson's behavior again and again, but was any part of her angry about him getting off with barely a slap?

Either way, KC knew he wouldn't be back any time soon. It'd tear her up if she had to shoot him, but she would if she had to. He'd learned that tonight and wasn't likely to press his luck any time soon.

By the time KC cleaned up the glass, covered the window with plywood, and emptied the trash, it was past one in the morning. She took her cell phone with her when she crawled into bed. It was too late to call Emma, but she dialed the numbers anyway. She was emotionally wrung out and needed her.

"Wha?" Emma's voice was sleep-filled and adorable.

"Hey." Now that she had Emma on the phone, she didn't know what to say.

"Hey," Emma replied. She could hear her smile through the phone. "What's up?"

"I miss you." There was so much more, but it all boiled down to that one simple truth.

"Did something happen?" Emma woke up a little with each passing moment.

"Why do you ask that?" She found simple joy in sharing a quiet moment over the phone with Emma. She wasn't ready to give that up by talking about Jackson.

"Because you don't normally call me at…Jesus, one thirty in the morning. What's going on for real?"

"Em, I wouldn't have to call if you were here where you belong."

The hitch in Emma's breath made her smile. It was proof that Emma missed her, too.

"I want to be." She remained quiet, content to listen to the sound of Emma breathing. She fell into time with her, matching Emma's inhale and exhale with her own.

KC broke the silence. "There are so many things I need to tell you. But right now I just want to be with you."

"KC…" The way Emma said her name caused an ache to bloom inside of her.

"I know."

"Are you ready?" Emma barely whispered the question.

"I think so."

"Make me believe you."

"I told my family about you. About us. Or about the us that I want." She fumbled over her words. Emma had offered her an opening and she was fucking it up.

"What did you say?"

"I told them that I want to date you," she said simply. There was no point in mincing words. She'd made up her mind. It was time for Emma to know it.

"You do?"

"Yes. That and a whole lot more." She laughed. "I didn't tell them that part."

"Okay."

"Okay?" She couldn't believe it. Last time she'd seen Emma, she'd stomped away down the road, none too pleased with her. Now she was willing to set that aside and go on a date.

"Okay. I'm willing to try."

"Really?" She didn't want to talk Emma out of it, but she'd never felt so lucky. Luck apparently had a dampening effect on her vocabulary and speech.

"Yes, really. Let's date." Emma's choice of words reminded her of high school, and she let out a happy, relieved giggle.

She recovered quickly and asked, "What are you doing tomorrow night?" She was giddy, and she didn't want to take the chance that Emma was sleep-addled and would change her mind as soon as she woke fully.

"You tell me."

"I'll pick you up for dinner at six, okay?"

"Mmm, but before that you need to come over and help me pack. You've neglected me long enough." Emma was coy and forceful at the same time. KC liked it.

"I agree."

"KC? Not that I'm unhappy, but is that really why you called?"

She and Emma had a date. As far as she was concerned, nothing else mattered.

"Jackson showed up tonight. I had to call nine-one-one." She tried to sound nonchalant. She didn't want to upset Emma, but she also didn't want her to learn about Jackson's drunken late-night visit via the grapevine. She couldn't afford to be caught with another secret. Even though she wanted to give herself a rest from thinking about Jackson, this was important enough that Emma deserved to hear it from her.

"Are you okay?"

"Much better now."

"Want to tell me about it?" Emma asked. Her voice was sweet and honey-thick with sleep.

KC wanted to lie awake and listen to the sound of Emma's voice. It comforted her, calmed her heart, but sleep was creeping in on her, like a black fog, heavy and pressing. "Later. Let's get some rest now."

"Mmm."

By unspoken agreement, they didn't disconnect the call. She fell asleep to the sound of Emma breathing soft and steady through the phone.

Chapter Fifteen

KC waited on the front porch for Emma to answer. The last time she rang Emma's doorbell, they were both little. Given the tenuous new developments in their relationship, she defaulted on the side of good manners this time. She pushed the button and waited. It seemed more respectful somehow. She scuffed her boots against the painted hardwood and set the bag of breakfast sandwiches and cardboard carrier of coffee cups on the porch swing.

It was time to conduct a quick hygiene check. She blew into her cupped hands and sniffed quickly. Minty fresh. Next she pulled out the collar of her shirt to check on her deodorant. It was working in all its powdery scented glory. Moreover, she could still catch the slightest hint of CKfree, her perfume du jour. She'd started wearing the CK line back in high school when Emma handed her a bottle of One and told her she had to wear it because it was her namesake. Sort of. It had been a solid recommendation and KC had evolved with the line.

She waited an eternity between ringing the bell and Emma opening the door. It was still early and the temperature hadn't yet risen above eighty. She started to sweat. What if Emma changed her mind? Not many hours had passed since their phone call, but the world could change in the course of seconds. A few hours was more than enough for Emma to come to her senses and realize she was better, deserved better—

"Hey, you. Come on in." Emma stood just inside the door, looking fresh and lovely and perfect.

KC tucked her hair behind her ears, a newly developed nervous habit, picked up their breakfast, and stepped in. She passed too close and lingered too long. Emma was a magnet and she was helpless to resist. She should have been polite, given Emma room to breathe without inhaling her toothpaste, but she couldn't bring herself to move away.

"Hi." She pressed a shy kiss to Emma's cheek and internally berated herself for not going for her lips. "I brought breakfast." She held the bag aloft and smiled hopefully. Food and coffee were always a safe bet with Emma.

Emma eased into the room, brushing across her body as she moved. KC held perfectly still, not even daring to breathe. She'd parked herself too close to Emma, and it took an extreme effort to let her move away without dropping their food and pulling Emma close again.

"Come on." Emma led her to the kitchen and took the bag and coffee from her. "Thanks." She set them on the table then faced KC fully wearing a small smile that made her look like she knew a secret. A happy secret.

Emma wound her arms around her waist and pulled her into a hug. She sighed happily and relaxed for the first time since their shared dance in Austin.

"Can I kiss you?" Emma asked, her breath hot and hopeful against KC's neck.

"God, yes." She sounded too eager. Too relieved. And too much like she'd learned nothing. She pulled away but held Emma's hands in hers. She couldn't give up contact completely. "But we should talk first."

"Yes. We should." Emma turned two kitchen chairs to face one another and sat. She gestured to the other, indicating KC should join her. They sat close enough to touch.

She unwrapped Emma's sandwich first and handed it to her, then her own. She took a bite and chewed carefully. She'd thought about nothing except being with Emma, talking with her, and once again she found herself speechless when she should be following through.

"I think," Emma sipped her coffee, "I think you should go first."

She nodded. "Makes sense." After all, Emma had said what she needed to in Austin.

She took a deep breath. "First, you need to know I'm not playing. I wouldn't risk our friendship if I didn't think this could go somewhere." She chose her words carefully. She didn't want to sound like she had a U-Haul waiting in the driveway. She loved Emma but wasn't sure exactly what that meant anymore. Co-habitation might be a part of their future, but she wasn't ready to promise forever. "I want this to work. I don't know what will happen, but I'm…I'm here."

Emma surged forward and caught her in a forceful kiss. It started sloppy and lacked technique and migrated to a slow, languid exploration. Emma eased her tongue into her mouth and she forgot all about talking. She forgot her own name. Hell, she forgot to breathe. All that existed was Emma and her lips and her silky, smooth, erotic tongue. She grabbed Emma's shoulders to pull her closer. She wanted to climb inside of her.

"Oh, hello, KC. I thought I heard the doorbell." Emma's mama breezed past them like it wasn't unusual to find the two of them connected by their tonsils.

She flew back and sat in her chair, completely dazed and hoping for a miracle. Her mouth would start forming words at any moment, she knew it. Emma pointed at KC's mouth, then used her thumb to show her there was something on her lip. She ran the back of her hand over her mouth and wipe away a generous amount of drool and dignity.

"Hi, Mrs. Reynolds." She finally found her voice, but it was a much squeakier version of her normal self. Her heart pounded. The combination of being worked up suddenly, then dropped just as quickly, left her spinning.

Mrs. Reynolds rinsed out her coffee cup and set it in the sink. "Are you here to help Emma pack?"

She nodded. She was still trying to catch her breath, so a nod would have to work.

"I don't know why she's in such a hurry to put her things in boxes. She's not leaving for another two weeks."

"That's not very long, Mama," Emma said.

KC's mood shifted from giddy to somber. "No, it's really not."

"Yes, well, I have a house to show." Mrs. Reynolds dropped a kiss first on KC's head, then Emma's. "I'll see you girls in a few hours."

When the side door that led to the garage clicked shut behind Mrs. Reynolds, KC sagged in her seat. "Fuck." She laughed to let out some nervous energy. It worked like the release valve on a pressure cooker. If she didn't release some tension, she might very well explode. "I guess I should have asked if your mom was home."

"I should have said something." Emma smiled and took a bite of her sandwich.

"So, are we done talking then?" She hoped not. She still wasn't sure what it all meant.

Emma shook her head, chewed faster, then swallowed. "I don't think so, but maybe we can just talk about things as they come up?"

She liked that idea. "Okay. If you ever question anything, promise you'll ask me."

Emma set her sandwich on the paper wrapper, wiped her hands on a napkin, then took KC's hand in hers. KC was all in favor of handholding.

"There is one more thing." Emma hesitated. "I won't share. If we're doing this, you don't get to see other people." She spoke quietly, but her gaze never wavered.

"Of course not." She understood Emma's point, but it hurt. Apparently, Emma believed she was ready, but only to a degree. She still had to work through a layer of distrust before she'd believe KC was capable of being in a committed relationship. How long would it take for Emma to trust her? Would Emma always be waiting for her to fuck up? She debated pointing out that she'd always been monogamous in relationships; she'd just never demanded the same from others. Somehow, that didn't seem any better so she kept the comment to herself.

She held Emma's hand tight and kissed her as gently as she knew how. She used that brief meeting of lips to communicate every ounce of love, devotion, and patience that she would never be able to adequately express with words. She pulled away before it could escalate into an expression of lust rather than love. She wanted her message pure and undiluted by hormonal influx.

Emma chased her lips when she finally pulled away. She brushed their lips together for one last, soft kiss, then sat back. Emma left her eyes closed for a few seconds. When she opened them, they were dark and needy.

"I don't think I'll ever get tired of that." Emma touched her fingers to KC's lips and smiled. "Ever."

"Me either. I can't believe we waited this long to start." She tried to tease, but given the reason they had waited, the joke fell flat. "We'll just have to make up for lost time." She winked and kissed Emma quick and easy, like they'd been doing it for years. It occurred to her that technically they had been. She and Emma had shared a casual physical layer to their relationship forever, but she had been blind to what her need to constantly touch Emma really meant.

"We should go upstairs."

She smiled far too eagerly. She'd been in Emma's room lots of times. The mere mention of it shouldn't make her heart race out of control. "Okay." She stood quick enough to knock her chair backward.

Emma laughed. "I appreciate your enthusiasm, but I'm only inviting you to pack boxes."

"Right." Heat rose through her head. She hated to blush. She grabbed her coffee and made a beeline for the stairs.

Emma touched her arm, a gentle request for her to stop. Emma kissed her lightly and said, "I think you're adorable."

Great. Adorable was a far cry from sexy. But it was better than annoying and obnoxious, so she said, "Thanks."

Emma laced their fingers together and they walked to her room hand in hand. Boxes lined the hall leading to Emma's bedroom, and the reality of Emma's impending move set in. It was easy to talk about in theory. Since returning from her four years of college in Las Vegas, Emma had talked nonstop about moving to Austin. It was a fantasy. Faced with the physical evidence that it was happening, KC stopped short.

"You're really leaving."

"I am."

"Well, I think that sucks."

"The timing could be better."

"You could stay?" She knew the answer before she asked the question, but Emma needed to know that she wanted her here.

Emma smiled and shook her head. "You could come with me."

It took everything in her to not scream *Yes!* the second the invitation was extended. But she thought about her family, about everything they were going through, and especially about how much of herself she'd given up to be with Lonnie. She wasn't very fond of that version of herself, and Emma had made it clear she didn't like that part of her either. As much as she wanted to, following Emma to Austin was the wrong thing to do. At least for now. She needed to be sure of herself before she got lost in another woman again. Even Emma.

"I wish I could."

"Me, too." Emma looked as sad as KC felt.

"But Austin's close. I'll visit so much you'll get sick of me."

"Ha. I doubt that."

"And you'll come home on the weekends, too."

Emma hesitated, then said, "I don't know, KC. I'm going to be busy. This new job is going to be really demanding."

"So demanding they'll expect you to work weekends?"

"Probably, yeah." Emma shrugged. "The news doesn't wait for Monday."

"What'll happen when I come visit then?"

"You'll get to know Austin while I'm at work, and you'll get to know me when I'm not." Emma smiled seductively and KC almost forgot how frustrating their conversation was proving to be.

"I don't want to drive five hours to get to know Austin." She fought to keep her voice level. None of this was new information. She knew how demanding Emma's new career would be. She knew how much Emma wanted it. And she knew how much Emma had sacrificed and was willing to keep sacrificing, in order to make it work. It was unfair to whine about it at this point.

"Of course not, but it might be the best I can do. Not everyone can have a job like yours, KC."

"What does that mean?" When she chose her job, it had been a matter of right time, right place. She hadn't gone looking for it so much as she'd stumbled across it and recognized a good thing when she saw it. Emma had always been driven, always talked about a future in television production, whereas KC wasn't particularly passionate about anything. She'd decided on a degree in English lit because she liked to read and writing essays came easily. Not until three weeks away from graduating did she really consider that school was ending and she'd need to do something with her degree.

She got a Masters of Education to make her employable but didn't get excited about education until a friend mentioned the online K12 program as a potential employer. She'd been lucky. Some other teachers spent much of their time trying not to scream about their working conditions. Still, that didn't mean it was a pushover job, so Emma's jab confused her.

"It means that while you get to telecommute, set your own schedule, and have summers and holidays off, the rest of us have to report to an office and be accountable for the time we spend there."

"I don't have the summer off." Her defense was weak and she sounded petty, but the words still came out. "I'm teaching summer classes."

"But you don't have to."

"I do if I want to eat." Her employer was ideal in terms of flexibility, but unlike some schools that spread the pay over twelve months, KC didn't get paid if she didn't work. Period.

Emma sat heavily on her bed and held out her hand, an extended olive branch inviting KC to meet her halfway. KC sat next to her and pulled Emma's hand into her lap. She traced random patterns over the back of her fingers.

"I know the timing sucks, but what else can we do? I'm committed and I have to go. You can't leave here. We need to work with what we have or this will never last." Emma kissed her hand. "And I really, really want this to work."

"Can we define exactly what *this* is?" KC asked.

"What do you mean?"

"Are you my girlfriend? Or are we dating? We never really decided that part." She never moved this fast in a relationship. She was quick to escalate the physical and held back the emotional. With Emma, the opposite needed to happen. If she slept with Emma only to discover it was a game, it would leave her completely gutted.

"What do you want?"

"I want you to be my girlfriend. I want to know that while I'm here and you're there, you'll say no when some cute girl asks you out." She pictured Maria and grimaced. Emma had a pre-existing dating pool in Austin.

"I promise."

"Yeah?" Relief flooded her. Emma always kept her promises. "Me, too."

"Good." Emma pulled her into a hug and nuzzled her cheek against hers. "We can make this work."

"We have to." KC agreed because she didn't have any other choice.

KC felt even stranger when she rang Emma's doorbell the second time in one day. They'd worked together through part of the afternoon, but she'd left a few hours ago to get ready for their date. Emma had offered to come along then to save her the trip, and when she declined, Emma offered to meet her at the restaurant. Frankly, Emma's need to be practical was screwing with KC's groove. She wanted to woo Emma, and wooing rarely aligned with practical.

She juggled two bouquets and a bottle of wine into one arm and straightened her hair with the other hand. She hoped to God Emma liked what she'd done with it, because it would take years to grow back to its former length. That afternoon, she'd left Emma and gone straight to her daddy's barber. No messing around with an in-between bob. She'd had it all cut off and gelled it straight up. Emma needed to answer the door and tell her if this haircut had the same effect as the last time she had short hair.

Instead of Emma, Mrs. Reynolds answered the door. "Oh, KC. Come in." She held the door open with a bemused smile.

KC stepped across the threshold but didn't go any farther. She had a point to make about her intentions, and charging up the stairs to continue where she and Emma had left off earlier in the day wouldn't send the right message. "Thank you, ma'am. These are for you." She offered Mrs. Reynolds the smaller of the two bouquets and the bottle of wine.

KC had never worked so hard to impress a girl's parents before and was traveling uncharted territory. But she remembered Owen's moves back when he'd been courting Kendall. He'd arrived to their first date with a firm handshake for her daddy, a box of chocolates and flowers for her mama, and flowers for Kendall as well. Her daddy had been impressed, her mama swooned, and Kendall promptly fell in love.

Mrs. Reynolds took her gifts and her smile grew about a mile. "Thank you, KC. Emma will be right down." She headed toward the kitchen but then turned back. "Your new haircut looks fetching."

KC ran her hand through her hair and could feel a blush rising in her cheeks. "Thank you, ma'am." She hoped Emma responded as well as Mrs. Reynolds. "I'll wait right here for Emma."

A few hours ago, she had been upstairs with Emma. Yes, they'd worked hard packing her belongings, but they'd also spent plenty of time getting to know each other in a new way. She'd never kissed anyone so much in such a short period of time. She was officially addicted. The memory made her blush harder, and she felt awkward waiting in the foyer of a home she practically grew up in. Mrs. Reynolds's light laughter in the other room as she filled a vase with water didn't help at all.

KC heard Emma on the stairs before she saw her. When she came into view, KC grinned like a fool. She couldn't believe how lucky she was that a girl like Emma had agreed to date her, and she was infinitely relieved that she hadn't missed the opportunity completely.

Emma wore faded denim jeans, polished boots, and a plain black T-shirt. KC was in love. As much as she liked it when Emma put on her pretty red dress, she loved Emma like this, with her hair flowing down her back and dressed to enjoy herself. This was the Emma she had fun with.

"Hey." KC barely managed a whisper. The weight of what they were doing settled in her chest, and it felt good and solid. Emma, perfect and beautiful, wanted her, and she'd be damned if she was going to blow it. She stepped forward and met Emma at the foot of the stairs. She held out the flowers and said, "You look great."

"So do you." Emma ignored the flowers and played her fingers through the tips of KC's hair. She kissed KC lightly. "Did you do this for me?"

She shrugged. "Do you like it?" The haircut had been as much to declare a change as to please Emma.

"I love it." Emma continued to toy with her hair for a few more moments, then seemed hit by sudden awareness that she was still holding flowers. "Are those mine?"

She nodded and swallowed. She shouldn't be so damned nervous. "Yes."

Emma kissed her again and lingered on her lips just a fraction longer. She left behind the sweet taste of strawberry lip gloss. KC had never noticed the flavor before. She released the flowers to Emma and smiled, dumbstruck by Emma's kisses.

"I'll put these in water." Emma laughed and joined her mama in the kitchen.

Perfect. Now they're both laughing at me. Their laughter was good-hearted, but she was still embarrassed. No amount of laughter, however, would convince her that Emma wasn't worth the effort.

"Ready?" Emma returned and took her hand lightly.

"KC?" Mrs. Reynolds followed them to the door. "You don't keep Emma out too late, you hear?" The glint in her eyes assured KC she was teasing, but she took the warning seriously.

In her most somber voice, she said, "No ma'am, I won't." She wanted to take Emma home and keep her close through the night, but she couldn't. The easy affection that allowed them to sleep in the same bed without escalating to a sexual encounter was long gone. She wanted Emma in the worst way, and she wouldn't let herself give in until they were both sure it was the right time.

Emma giggled and dragged her out of the house and into her car. "You're being so serious. It's adorable."

"That's twice today you've called me that."

"I can't help what's true."

She still wasn't sure adorable was what she was aiming for. "Thanks, I think."

"Oh, trust me. It's a compliment." Emma punctuated her sentiment with a long, deep kiss. "You brought my mama flowers and wine. That's adorable."

"I was trying for charming and debonair, not adorable," KC grumbled.

"Oh, it's all those things, too. She's wishing she was in my place right now." Emma's expression changed and she immediately sobered. Mrs. Reynolds was the same age as Mrs. Truvall.

"Well, that's too bad." KC tried to re-inject a little of the previous lightness to their mood. "Because from now on, you're the only one who gets to be in your place." She smiled and wiggled her eyebrows.

"What?" Emma laughed. "That made *no* sense."

"What I meant was, you're the only one I want to be with." She said the words seriously, with as much sincerity and honorable intent as humanly possible. "And that makes all the sense in the world."

"Yes, it does." Emma stopped laughing, but her eyes sparkled with happiness. "Where are you taking me?"

She started the car and backed out of the driveway. "Wait and see." She took Emma's hand and kissed her knuckles. Fairmont was a small town. There were only so many options for dinner, and it wouldn't take Emma long to figure out where they were headed. Still, KC wanted to enjoy teasing her for a while longer.

Emma pulled their joined hands into her lap and smiled. "That's how it's going to be? We're dating so suddenly you're all butch? Showing up with flowers and wine and a new haircut? Taking me to a mystery dinner? Are you going to order for me, too?"

New haircut or not, KC couldn't pretend to be the one in control. As far as she was concerned, Emma called all the shots. "Do you want me to?"

"God, could you be any sweeter?" Emma stretched across the console and kissed her on the cheek.

While they flirted, she navigated the streets and angled her car into a street-side parking space in front of Gloria's Steak and Seafood. It was one of the few places in town that served wine and beer along with some truly kick-ass steak.

Emma laughed. "You actually could order for me here." Emma always ate the same thing: rib eye medium rare, with a salad and a cheddar biscuit. Sometimes, for fun, she'd add a skewer of shrimp on the side just to mix it up.

"I could, but I won't." She smiled. She aimed for the lopsided grin that girls seemed to like a lot but wasn't sure it worked. She was too damn happy to keep half her mouth from smiling tonight.

Before she opened the car door, she ran her hands through her hair one last time. She was debuting a new haircut in the most popular dinner restaurant in town. She was nervous. "Do I look okay?"

Emma gave her a smoldering look that made her want to turn around and take Emma to bed immediately. "You look really sexy."

"So do you." She cupped the back of Emma's neck and eased her fingers into Emma's hair. She kissed her gently and with promise. There would be plenty more kissing in their future, but first they needed to get through dinner. "Let's go in."

On the walk to the entrance, she wished she could hold Emma's hand. She had to restrain herself from grabbing it.

In fact, she couldn't think of anything else and was proud she made it from the car to the entrance without tripping over herself. Given the ball of nerves rolling in her belly, she expected to lay herself out flat at any given moment. She held the door open for

Emma, and as they were entering, they ran into Lonnie, Glen, and Leann.

"Well, hello, girls." Glen greeted them with friendly enthusiasm, and she felt like an even bigger jerk for running around with his wife behind his back

She swallowed a surge of guilt, adding it to the already sizeable amount of tension in her stomach. "Good evening, sir. Mrs. Truvall. Leann." She nodded to all three in turn. "How was your dinner?"

"Delicious as always," Glen said. He appeared oblivious to the wall of irritation coming from Lonnie and Leann. Leann focused her glare solely on KC. She couldn't blame the kid. She would glare like the devil if she found out her mama was having an affair, too. Lonnie looked at KC's hair, smiled unkindly, and shook her head. KC's stomach tightened. Emma didn't deserve whatever anger Lonnie had inside her aimed at KC.

Lonnie asked, "Are you girls on a date? How sweet."

"Thank you, ma'am." Emma answered with an equal amount of venom. "It's been a long time since KC's had someone she could take out for dinner. I'm enjoying the attention."

She needed to get Emma inside before the two of them went at it right there in the vestibule. She smiled at Glen and said, "We won't keep you and your family any longer, sir. Have a good night."

"All right, KC, we'll see you for dinner tomorrow." Glen led his family onto the sidewalk and let the door swing shut behind him.

Shit. She'd forgotten all about Sunday dinner. Her mama expected Emma to be there, and KC still hadn't mentioned it. If meeting for a few seconds in a public business was that tense, she couldn't imagine an entire meal with both women present.

"Are you okay?" She wanted to work her arm around Emma's waist and pull her close. Being reminded of Lonnie couldn't be easy for Emma.

"Yeah. I'm just trying to figure out what you ever saw in her."

KC didn't answer until after the hostess had seated them. She gave them a secluded booth with a view of the street. As KC slid into the seat, she noticed Shannon Lewis, one of Glen's employees, two booths down dining with her family. She stared out the window at Glen with a look of sad desperation.

When KC turned her attention back to her own table, she found Emma staring at her intensely. She smiled nervously. "What?"

"Are you sure, KC?"

"Sure? Of what?"

"Of this. Of us. Are you sure, *really sure*, that you're ready? Maybe you should try being single for longer than a week."

She took a deep breath. She hated constantly feeling like she had to defend herself, but what else could she expect? She'd set herself up to be second-guessed and scrutinized; she couldn't throw a fit when it happened. "I'm not sure what you're asking. Am I ready to drop to one knee and promise forever? No. I'm not. But because it's you, that thought doesn't freak me out completely. And that means a lot to me. It should mean something to you, too. I don't know for sure that this is going to work. But I know that I want to find out. I think we'll be amazing together and I want to try."

Emma shook her head. "But are you ready for this? For everything that goes with being in a relationship with me? I'm not someone you can hide away from your family for the next year."

"I know that, Emma. And I'm not going to try. I've already told my family. I asked you on a date. I rang your doorbell and greeted your mama with respect, and if she wants, I'm prepared to talk about my intentions. I walked into this building wanting to be able to hold your hand. And the way I've been looking at you tonight will fuel beauty-parlor gossip for months."

"I know." Emma shook her head. "This was all just a lot easier for me to deal with when I ignored my feelings for you. Now that you know how I feel, I can't pretend that it doesn't hurt to think about you with Mrs. Truvall. Seeing her makes me question everything. I'll be devastated if you tell me in two months that you've changed your mind."

"So what? We don't try?"

"I didn't say that." Emma shook her head slowly and gave her a smile that somehow communicated that she was sad and that she thought KC was insane for suggesting they stop.

"Emma, tell me what you need from me. If you want me to stand on the table right now and announce that we're officially dating, I'll do it. I was Lonnie's secret for too long. I'm not willing to hide in someone else's closet again. And I'm certainly not willing to put you in one." She debated switching sides of the table. She wanted to slide into the booth next to Emma, put her arms around her, and promise that they were going to be okay. "Tell me. Whatever you want."

"Just be patient with me, okay? I've spent a long time hiding my feelings. It's going to take a little while for me to trust them being so exposed."

"I can do that." She sensed Emma was still holding back, so she pushed for more. "What else?"

Emma inhaled heavily. "Okay, you went from crazy for someone else to crazy for me in two seconds flat. I don't understand how that's possible. I've been in love with the same person for years."

She looked around. She didn't want to have this conversation in the middle of Gloria's. The waiter would come around for their order any second. Nothing about the setting screamed intimate, heart-felt conversation. But if she didn't seize the moment, the rejection she sensed simmering beneath Emma's skin might be brought to the surface by fear. It looked like she didn't have a choice but to say what needed to be said right here, right now.

"You want to know about Lonnie?" She asked the question quietly. The restaurant was full of people they both knew. Odds were nobody was listening, but that didn't mean she wanted to take the chance and accidentally share her business all over town.

Before Emma could respond, the waiter showed up as predicted and they placed their orders. She was less enthusiastic about the steak than she had been when she picked Emma up earlier.

When Emma didn't respond even after the waiter left, she continued. "Remember how you used to have a crush on Mrs. Lowenstein?" Mrs. Lowenstein had taught geometry their senior year of high school. "You would go to class early and stay late. You'd ask for special meetings for her to clarify assignments you understood perfectly. You were head over heels, right?"

She waited for Emma to agree, which gave her a chance to group her thoughts. "And you felt it with some very real desperation, but the emotion itself wasn't real, right? And you carried that crush, or the idealized memory of it, to Las Vegas with you after you graduated. And eventually it faded naturally over time. But say you came back from college and discovered that Mrs. Lowenstein was just as into you. Would you go for it?"

"I don't…"

"Be honest with yourself. Your teenage fantasy shows up and wants to take you to bed. You wouldn't let yourself be seduced?"

Emma shook her head. "That doesn't explain why you kept going back for a year."

Ouch. "You're right. I don't know what to say. It was just easy." KC didn't like to think too hard about Lonnie, about what their affair said about KC. What kind of person was willing to hide something that important from her best friend, from her family? It didn't speak well of her, and yet KC knew it had been something she needed. As desperate and sad as that sounded, she thrived under Lonnie's attention. Lonnie was the first person in this damn town to make her feel like she was okay, because even *normal* folks sometimes want things they're not supposed to. That, combined with her constant lust for Lonnie, was enough to keep her from thinking about how fucked up it was to keep that kind of secret.

"Okay." Emma nodded slowly. "I don't like it, but I guess I can see that."

"Lonnie was a crazy teenage crush and we never should have taken it any further. Once it started, there just wasn't a good-enough reason to stop. No, that's not right. There was plenty of reason, but I was too selfish to see it. It took me a long time to realize the risk I was taking with my family. I'm embarrassed about that. But it's over and done, and I'll never do anything like that again."

"Go on."

She exhaled and took a drink of water. She was halfway there. "When I finally ended things with her, I realized that the emotion I'd entered the affair with was false. It was shallow and immature and I outgrew it a long time ago. I just wasn't ready to let go."

She had worked through all of this in her own mind over the course of the past few weeks, but hadn't said any of it aloud. She felt foolish for having let something so superficial persist for so long.

"I don't know where we're going. I can't make any promises. But I can tell you that my feelings for you are real, and they are worth exploring." Even though she loved Emma, she wasn't willing to use that word in this instance. It had too many layers of meaning, and she didn't want to imply a deeper level until she knew for sure herself.

"You didn't even know I was alive."

"Oh, Emma." That couldn't have been further from the truth, but she didn't know how to change Emma's mind. However, this conversation was too important for her to just give up. "I was devastated when you stopped talking to me in high school. I spent three months in silent hell because I was sure you'd never speak to me again. I promised myself that if you ever decided we could be friends, I would never say or do anything to make you feel uncomfortable around me. It wasn't a matter of not feeling anything for you. It was more a matter of you reminding me that I was allowed."

Emma stared at her without speaking.

"Please tell me you understand." She was damn close to pleading.

Emma nodded and started to respond as the waiter set their dishes on the table. When he left them, Emma finished. "This isn't going to be easy. For either of us. I've wanted you for so long and convinced myself that I'd never have you. It's hard to believe that all I needed to do was just ask."

KC couldn't stop herself from stretching a hand across the table. The slightest touch from Emma calmed KC, cleared any uncertainty from her mind. She wanted to offer the same to Emma, a nonverbal reminder that they'd be okay if they remembered to talk things through.

Chapter Sixteen

KC followed Trina down the church aisle. She didn't normally sit next to her sister, but since she was carrying Buddy she had limited options. Trina selected a pew in the middle where Kendall, Owen, and their children were already seated. Trina sat next to Kendall and turned to KC. "Sit with us, okay?"

"Yeah." She joined them and hoisted Buddy onto her lap. It wasn't her usual spot, but Emma should still be able to find her. Their church wasn't *that* big.

"Thanks." Trina faced forward, so it was unclear if she was speaking to her or Kendall. She suspected both. Kendall took Trina's hand and held it, but didn't respond.

This was Trina's first time at church since she'd left Jackson. She'd skipped the service last weekend while KC was away in Austin. Given Trina's position, she probably felt safer when flanked by both her sisters. Had they just arrived at a new Sunday seating arrangement?

"Here you are." Emma slid in next to her, filling the pew. "Why aren't we sitting in the back?" The last few rows were home to the young and single, like her and Emma. Families took up the middle.

She shrugged and nodded toward Trina. "I hope it's okay."

"It's perfect." Emma briefly touched her hand and then leaned around her to say hello to everyone else.

The music started and the choir stepped onto the risers, signaling that the service was about to begin. During the opening notes of "Glory to the Redeemer," a few stragglers entered through the side door that led directly to the parking lot. KC hoped they had better luck finding a space than she did when she arrived at this time.

Jackson was among the latecomers. Instead of his usual Sunday suit, he wore rumpled black slacks and a button-down shirt. The top two buttons were open and his tie hung loosely around his neck. He stared at Trina and Buddy for several long moments, then finally selected a seat directly across on the opposite side of the aisle.

KC shuffled her hold on Buddy and then grasped Trina's free hand. Feeling a slight tremor in Trina's grip, she whispered, "It's okay."

Trina nodded once and didn't look in Jackson's direction again. KC squeezed Trina's fingers and listened to the choir sing. She wished she could follow Trina's lead and simply not look at Lonnie, but their relative positions made that impossible. The only way for her to avoid seeing the choir would be to turn her head away, which would draw attention from every one, including her mama. She took a deep breath and stared straight ahead.

When Buddy started to fuss, Emma took him from her. She bounced him on her knee like it was the most natural thing in the world, then pulled a baggie of Cheerios from her pocket and showed them to him. He smiled and reached for them. Emma held the bag and fished them out for him one at a time. She kissed Buddy's hair and smiled.

Trina squeezed KC's hand and mouthed, "Thank you."

Her heart felt full to bursting. She was surrounded by the people she loved, and life was moving in the right direction. She was doing good for those who mattered. Emma smiled and played quietly with Buddy. KC's heart squeezed tighter. After this, they had one more weekend together. Then Emma would be gone. She wished she could capture this moment and hold it just a little longer.

After the service, Trina reclaimed Buddy and headed to the restroom. Kendall followed her. KC lost track of Jackson in the after-church press of bodies, but figured Trina was fine with Kendall acting as watchdog. She did see Shannon Lewis slip out the side, with Glen not far behind.

"Let's get out of here." She rested her hand on Emma's low back.

"Don't sneak off yet." Her mama grabbed her in a hug. "I haven't seen you in forever."

She dutifully kissed her mama's cheek and said, "You saw me Friday."

"Hush." Her mama swatted her arm, then pulled Emma into a hug as well. "Emma, honey." She held Emma a little longer than necessary and KC squirmed. Finally she let her go and said, "I'm just so happy for you two."

"Thank you, ma'am." Emma blushed, and it was fun to watch her suffer through the scrutiny she had been subjected to when she'd picked Emma up for their date the night before. "We're still feeling it out, but I'm pretty happy, too."

Lonnie stood next to her mama looking a little too disinterested for her lack of attention to be real. KC wanted to take Emma by the hand and lead her away but couldn't justify being overtly rude. "Hello, Mrs. Truvall. You sounded lovely today, as always."

"Why, thank you, KC." Lonnie's sweet smile left a saccharine residue on the words. She obviously wanted to get out of there as much as KC did.

"All right, we'll leave you girls alone," her mama said. "Emma, you are joining us for Sunday dinner, aren't you?"

KC couldn't decide who looked more shocked at the announcement, Emma or Lonnie. It was going to be a fun afternoon.

"Mama, I'm sure Emma has other plans." She tried to give Emma an out.

Lonnie narrowed her eyes and smiled. "Well, we'll sure miss you, sugar."

Emma stepped closer to her. "As it turns out, I'm free for the afternoon. I'd be delighted to join you."

"Perfect." Her mama just about squealed like a schoolgirl. How long had her mama been wishing for her to date Emma? Or maybe it was just a desire to see all her girls happily settled, and this was the first hint KC had ever given of heading that direction.

"What's perfect?" Kendall joined them. Trina was nowhere in sight.

"Where's Trina?" KC asked. One of them should be with her.

"I don't know. I thought she was with you." Kendall looked around, her brow furrowed.

"You didn't go with her to the bathroom?"

"No. I needed to speak to Melissa's Sunday-school teacher." Melissa was Kendall's oldest daughter.

"Oh. I'll be right back." She started walking before Kendall finished, Emma following her.

"I'm with you." Kendall fell in step.

They found Trina standing just outside the restrooms. Buddy was on her hip and she was talking quietly with Jackson. Tears ran down Jackson's face, and Trina looked thoughtful and resigned, but not afraid.

"Everything okay here?" KC held out her hands to take Buddy, but Trina stopped her.

"We're fine. Jackson wants to see his son." Trina sounded eerily calm.

Trina might have been calm, but that statement had the opposite effect on KC. "What?" She tried to channel whatever Zen Trina was demonstrating, but she fell short. Jackson was volatile and, as far as she was concerned, had no business being near Buddy until he sorted himself out. Emma touched her arm, which helped settle her breathing.

"We were just trying to sort out the best way to make that happen." Trina's voice gained strength with each word. "He knows how I feel about him being alone with Buddy right now, but we're trying to find a compromise."

"Whatever you want, Trina. I just miss him." Jackson sounded broken. If she hadn't seen his whiplash-quick transformation from enraged to remorseful for herself, she might have believed him a changed man.

Trina turned toward Kendall and her, her face set in a strong line. "Why don't you all let me talk to Jackson alone? This is between us." When Kendall started to protest, Trina cut her off. "I'll be fine."

"Okay." Kendall nodded as her mouth curved into a knowing smile. "We'll be just over there." She led KC and Emma away.

"What the hell just happened?" KC asked.

Emma slapped her arm. "KC, language."

"Sorry." She flashed on the image of her and Emma together twenty years in the future. She would still say the wrong thing, no doubt, and Emma would be there correcting her. The thought made her impossibly happy. "But seriously, what just happened?"

Kendall studied Trina. "I think our baby sister might have found her feet."

"I can't believe you didn't tell me about this." Emma didn't sound nearly as angry as she expected.

"I didn't think you'd want to go. I was trying to save you from an awkward afternoon." *With my ex-lover.* They were sitting in Emma's car outside KC's family home. By the look of the driveway, they were the last to arrive.

"You don't get it, do you?" Emma took her hand. "You know how hard you tried to impress my mama last night? It worked. Now I want a chance to do the same with your folks."

"My parents aren't the only ones in there, Emma."

"I'm not going to crawl away every time Lonnie Truvall shows herself. She needs to know that you're off-limits."

"She does."

"Really? You think she won't come calling for you the second she has the inclination? Just because you said no doesn't mean she believed you."

"Oh, hell, you're not going to talk to her, are you?"

"I'm not planning on it. I just want her to see us together." Emma climbed out of the car and leaned back in the open door to finish speaking. "That's enough for me."

"Fuck," KC muttered as she got out of the car. This afternoon was going to be a disaster.

"Yes, before you ask, you can hold my hand." Emma took hold of her. Under other circumstances, she would probably have enjoyed Emma's commanding touch, but as she walked up the front stairs all she had time to do was brace for impact.

They entered to find everyone present except Glen. The Truvall family car was in the driveway, so his absence was conspicuous. After she said her hellos, she asked, "Is Mr. Truvall coming?"

In retrospect KC realized she probably shouldn't have asked, but Lonnie was a handful even with Glen present. KC didn't want to find out how difficult she could be when her husband was missing from their regular Sunday dinner.

"He had a minor issue at the store. He'll be along shortly." Lonnie sipped her whiskey and carefully avoided looking at Emma.

"Inventory?" Emma asked the question with an arched brow.

KC squeezed her fingers and telepathically screamed for Emma to stop.

"Mmmm." Lonnie regarded Emma levelly. "Tell me, Emma, when are you moving to Austin?" She smiled with far too many teeth.

Emma held Lonnie's gaze. "In about a week."

Lonnie inclined her head to the side. "What will our poor KC do without you here to entertain her?"

KC choked on her own fear. They were about two seconds away from a full-on catfight. She wrapped her arm around Emma's shoulders and held on for dear life.

"I'll be wearing out the road between here and Austin, that's for sure." She kissed Emma on the cheek. Before she pulled away, she whispered in Emma's ear, "Please, Em."

"Oh, you two are so sweet." KC's mama clapped her hands together. "Lonnie, didn't I say they would be adorable together?"

"You sure did." Lonnie drained her glass.

"KC, I have to admit, I didn't think I'd like your hair when you told me about it over the phone yesterday, but it really is attractive on you." Her mama smoothed the spiky part of her hair.

"Quit it." She ducked out of reach. "It's supposed to look like that."

"I know. I just think it'd be so much nicer if you'd get it to lay down properly." Her mama eyed her critically. "What do you think, Lonnie?"

"It looks very becoming." Lonnie smiled archly. "If you don't mind the whole town *knowing*."

"Knowing what?" Kendall stood, hands on her hips. It was unclear if she didn't realize what Lonnie meant or if she was defending KC.

"That I'm gay, Kendall." She touched Kendall's arm lightly. She appreciated Kendall's self-appointed need to act as guardian, but she didn't need protection from the truth. "They already know, Mrs. Truvall. Secret's been out for a long time."

"And with that, it smells like dinner is ready. Let's get it on the table." Their mama headed toward the kitchen, and her daughters fell in line behind her. The subject was officially changed.

"Come help us?" KC asked Emma. No way was she was leaving her in the living room with Lonnie. Even with the men and children to act as a buffer, they wouldn't both survive.

Emma stared at Lonnie a moment longer, then smiled at KC. "Absolutely."

All the side dishes were already laid out on the sideboard and ready to be served. KC's mama pulled a ham from the oven and said, "This is the only thing we were waiting for."

"We have a full house today," Kendall observed. "Wish it was cool enough to eat outside."

"That would be nice." Trina pulled plates from the cupboard and took them to the dining room.

KC followed with utensils. "Em, grab the glasses?"

They propped open the door between the kitchen and dining room while they set the table.

"We're all here, Trina. Tell us what happened with Jackson," Kendall called from the kitchen, where she helped slice the ham.

"I told you already. He asked to see Buddy."

"There's more to it than that. Last time you saw Jackson, you couldn't stop shaking." KC spoke gently. She didn't want to advertise Trina's business, but she was amazed at the change in her demeanor toward Jackson.

"Yes, and I decided then that I wasn't going to let him have that power over me any more. I just kept breathing and reminding myself we were in the middle of the church. No way Jackson would do anything in front of the whole congregation."

That made sense. Jackson was big on appearances. "Still, you looked so—"

"I had to prove I could talk to him without falling apart," Trina said. "I can't hide behind you all forever."

KC reassured her. "Yes, you can."

"I'll happily kick his ass forever." Kendall spoke at the same time as KC.

"I know. And I appreciate it. But I have to think about Buddy. It's best for him if we can communicate without a mediator."

"That doesn't mean you should ever be alone with him." Emma focused on the glasses as she spoke. They were speaking candidly about a difficult topic, but that didn't mean they were easy words to say.

The color drained from Trina's face at the suggestion. "I'm definitely not ready for that."

"So what did you work out?" KC asked. "About Buddy."

"Buddy misses Jackson so much. I can't justify keeping him from his daddy."

"That's understandable." Their mama wiped her hands on her apron and pulled Trina into a hug. "You have to think about what's best for your baby."

Trina took a deep, shaky breath. "Right. So, I'm going to take him to Jackson's mama on Saturday. Jackson can visit him there."

This seemed a reasonable solution to KC. Mrs. Monroe loved her son, but she followed her convictions. Right was right, regardless of who was involved. And Jackson's treatment of his wife was just plain wrong.

"That sounds good." Kendall nodded thoughtfully and the rest murmured their agreement.

"Now that that's settled, it's time to eat." Her mama said the last part loud enough for those waiting in the living room to hear.

"Look what the cat dragged in." Her daddy walked in with Glen and clapped his hand against Glen's shoulder. "Tough business that keeps you from family on a Sunday."

Lonnie brought her highball glass to the table. A poor substitute for the iced tea KC's mama made, but Lonnie's eyes were already fogged with drink. She was well on her way to sloshed and didn't appear willing to slow down just because mealtime had arrived. Lonnie glared in turn at Emma, KC, and Glen.

Emma tensed when Lonnie entered. KC kissed her cheek and said, "We're okay, right?"

Emma claimed her hand and held it tight. "Why wouldn't we be?"

Leann sulked into the room. She hadn't said a word to KC since she'd revealed that she knew about Lonnie and KC's affair. KC doubted she would start talking today.

Between them, they were building toward a large explosion. KC hoped they made it through the main course first, because she loved her mama's ham.

They survived the meal without bloodshed. As if by unspoken agreement, they all referred to their childhood Sunday-school lessons for how to proceed—if you can't say anything nice, say nothing at all.

The rest of the family kept the conversation moving along while KC waited quietly for either Lonnie or Emma to blow. At that point, KC's money was on Lonnie speaking first, based solely on the amount of Jack Daniel's she'd consumed.

"I'll take care of the dishes, Mama." Maybe that would keep her and Emma out of the line of fire for the rest of the afternoon.

"Nonsense. I want to talk to you and Emma while you're here." Her mama looped her hands through KC's and Emma's arms. "Come on now."

Lonnie saluted them with her glass. "That's right. It's Leann's turn. I'll help her. You go tell your mama all about your new girlfriend."

"Thank you, Mrs. Truvall." She escaped while she had the chance.

Her mama settled on the couch between KC and Emma and opened the family photo album. Under normal circumstances, this would make her want to run away, but any embarrassing photos her mom might produce probably had Emma in them as well. That took the sting out.

They looked through the album, with KC making the appropriate noises of outrage and Emma giggling as she thumbed through the pictures. When they got to the end, Emma said, "Is that all?" She looked genuinely interested in more, and KC thought about all the ways she could punish her later.

KC rolled her eyes. Emma knew exactly how many albums they had full of childhood pictures.

"Oh, no, honey, that's the tip of the iceberg." KC's mama was thoroughly charmed. "KC, run upstairs and grab another one out of the hall closet. Get the one from 1996, the year you girls were ten."

There was no point in arguing. Escape wasn't an option. "I'll be right back."

KC found the album quickly and was halfway through the return trip down the hall when Lonnie crested the top of the steps.

"There you are, sugar. I was afraid I'd never get you alone today." She slurred the words slightly as she made her way down the long hall, placing her feet with an overt amount of care. She'd reached the stage of inebriation where she could no longer keep track of her limbs properly.

KC backed away and held up her hands. She wished a second staircase would appear at the other end of the hall. "Lonnie, I think you've had too much to drink."

"Don't be silly. I haven't had nearly enough." Lonnie smiled lazily. "I miss you. Why have you been ignoring me?"

"I'm not ignoring you." If she wanted to, she could make it around Lonnie, but there was no guarantee Lonnie would remain on her feet if KC pushed past. She waited.

Lonnie stopped at KC's old bedroom and gripped the doorknob. "What do you say? One more time?" She rested her head against the door. "We had a lot of fun, didn't we?"

"We did." KC spoke gently. Despite their history, she cared for Lonnie. She was a lifelong family friend and KC didn't want her to suffer like this. "But that's over now."

"Why?" Lonnie reached out, beckoning her closer. "She doesn't have to know. It can be our secret."

She stood her ground, not even tempted. Lonnie held no appeal; she had nothing KC wanted. "No. I won't do that to Emma."

Lonnie smiled cruelly. "And what about after she moves? I'll be right here when you need me."

"That's not going to happen." She shook her head. "I won't cheat on Emma."

"Sugar, *everybody* cheats. It's a fact of life." Lonnie waved her hand like she'd just revealed a winning poker hand.

"Not everybody." She shook her head. Lonnie's version of the truth was too bleak for her to assign it to her own future. There had to be good people in the world, people capable of honoring their vows. Love and devotion had to be more than just myth. Her parents seemed to have it, as did Kendall and Owen, but she didn't want to dig deep enough to prove whether that was real or not. She wouldn't be able to take it if they weren't as devoted as she thought.

"Why did you pick now to get a conscience? I need you, dammit."

"No, you don't." She stared at Lonnie, trying to reconcile what she knew about Lonnie with the broken woman before her. There was no way ending their affair had sent Lonnie into this morose state.

Tears pooled in Lonnie's eyes but didn't run over, and she dropped her head into her hands. Lonnie's shoulders shook and

KC's resolve to remain distant cracked. Regardless of her leftover, misplaced urge to comfort Lonnie, KC wasn't the right person to do it. "I'm sorry, Mrs. Truvall. Let me get my mama for you."

She retreated down the stairs, photo album in hand. When she got to the living room, she said, "Mama, Mrs. Truvall needs you upstairs. She seems a bit emotional."

"Oh, dear." Her mama cast a sideways glance at Glen. "I hope everything is all right."

"I'm sure she'll be fine. In the meantime, I need to get Emma home. I promised her mama I wouldn't keep her all day."

She told the rest of her family good-bye and escorted Emma outside. When the front door closed behind them, she pulled Emma into a tight embrace and held her for several moments. She needed a moment of emotional reprieve, and in Emma's arms was the safest place she knew.

"Everything okay?" Emma stroked her hair and brushed light kisses over her cheek.

"It is now."

Chapter Seventeen

"Mama? You home?" KC poked her head in the front door and called out. Her parents never locked their door, despite Kendall's best effort to get them to start. Her daddy said if someone wanted to come in without his permission, they could discuss it with his Smith and Wesson. It was a conversation she wanted to avoid, so she was very vocal when she entered their house.

"I'm in the kitchen, KC."

Evelyn Hall spent a good portion of her time in the kitchen. When KC was younger, she asked her why. The thought of her poor, oppressed mama slaving away to cook for her daddy didn't sit well with KC. Any man who wanted to eat bad enough should figure out how to fix a meal or two if properly motivated. As it turned out, her mama simply loved to cook. She'd explained that if she'd ever pursued a career outside of her home, she would've been a chef. Early in their marriage, her daddy had tried to help, and she'd banned him from her kitchen.

"What are you up to today, honey?" Her mama stood at the stove stirring a large stockpot, surrounded by sterilized jars, her water-bath canner boiling on the back burner.

"I came by to talk to you." She kissed her mama hello on the cheek, then peered into boiling pot. "What are you making?"

"Strawberry jam. I spent all day yesterday picking berries."

"You should have called me. I'm between sessions." Spring session had ended after finals, and summer had yet to start for her.

Picking strawberries wasn't on her list of favorite things to do, but helping her mama was.

"You know I don't like to bother you girls. You have lives of your own to live. Especially you, right now, with Emma leaving soon."

"That's kind of what I wanted to talk to you about." KC braced herself for what she needed to say. After Lonnie had ambushed her on Sunday, she'd realized she'd never be able to fully grow beyond that part of her life until she owned up to it. At this point, all the people who really mattered knew about her and Lonnie except her mama and daddy. She could talk to her mama, and her mama would talk to her daddy for her. All of her truly important conversations between her and her daddy took place via her mama. She didn't see any reason to break with tradition this time around. The tricky part in this case would be telling her mama about her part in the affair without naming Lonnie.

"Don't tell me, you've decided to stop being stubborn and you're moving to Austin with Emma." Her mama spooned a bit of jam out of the pot and held it out. "Here, taste this."

She dutifully tried the fruit and nodded. It was delicious, as always. "No, Mama, I'm not moving. Not any time soon, anyway."

"Hold on, honey. I need to get this into the jars." Her mama ladled with unerring precision. She never missed a drop. One year KC had tried to fill the jars in an effort to help. She'd dropped jam on the glass threads, and they'd spent forever cleaning them up so the lids would seal. That was the end of KC pouring the jam.

She followed behind her mama, spinning the metal flats and rings onto the tops of the jars. When she was done, her mama placed them in the canner and set the timer. "Now then, if you're not moving, what brought you over here?"

She'd rehearsed what she wanted to say over and over in her head the night before, and again on the drive that morning. It was important that she tell her mama everything, but even more important that she let her know in a way that wouldn't destroy her.

"I need to tell you about the relationship I was in before Emma." The word *relationship* was a bit of a stretch. She realized that now.

But she wasn't ready to trot out a term like *fuck buddies* just yet either. *Affair* was the most appropriate way to classify what she'd shared with Lonnie, but she needed her mama to hear what she had to say completely before she got caught up in the bad parts.

Her mama poured them both a glass of iced tea and led her to the breakfast table. "What about it?" She asked the question while looking down into her glass.

"I just…" She took a deep breath. "I saw her for a year and kept it from you. I know you must have questions and I want to clear some of that up, if I can."

"Okay." Her mama met her gaze and held it.

"The other day I said I couldn't tell you who it was because she's not out, and that's true. But there's more to it."

"Go on."

"Well, for starters, she's older than me." She took a drink of her iced tea and wished for something stronger. If she could get her mama past the age difference, then she'd tell her about the married part.

"I see. How much older?"

"Around your age." Lonnie was two years younger than her mama.

"I don't understand. Why in the world would you do that?"

She shrugged. "She's beautiful and sexy and I've had a crush on her for as long as I can remember." As much as she hated herself for the affair now, and hated Lonnie for refusing to let go, her feelings about Lonnie at the start hadn't changed. At forty-six, Lonnie's age the first time they slept together, Lonnie had been lush and gorgeous and so very eager. She was responsive and pliant to KC's touch. That part remained throughout their affair. In the beginning, she'd also been timid and unsure, reluctant to reveal the flaws on her body.

Learning the landscape of Lonnie's body, while at the same time teaching Lonnie to trust herself about what felt good, had been a revelation. Now that their affair was over and she was ready to move on, it was easy to forget what it had first been like, but at the time she had been drunk on the sweetness of it all. She'd consumed

Lonnie like a bottle of cheap wine. However, she didn't think her mama wanted to hear all that.

"Well, I don't know what a woman my age would want with someone half her age. Just the thought exhausts me. But that doesn't seem like enough for you to have kept it a secret for a year."

This was her moment of truth, her chance to come clean. Her voice shook when she said, "She's married."

"Oh, KC." Her mama shook her head. "What were you thinking?"

"I know, Mama. It was wrong. I can't explain why I did it." All the reasons, the justifications, which had felt tangible enough to touch at the time, fell apart under scrutiny. She'd fucked Lonnie because she wanted to. She was selfish and didn't consider the very long-reaching effects of that selfishness. There was no other way to describe her behavior and no way to justify it.

"Why are you telling me this now that it's over? You have Emma."

There were so many reasons she didn't know how to explain them all. A large part of her needed her mama to hug her and tell her she was going to be okay, that even though she'd made a mistake, the important part was to own it and then do better. But she wasn't a little girl, and she wasn't confessing to taking a cookie without permission. Also, it was better to self-identify than to be found out later. Too many people knew about her affair with Lonnie, and she didn't want one of them to tattle to her mama before she could tell her herself. Most important, though, was what it meant in her relationship with Emma.

"I'm not proud of it." She shook her head. "Emma knows and it upsets her. For a while I wasn't sure she'd be able to get past it, but she's trying, and I think that's because she sees that I've changed. I want to be better. I want to be the kind of person who deserves someone like Emma."

"Does Emma think you will be unfaithful to her?"

"Mama, I would never cheat. Ever." This wasn't about Emma; it was about her and the core of her character. She didn't have it in her to step out on someone.

Her mama shook her head. "It doesn't matter if you would or not. You disrespected someone else's wedding vows. Those are sacred. Emma has to be questioning if you would honor your own."

"I haven't asked. I hope she doesn't feel that way." She had promised to be monogamous, but she'd been afraid to ask Emma if she believed her. She couldn't bear the thought of hearing Emma say flat out that she didn't trust her. "Emma and I agreed to be exclusive, and I wouldn't promise her that unless I intended to honor my words."

"Good intentions aren't always enough, KC."

"I know." She wanted to be able to wipe the slate clean, to move back in time and erase the affair completely. Since that wasn't possible, all she could do was hope Emma would stick with her long enough for her to be able to prove she was good for her word.

"Is this why you're not moving?"

"It's not what you think. Emma asked me to go with her, but I said no. For now." She had used the excuse that her family needed her. She'd believed it at the time, but with every day that passed, Trina proved more and more that she was perfectly capable of taking care of herself. She'd put up with Jackson for too long and wasn't going to fall into that trap again. KC was proud of her.

"Does she understand?"

"I think so." She smiled. "I hope so. I told her I needed to stay for Trina, but I also need to make sure I'm ready for what comes next. Emma isn't the kind of girl I can string along. If I move in with her, I need to be prepared to stay forever."

"And you don't think you can do that?"

"I'd like to think so, but it wasn't very long ago that I was seeing a married woman and thought that was perfectly okay." She hated saying those words, laying it out that clearly. She'd rather her mama not know all her bad secrets.

"I don't believe that. You may have done it, but some part of you knew it was wrong."

"I suppose. But Mama, that's why I can't go with Emma yet. Even if I was willing to admit it was wrong, I wasn't willing to stop. I wanted Lo—her. And I didn't care about anything else."

She choked on her near slipup with Lonnie's name. The only thing saving her was that her mama wasn't likely to ever think of her calling Mrs. Truvall by her first name. She chided herself about being more careful. Her need to talk things through with her mama didn't mean she was allowed to selfishly destroy other lives.

That's exactly what would happen if her mama found out the woman she'd been talking about was Lonnie. Her mama would be lost without her friend. And while Lonnie and Glen might survive any number of infidelities on both their parts, that didn't mean Glen could overlook his wife having a lesbian affair with a woman half their age.

"KC, do I know this other woman? The one you had the affair with?"

KC swallowed and nodded. "Yes, Mama." Maybe her mama picked up on more than she realized.

"Is it a friend of mine?"

That was the twenty-thousand-dollar question. If KC asked Kendall, the answer, without hesitation, would be no. If she asked Lonnie, she'd say yes just as quickly. KC thought about what her mama would say and realized the answer would probably change if she knew the whole truth.

"Yes, ma'am." There was no getting around the fact that, regardless of possible future changes, Lonnie was her mama's friend before she was KC's lover.

"And you won't tell me who it is?"

"It would do more harm than good for me to do that." To her ears it sounded like the coward's way out. She remembered Kendall telling her that she wasn't allowed to be selfish any more, that revealing Lonnie's name to her mama would be pointless and painful. She bit her lip and hoped the answer would suffice.

"I understand." Her mama stood. "I need to get the next batch started. Help me."

KC pushed away from the table, uncertain that she'd said all she needed to. The topic felt much larger in her head. Surely she needed more words to fully discuss it. She met her mama at the counter and measured out white sugar into the pot of strawberries.

Her mama added the pectin, stirred, then put the mixture on the burner.

She touched her mama's arm. "Are we okay?"

"Of course we are." Her mama smoothed her hair away from her face. "KC, I may not like it, or even understand it. But I do know this conversation was hard for you, and I'm proud of you for telling me." She pulled KC into a hug. "Just promise me one thing."

She sucked in a breath through her tears. She hadn't realized how much keeping this a secret from her mama had been pressing on her. The knowledge that she was still loved, possibly on the way to forgiven, meant everything to her. "Anything."

"Promise you won't ever do anything like this again. Life is too short for secrets this big and harmful."

"I promise." KC felt relief and dread in equal measure. Her mama still loved her, forgave her for being selfish, but expected her to learn from her mistakes and not repeat them. Making the promise was easy. Now all she had to do was keep it. She didn't have the best track record, but God help her, she was going to try her damnedest.

Trina fed bullets into the cylinder of her revolver one by one. Her ear protection circled her neck, ready for use when the range master signaled the start of the next round. "Emma, did you find a place yet?"

Emma and Trina had teamed up together and dragged KC along for an afternoon at the firing range. Their daddy had taught them all to shoot when they were little, so she was expected to enjoy blasting up tiny paper targets, but it held little appeal. She could think of at least a hundred other things she'd rather do with her Saturday than play with guns.

She had given in to Emma's request when she asked for the third time. Her willingness to participate came about as a combination of a desire to please Emma and an even stronger desire to be pleased by Emma. Emma had been kissing her neck at the time, and somehow her answer got messed around from no to yes. Earlier in the week

Emma had discovered the perfect spot low on KC's neck that turned her brain into applesauce. It was a weapon she feared would be used against her during future negotiations in their relationship.

She pulled Emma's ear protection away from her ears and said, "Trina wants to know if you found an apartment yet."

Emma took the earmuffs from her and dropped them around her neck. "Yeah. I signed the lease yesterday." She'd completed the paperwork via fax.

"Did you settle for one of the places you and KC looked at?" Trina asked.

"No. I found a place online that's close to work, is in my price range, and only has a six-month lease."

"How do you know you'll like it?" Trina finished loading her gun and snapped the cylinder into place.

Emma snorted. "I don't expect to. I hate apartments, but I can't afford to buy yet."

"What about you, KC?" Trina asked.

"What?"

"Can't you afford a house?" Trina jumped in the middle of a topic that KC and Emma had been studiously avoiding for the past week.

"Probably." Suddenly she wished she'd brought her nine-millimeter along. When she'd realized what she'd agreed to, she'd purposefully left her own firearm at home in protest. Shooting was not on her list of favorite things, but if she'd brought it, she'd have something to focus her attention on besides the conversation.

Trina had all the reason in the world to refamiliarize herself with her revolver. She needed to trust herself, trust her aim and her ability to pull the trigger, just in case the need ever arose. Jackson hadn't been back to their house, but today was his first official visit with Buddy. That had to be playing hell with Trina's nerves. But Emma's interest baffled her. Handguns were less common in Austin. It wasn't like she intended to carry one as her personal form of self-defense when she moved to the city.

"Mmm." Trina didn't pursue the question any further. She lined up her sights on the target and mimed shooting through her six bullets. "Jackson and I used to go shooting before Buddy was born." She set the revolver on the ledge, barrel facing out, and rested her hands on her belly. She was nearing her third trimester.

"Why'd did you stop?" Emma asked.

Trina laughed. "They wouldn't let me bring the baby here, and I couldn't bear to be away from him."

"Think you'll come after this baby gets here?"

"Probably. Sometimes I wonder if things would have been different if I'd kept coming." Trina's thoughts were far from their conversation. She stared into the distance over KC's shoulder.

KC wished Trina wouldn't play what-if. "Could you use that gun if you needed to?"

"I don't know." She shook her head. "Doubt it. But easier now than then, that's for sure."

The light changed, indicating the next round was about to begin, and they all moved their protection back to their ears. When they received the go-ahead signal, Trina emptied her cylinder, six shots in rapid succession, nice and easy with no hesitation. When she pulled the target home, it showed a cluster of six holes in the center.

They pulled their hearing protection off at the end of the round.

"Sure you don't want a turn, KC?"

"No, thanks. Emma's next." They'd reserved only the one lane to split between them. It was cheaper than two or three separate lanes. "Who are you picturing when you pull the trigger?" KC expected Trina to say Jackson and probably shouldn't have asked the question, but curiosity got the better of her.

Trina smiled wryly. "Me a month ago. I never want to go back to being that person." She folded the target and slipped it in her back pocket. "I'm done whenever you are, Emma."

Before the next round started, KC asked, "Have you had a chance to talk to Leann?" Things had been so hectic between them, KC had almost forgot about Lonnie's daughter.

Emma nodded. "We've met for coffee a couple of times. She's really angry about some things, but she seems to understand that it gets better from here. It's tough being a gay teen in Texas, but it's not permanent." She grinned.

"Did you tell Mr. Truvall?" KC knew she couldn't put herself in the middle of that conversation again but didn't want him to worry unnecessarily.

"Leann promised she would."

"Good." It felt like inadequate closure for an awkward chapter in KC's life, but it was the best she was going to get.

"Let me empty this clip and we can go," Emma said.

Emma popped off her ten plus one at a slower pace than Trina. She reset herself between bursts and squeezed through the trigger gently. When she pulled her target back, her shots were all over the paper. KC didn't take time to count, but she wouldn't have been surprised if one or two had missed altogether. She was thankful Emma didn't have the same motivation for accuracy that Trina had.

"Looks like I need to keep practicing." Emma counted the holes but didn't comment on the number.

"I'm sure there's a range in Austin." KC was teasing her.

As they walked toward the exit, Trina poked Emma's arm and asked, "What's that?"

KC pulled Emma's shirtsleeve up higher so that Trina could fully view the nicotine patch on Emma's arm.

"I'm trying to quit."

"In the middle of a move? And starting a new career? Damn." Trina let out a low whistle.

"The only time I really smoke is when KC does something especially stupid." Emma laughed when she said it, but KC didn't think she was joking.

"Too bad they don't have a quit-being-stupid patch for KC, huh?"

"She's doing okay." Emma smiled in a way that made KC wish they were alone.

Trina laughed. "It's only been a week. Give her time."

"Not funny." KC pulled Emma into a hug. "I'm going to ride home with Trina. I'll see you tonight?"

"Count on it."

KC helped her into her Mini, then watched her pull away before climbing into the passenger seat of Trina's car.

"How big of a hurry are you in?"

Trina shrugged and adjusted her sunglasses. "I got time."

"Let's swing past Longhorn Chevy."

"First a new haircut, now a new car. What's next?" Trina started the car and pulled out into traffic.

KC imagined her future with Emma and happy warmth filled her. When she'd looked to the future before, all she saw was a big blank page, waiting to be written. It filled her with uncertainty. Now, she still saw a blank page, a story waiting to be written, but Emma was with her, their joined hands holding the pen together. The uncertainty gave way to hope and anticipation. The hair and the car were window dressing in a much bigger picture. "The rest of my life."

Chapter Eighteen

KC pulled into Emma's driveway a few minutes early. She let the engine idle, the powerful thrum of the eight-cylinder four-wheel drive a world away from that of her old Accord. The dealer had taken much longer than she anticipated. The Chevy Tahoe was her first brand-new vehicle, and the amount of paperwork involved staggered her. At the end of it all, she was pretty certain she'd signed over all of her present and future offspring, along with three Nubian goats.

She'd driven straight to Emma's after they finally handed her the keys, not having enough time to swing past her house to clean up, let alone pick up flowers. She hoped it wasn't too much of a letdown after their last date. She didn't want to disappoint, but she'd reasoned that on time and empty-handed was better than late and bearing gifts. She hoped she'd made the right choice.

Before she could overthink it, Emma burst through the front door and ran out to greet her. She opened the driver's side door and pulled KC into a hug.

"Oh, my God, no wonder you tried so hard to get rid of me this afternoon. This is beautiful." Emma inhaled the new-car smell. "I want to drive."

"I should go in and say hi to your mama before we go." She reached to turn off the engine, but Emma stopped her.

"No, she's at my grandma's. If you really want to say hello, you can call while I'm driving." Emma pushed at her arm.

She laughed and climbed over the console to the passenger seat. "Did you grab your license?"

"I'm good." Emma smoothed her hands over the leather seats. "This is hot."

"Hot? Emma, you're twisted. This is a family vehicle." She mentally clapped her hand over her mouth a split second after the words left it. That wasn't the way she'd envisioned telling Emma why she'd picked the SUV instead of a smaller, sportier alternative.

"I know." Emma climbed behind the wheel and winked at her. "Want to make out in the backseat later?"

Hell, yes, she did.

Emma backed out onto the street. "Where are we going?"

"I originally planned to take a picnic and drive out past the Decker farm, but I ran out of time." The backseat was regrettably lacking a picnic basket. The Decker family owned a good amount of land south of Fairmont. Beyond that stretched mile after mile of open road and not much else.

"Alternative plan. How 'bout we swing past Church's and grab some chicken. Then we can go for that drive."

Emma turned off the air conditioning and opened all the windows, including the sunroof, and reached for her hand. She laced their fingers together and pulled KC's hand to her mouth. "This is a beautiful car." She kissed her knuckles, then dropped both hands, fingers interlaced, into KC's lap.

"I'm glad you like it."

"Did you get it because of me?"

She smiled and considered her answer. How ready was she to have this conversation? She wasn't even really sure of the answer herself. She opted, as was her promise to Emma, for the truth. No secrets allowed. "It'll make the drive to Austin easier."

"Yes, but that new Camaro you've been talking about would have done the same."

"Can't fit any boxes in a Camaro."

"I'm renting a U-Haul."

"Well, now you don't have to, do you?"

"This won't hold all my stuff."

"I'm going to make more than one trip." KC shrugged. Her reasons for staying in Fairmont were shrinking by the day. It was getting increasingly harder to convince herself not to move to Austin with Emma. But she wasn't ready to lose herself in another person yet. Not until she had a better grip on herself—who she was and what she believed.

"Lots of trips is an argument against a vehicle of this size, not in favor of it. The gas mileage is going to be a killer."

"But it has great safety ratings." KC considered that a worthwhile trade-off.

"Since when do you care about safety ratings?"

"One of us has to, and if you're going to continue driving that Mini, I guess it's up to me."

Emma pulled over suddenly, leaving the SUV angled awkwardly on the side of the road. She put it in Park, killed the engine, then scrambled over the console to straddle KC's lap.

"That is the sexiest thing I think I've ever heard." She held KC's face in her hands and kissed her hard and quick.

She wrapped her arms around Emma's waist. "Yep, twisted."

She smiled into the next kiss, then slowed Emma down and dragged out the connection. If considering a vehicle safety rating earned her this reaction from Emma, what would she get if she brought up childproofing electrical outlets?

After tugging Emma's shirt free from where it was tucked into her pants, she eased her hands under the fabric. Emma's skin was hot beneath her touch, and she moved her fingers in slow, lazy figure eights. Kissing Emma was like a symphony. Joy and beauty suffused her. She was overwhelmed, blessed beyond belief by Emma's generosity and patience.

She parted her lips and Emma's tongue slid into her mouth. Emma kissed her, greedy and hard. She sucked KC's tongue, then swirled her own around, over, under, everywhere, until KC was lost. When she moaned, it started deep in her gut and traveled through her like a wave, only to land inside Emma's mouth and be echoed back to her. Emma took control effortlessly and gave it back just as easily. KC's lungs grew tighter with every second, but she refused to break away. Emma stole her breath, leaving her light-headed and desperate, and KC surrendered to it like a sailor to a siren's call. Passion flared hot at her core.

Emma gasped for breath, her mouth warm and wet against hers, but no longer kissing. "God, I want you."

Emma fumbled with the opening of KC's jeans, and the moment the button let go, KC snapped to reality. "Emma." She panted, unable to catch her breath. "Emma, wait." She grabbed Emma's hands, holding firm, and took a deep, steady breath, then another. The spell receded enough for her to remember how much she respected Emma. This wasn't a random hookup. It was a love of a lifetime, and KC wanted to honor that the best way she could. Desperate humping on the side of the road didn't even come close.

Emma slumped against her, and the additional pressure was delicious. The movement thrust Emma's pelvis onto their joined hands, and she could feel Emma's heat through the fabric. Emma groaned and thrust against her hand. "Please."

"Emma, look at me." She waited until Emma opened her eyes and met her gaze. Her pupils were nearly black, with only the slightest ring of blue at the edges. "Not here. Not like this."

She didn't want to remember their first time together as fumbled groping in a car, even if the car was big enough for them to stretch out comfortably. She wasn't willing to have a member of law enforcement knock on the window and tell them they were illegally parked, then give them a ticket for indecent exposure and lewd and licentious conduct in public. That wasn't the memory she wanted for the first time she touched Emma intimately. She wanted to work Emma up, make her plead, then watch as she came. She wanted to revel afterward, to hold Emma while they basked in the afterglow. As much as she liked her new SUV, it wasn't the right place.

Emma pressed her forehead to hers, inhaled deeply, and lifted her hips so she was no longer riding KC's knuckles. "You're right."

"I'm sorry." She pressed a light kiss to Emma's temple. She craved so much more, but the part of her that loved and respected Emma wouldn't allow her to give in.

"Fuck Church's." Emma groaned as she dragged herself away from KC. The separation bordered on painful, and she fought to not pull Emma back to her. Emma kissed her one last time, then shifted to the driver's seat. "I'm taking you home."

❖

Emma drove them back to her house, the only real option. Her mama was gone for the evening, and Trina and Buddy were both at KC's.

Emma killed the engine and held out the key to her. "You better put this on your key ring before it gets lost."

"I've already got one." She showed Emma her keys, complete with the new fob for the Chevy. "Why don't you keep that one?"

Emma squealed and snatched her hand back before she could change her mind. She laughed. The night so far, even though she'd showed up without flowers and their picnic had been aborted, was perfect.

She took a deep breath. "Ready to go inside?" KC asked the question with the grave attention she felt it deserved. This was a milestone. She wanted to be absolutely sure Emma was on board. Under her careful scrutiny, Emma's giddy laughter transformed to serious anticipation.

"Absolutely." Emma pocketed the key with a grin, then leaned over the console and kissed her.

Emma might have intended the kiss to be light and easy, but that wasn't what happened. KC's mouth opened reflexively and she teased her tongue over Emma's lips. It was a gentle hello, an exploration of her new favorite playground, and she moaned at the contact. She pushed forward, taking Emma's mouth forcefully. She wanted to be inside Emma with a consuming desperation.

When Emma surrendered to her, she glided into Emma, licking along her tongue, the roof of her mouth, learning the heat inside of Emma. She explored until she was breathless and retreated with a gasp. Emma drove forward, filling the opening before she had even created it. She sucked Emma's tongue into her and hummed. Emma tasted sweet and minty, like the essence of life lived inside her, and she couldn't get enough. She wanted her mouth on every part of Emma.

Emma took her time, slowed the kiss to a deep, passionate journey without boundaries or deadlines. She savored the feel of Emma's tongue inside her mouth, sucked the flavor of Emma into her. She whimpered when Emma pulled away. Emma made her head spin in the best possible way. With their kiss, the world was reduced to one overpowering thought. Emma was the answer to every question she had ever asked. Emma was her only truth.

Rather than open her own door, Emma crawled into her lap again and nipped at her lips, then opened the passenger door.

"Coming?" Emma asked as soon as both her feet touched the ground. Then she turned and ran into the house.

KC fumbled with her seat belt and almost fell on her head trying to get out of the SUV. Sexy women made her clumsy, and Emma was off the charts. She hoped she would survive the night without major injury.

Emma watched from the front porch. When she saw that KC had made it safely out of the vehicle, she giggled and ran inside and up the stairs. KC took a moment to center herself. She locked and armed the alarm on her new Chevy, straightened her clothes, and gave herself a pep talk. This was Emma. She knew her. She loved her. Emma was everything she wanted. All she had to do was make it safely into the house and up the stairs.

She almost hyperventilated when the gravity of what they were about to do hit her fully. The knowledge that Emma was waiting for her simultaneously calmed and excited her. Her heart raced, but her thoughts cleared. She saw her life, their future, with amazing clarity. She took a moment to calm herself and then followed Emma inside.

"Em?" She called out when she made it through the front door, then stood at the base of the stairs and waited for the answering call. She couldn't charge up the stairs like a lumbering pubescent boy, too eager to fill her own needs to hesitate for even a moment to consider Emma's. Emma deserved better from her, so she waited. She wanted to make absolutely certain she was invited to proceed.

"I'm here, KC. Don't make me start without you." Emma's voice floated down to her and swamped her with desire. She locked the front door and climbed the stairs.

Her heart beat harder with each step until she trembled from the strain of holding back. She wanted Emma, and the effort to keep herself from running like a bull to Emma was taking a toll. She stumbled on the last step, eager and clumsy.

The door to Emma's room lay open, and she shut her eyes as she stepped into the room. She didn't know if she was truly ready for what waited for her and needed a moment to reflect. They were about to cross a line from which they could never retreat.

She held her breath and opened her eyes. Emma stood at the foot of the bed. Light filtered through the sheer curtains behind her, bathing her in an ethereal light. Emma bit her lip and shifted from foot to foot. Then she tilted her head and smiled.

"Hi," Emma said.

KC crossed the room and stopped when she was within touching distance of Emma. "Hi." She traced her hands lightly up Emma's arms and smiled when goose bumps rose on Emma's skin.

She leaned in until her lips were a breath away from Emma's. Very gently, very slowly, she brought her mouth to Emma's. She kissed her for the pure joy of the connection. She had no agenda beyond learning Emma. She tugged at the bottom edge of Emma's T-shirt and asked, "Can I take this off?"

In the past week, she'd had her hand inside Emma's shirt enough times that she knew what her breasts felt like in her palm: perfect. But this would be her first look as lovers. She held her breath in anticipation.

Emma nodded and covered KC's hands with her own. She helped pull her shirt up and over her head, then reached around to unclasp her bra.

"Wait." KC pressed their bodies together and moaned. She restrained Emma's fingers and said, "Let me. Please."

"Okay." Emma's voice shook.

She stared into Emma's eyes as she worked the clasp, one hook at a time. She could wait all night to go further so long as Emma continued to embrace her. When the last hook came undone, she released the fabric and it sagged around Emma's arms, held in place only by the connection of their bodies.

She stayed still, her body longing for more. Emma would complete her, and the thought humbled and elated her. She was so eager, but she didn't dare rush for fear that everything would shatter in her haste. She kissed Emma again, deeper this time. She let her lips and tongue explore, savoring the taste of Emma's lips, her mouth, her skin. She licked inside Emma's mouth, sweeping her tongue against Emma's, deep and languid. She was gone in soft, sweet mint.

Emma moaned into her mouth and grasped her shoulders tight, her nails digging through her shirt and into her skin. "Off." Emma worked the buttons on the front of KC's shirt. Her fingers proved nimble despite the urgent, lost cadence of her tongue against KC's.

KC let their kiss end naturally, riding it where Emma wanted until it tapered to a sweet, open-mouthed press of Emma's lips against hers.

"Can I see you?" Emma asked while they were still connected at the mouth, and her words resonated down KC's throat.

KC answered with a groan. "Yes. Anything."

She stepped back to finish removing her shirt, and when she did, Emma's bra slipped down her arms and fell to the floor. KC whimpered. "God, Em." She froze, immobile in the face of Emma's perfect beauty. Emma's breasts were just the right size for her hands, and the tips were small and pink and so very hard. Her mouth watered at the sight. Her instincts demanded that she drop to her knees and worship Emma, but she couldn't, not yet. She needed to fulfill Emma's request to see her, and she would as soon as her brain stopped misfiring.

"You're so beautiful." She bent until Emma's breasts were at eye level. She licked around the edge of one areola, then the other. When Emma moaned, she flicked her tongue over the tip and quickly sucked Emma into her mouth. She wanted to stay there, work Emma and coax an orgasm through her nipple. She caressed the other side with her hand, rolling the tip between her thumb and fingers.

"Please, KC." Emma tugged at her hair, her fingers clenched tight and digging in sharply. She pulled KC away with a slurping pop. She sounded desperate with want.

"What?" She was dazed. She'd had the barest taste of Emma and it wasn't enough.

Emma started in on her buttons again and worked through them with quick concentration. She pushed KC's shirt open with a growl. "This."

Emma jerked the shirt down KC's arms and stopped when she reached her elbows. She abandoned the shirt and reached for KC's bra. Unlike Emma, who had worn delicate light-blue lace that matched her eyes, she was wearing a sports bra. Once again, she wished she'd had time to change before their date. Undeterred, Emma pushed the bra up and KC's breasts bounced free.

"Finally," Emma said, and then, without preamble, she lowered her mouth to KC's breast and worked the nipple gently with her teeth. Her body pulled perfectly straight, like a puppet with a string running through its middle. She held Emma to her as the sensation traveled along an invisible cord, linking Emma's mouth directly to her core.

"Bed, please," she begged. It felt too good for her to remain in control of her faculties for much longer. Gravity was winning out over her ability to remain vertical.

Emma tugged harder, her teeth scraping the sensitive apex of KC's nipple. KC's knees buckled. "Please, Em."

Emma kissed her way up the skin of her chest and neck, skipping the section still covered by the bunched fabric of her shirt and bra. She sucked KC's earlobe into her mouth and worked it the same way she had KC's nipple. "I'm never going to get enough of you." She breathed the words like a prayer that filled KC like vapor. Her words, her love, were everywhere, yet nowhere all at the same time. KC echoed Emma's sentiment. Her desire for Emma would never be fully satisfied. She'd always want more, more, more.

Finally, Emma released her and KC almost collapsed under her own weight without Emma's arms around her, supporting her. She opened her eyes and saw Emma opening the button fly on her jeans.

Her head was tipped down and her hair fell forward, obscuring KC's view of her face. Light streamed around her, embracing Emma and cradling her beauty and youth. KC was struck with one clear thought—Emma was an angel.

She felt unworthy but eternally grateful that this lovely creature willingly shared herself with her. She reached for Emma to help with the rest of her clothes, only to be reminded that she was still fully dressed herself. Sort of. Her shirt hung off her arms, covering nothing but restricting her motion. She removed it hastily, then pulled her bra over her head. A splotchy red band circled her chest where the rayon material had bunched together.

She didn't feel sexy as she stripped out of her pants, hopping from one leg to the next, but when Emma raised her head after unfastening the last button on her jeans, she met KC's eyes with a look of such desire that KC flamed under her gaze. "We need to hurry." She could barely speak, her words nothing more than a desperate, scratchy squeak.

"Yes." Emma toed her boots off then shimmied out of her jeans. She stood before KC wearing only a pair of almost-not-there lace panties and white socks.

Laughter bubbled inside KC. The panties shattered every last one of her Victoria's Secret fantasies, but the socks made Emma *Emma*. Suddenly Emma was human and within her reach. She pulled Emma into her arms and kissed her solidly. "God, I love you." She spoke with carefree ease then froze when she realized which words had escaped without her knowledge or consent. The heavy weight settled into the air once again. "I mean…"

"Don't." Emma placed her fingers over KC's lips. "Don't try to take it back." Emma's eyes shone. She kissed KC with soft reverence, then whispered, "I love you, too."

She nodded and swallowed, choking back the tears that threatened to spill over. She and Emma had been building toward this one perfect moment for so very long, and it felt impossibly good to give a name to her feelings, to acknowledge the way Emma possessed her down to the very fiber of her soul.

"I'm so glad." She caressed Emma's face—her cheeks, her lips—following the touch of her fingers with her lips. Words were not a sufficient expression of her gratitude.

Emma allowed her time to simply feel her, to touch her grace, and when she finally pulled away, her eyes were dark and heavy with emotion. "Can we go to bed now?"

"Please." She stripped the rest of her clothes off, careful not to look at Emma as she did the same. They'd never make it all the way to the safety of Emma's bed if she did. The temptation to touch would be too great.

They settled together beneath the cover of Emma's blankets, and KC pressed her body fully against Emma's for the first time, uninhibited by neither their clothing nor their long-held self-denial. The sensation of Emma's skin against hers was glorious, a revelation.

KC took her time; she worked to memorize the landscape of Emma's body. She added every dip, every freckle, every line, to her catalogue of Emma. Emma trembled beneath her fingers, an isolated tremor on a placid lake of smooth, creamy skin. KC pressed her lips to a quarter-sized sweet spot just above Emma's right hip. The flesh there danced beneath KC's mouth and she sucked it between her teeth. Emma squealed and pushed at her, but she didn't relent. She wanted to own Emma at the source, starting with this small patch of skin. She sucked long enough for the skin to turn purple and dark. Emma grasped her head, pulling her tight against her until her entire face was buried in the smooth planes of Emma's abdomen. She gasped for air, then smoothed her tongue over the worried skin.

Emma panted and whined, a high keening that was worlds away from the soft sighs overtaking KC from the inside out. She was home and perfectly at peace. Emma tugged her hair and guided her up until their bodies were flush and slick with sweat against each other. She kissed KC with needy desperation, her tongue invasive and insistent. With that kiss she declared herself. Emma wanted everything, and KC flayed herself open so Emma could take what she wanted. She belonged to Emma.

"KC, please." Emma's voice was coarse and deep with want. "I need—" Emma kissed her again, brief, but no less invasive. "God, I need you."

Emma spread her legs and she fell into the opening between Emma's thighs. She slotted into place like it was her destiny, like the only possible outcome for her life had always been, would always be, to live in the infinite moment that led to Emma's ultimate happiness. She thrust her hips, a useless dry hump that gave neither of them any relief. She was desperate with wanting and pushed Emma open even wider until her pubis bumped into the wet heat at Emma's apex. Emma groaned and her eyes rolled back into her head. KC thrust again, feeling herself slip in the abundant wetness. She wanted to feel Emma beneath her fingers.

She thrust against Emma for longer than her body accepted as possible. Her own desire trembled and whimpered with its need to reach full crescendo. Emma's hip snapped up, over and over, rising to meet KC's every downward stroke. Finally, blessedly, Emma's body shook and jerked with orgasm and KC collapsed against her. She gathered Emma in her arms, stroked her hair, and comforted her as her body calmed.

"Wow," Emma whispered. "That was…" KC shifted to her side and indulged her desire to touch Emma where she lived.

She glided her fingers through the incredible wetness coating Emma's thighs and lower lips. She parted Emma and played in the slippery heat. She circled Emma's clit, then rubbed firmly over the top. Emma squirmed and moaned. KC laughed and pushed two fingers inside her, deep and effortless. "I'm not done with you yet."

"God, KC." Emma arched against her, back bent, hips digging into the mattress. Emma thrust up to meet her on the next stroke.

She set an easy pace. She built Emma up, pushing her toward orgasm again. Emma felt so good against her, looked so perfect in ecstasy, she couldn't imagine being satisfied after only one.

Emma dug her fingers into KC's shoulder. KC hissed and pictured the perfect crescent moons that would be left in her flesh. She thrust harder and faster. She felt Emma draw tight and clutch around her fingers. She massaged the fleshy swelling of nerve endings high inside Emma's vagina, coaxing all the pleasure in Emma's body to coalesce in that one perfect moment. She worked Emma through her orgasm, drawing it out and easing her down from the high.

Emma collapsed, limp against the mattress. KC withdrew gently and kissed Emma's temple. She settled into Emma's side, happy to have Emma in her arms, spent and yawning. The urgency of her own need slaked with Emma's satisfaction

"Okay?" She stroked Emma's cheek and tucked a stray hair behind her ear.

"God." Emma drew the word out in a long groan that turned into a yawn. "You're amazing."

Emma snuggled her head into KC's shoulder.

KC smiled. Her life was far more perfect than she ever deserved. "Sleep."

"Uh-uh." Emma shook her head sleepily. "I'm just catching my breath."

"I'm okay, Em. You rest."

Suddenly Emma's fingers were between KC's legs, pushing inside. Her cunt flared to life and she groaned.

Emma laughed. "You're okay? Feels like you're drowning." Emma drew her fingers to her lips and licked her wetness. Her eyes were still closed and she had a lazy grin on her face.

The image of Emma with KC's desire coating her fingers was too erotic for her to withstand. Her eyes slipped shut also. "God, Em, you're so fucking sexy."

"Yeah?" Emma's fingers found her opening again. "You should see me when I'm not completely spent."

Emma played with her clit, an arrhythmic motion that made her strain and gasp for more. Emma gently coaxed her higher and higher until she overflowed into the calmest, most fulfilling orgasm she'd ever experienced. Rather than a frantic search for more, she was overcome with the absolute knowledge that she'd arrived.

She pulled the blankets around them and held Emma as they slipped blissfully into sleep.

Chapter Nineteen

KC paced the length of her house. She should be working on the syllabus for the summer session. Instead, she was obsessing about her future with Emma.

"Sit down. You're keeping Buddy up." Trina had been trying to put Buddy down for a nap for the past ten minutes. The bedroom door had been closed, so KC didn't realize he would be able to hear her.

"Sorry." She grabbed her cell phone from the kitchen table and went out to the back porch. There she dialed Kendall's number and hoped she'd get her sister instead of voice mail.

"This is Kendall." She spoke with professional efficiency. During business hours, she generally picked up without checking caller ID.

"You got a minute?" KC asked.

"Give me a sec." Kendall lowered the volume on a news commentary playing in the background. "What's up?"

KC took a deep breath. "I want to move to Austin." Her heart pounded against her chest with excitement from having said the words aloud.

"So move." Kendall said it like it was the simplest thing in the world.

"That easy?"

"Why wouldn't it be? Did Emma say she doesn't want you or something?"

"No, she definitely wants me there." She thought back to their date Saturday night, the way she felt holding Emma in her arms as they fell asleep. It had been different than every other time they'd shared a bed in the past. This time they were sleeping together as lovers, not just friends. It had been a defining moment for their future.

"Then I don't understand the problem."

"What about Trina?"

"What about her?"

"Don't you think she kind of needs me?"

"Why would she?" Kendall sounded genuinely confused. Up until that point, KC had thought Kendall was playing devil's advocate, trying to get her to outline all the reasons why moving was a bad idea for her family.

"Kendall, she talks about Jackson all the time. She misses him. The other day she said she sometimes thinks about going back to him."

"And if she's going to do that, she'll do it."

"I can't just let her."

"Whether you're here or in Austin won't make any difference. As much as it sucks, we have to let Trina sort this out for herself."

"And if he hits her again?"

"Then we'll let Daddy go get her instead of us."

"I don't want Trina to get hurt again. And I don't want to visit Daddy in prison." Jackson wouldn't survive if their daddy collected Trina.

"KC, she's in counseling with Pastor Davis. They both are. Whatever happens next is between Trina and Jackson and God. And you can't put off starting your life with Emma because you're afraid of something that might happen. Trina might go back, but she might not. Only she can make that decision. You can't do it for her."

KC remained quiet. The thought of relocating frightened her, but not nearly as much as not being with Emma.

"You know what to do, now do it." Kendall disconnected the call.

She listened to the dial tone for a few seconds. Kendall was right; she did know what to do. She pocketed her phone, left a note on the kitchen table for Trina, then headed out to her new SUV. She needed to see Emma.

❖

KC found Emma taping the last few boxes in her room. At a glance it looked as though all that was left were her toiletries, a book on the nightstand, and a few clothes. Everything else was boxed, taped, and labeled.

"Have you figured out which of these are critical for the trip and which you can leave behind?" She leaned against the doorframe and smiled at the small scowl on Emma's face as she fought to unwind a crumpled section of tape.

"No. I need it all." Emma gave up and tore off the tape and balled it up. She threw it across the room and tagged KC in the chest. "I don't know why you won't let me rent a goddamned U-Haul."

"Because," she crossed the room and pulled Emma into a loose hug, "I'll need something to do while you're working all those weekends. A trip home to fetch your things will keep me from missing you too bad."

"What do you mean, a trip home?" Emma overemphasized the last three words.

She waited, the smile on her face growing with each passing second. She was helpless to stop it.

"Do you..." Emma took a deep breath. "Are you saying what I think you're saying?"

"Do you think I'm saying I'd like to move to Austin with you?"

Emma nodded, the movement jerky and uncertain. Her eyes shone bright with tears and hope.

"Then you'd be right."

The tears spilled over onto Emma's cheeks and KC was certain she was in a similar state, but she was too happy to care.

"Are you sure?" Emma's voice trembled. She was just as nervous and eager as KC.

"Yeah." She pressed a small kiss to Emma's mouth. They were both shaking.

Emma dropped her arms from around her and held out both hands for KC to take. KC forced herself to breathe as she clasped Emma's hands. They were totally going to do this, and she felt the same overwhelming excited calm that she always did when she thought of her future with Emma. Later, they would talk about the details. They'd talk about the house Emma wanted and what KC had learned about the market both in the city and farther out. They would talk about commitment and weddings and children. They would talk about forever. For now, though, she simply wanted to feel Emma, to capture the joy of this perfect moment.

She was finally saying yes to the right person.

About the Author

Jove was born and raised against a backdrop of orchards and potato fields. The youngest of four children, she was raised in a conservative, Christian home and began asking why at a very young age, much to the consternation of her mother and grandmother. At the customary age of eighteen, she fled southern Idaho in pursuit of broader minds and fewer traffic jams involving the local livestock. The road didn't end in Portland, Oregon, but there were many confusing freeway interchanges that a girl from the sticks was ill-prepared to deal with. As a result, she has lived in the Portland metro area for over fifteen years and still can't figure out how she manages to spend so much time in traffic when there's not a stray sheep or cow in sight.

She lives with her partner of seventeen years. Between them, they share a collection of six children, one dog, two cats, a mortgage payment, one sedan, and a cushy SUV big enough to hold the Lesbian Brady Bunch on their family outings. One day she hopes to live in a house that doesn't generate a never ending honey-do list.

Incidentally, she never stopped asking why, but did expand her arsenal of questions to include who, what, when, where, and, most important of all, how. In those questions, a story is born.

Her books include *Edge of Darkness*, *Split the Aces*, *Chaps*, and *Indelible*. They are available from Bold Strokes Books.

Books Available from Bold Strokes Books

Date with Destiny by Mason Dixon. When sophisticated bank executive Rashida Ivey meets unemployed blue collar worker Destiny Jackson, will her life ever be the same? (978-1-60282-878-0)

The Devil's Orchard by Ali Vali. Cain and Emma plan a wedding before the birth of their third child while Juan Luis is still lurking, and as Cain plans for his death, an unexpected visitor arrives and challenges her belief in her father, Dalton Casey. (978-1-60282-879-7)

Secrets and Shadows by L.T. Marie. A bodyguard and the woman she protects run from a madman and into each other's arms. (978-1-60282-880-3)

Change Horizon: Three Novellas by Gun Brooke. Three stories of courageous women who dare to love as they fight to claim a future in a hostile universe. (978-1-60282-881-0)

Scarlett Thirst by Crin Claxton. When hot, feisty Rani meets cool, vampire Rob, one lifetime isn't enough, and the road from human to vampire is shorter than you think… (978-1-60282-856-8)

Battle Axe by Carsen Taite. How close is too close? Bounty hunter Luca Bennett will soon find out. (978-1-60282-871-1)

Improvisation by Karis Walsh. High school geometry teacher Jan Carroll thinks she's figured out the shape of her life and her future, until graphic artist and fiddle player Tina Nelson comes along and teaches her to improvise. (978-1-60282-872-8)

For Want of a Fiend by Barbara Ann Wright. Without her Fiendish power, can Princess Katya and her consort Starbride stop a magic-wielding madman from sparking an uprising in the kingdom of Farraday? (978-1-60282-873-5)

Broken in Soft Places by Fiona Zedde. The instant Sara Chambers meets the seductive and sinful Merille Thompson, she falls hard, but knowing the difference between love and a dangerous, all-consuming desire is just one of the lessons Sara must learn before it's too late. (978-1-60282-876-6)

Healing Hearts by Donna K. Ford. Running from tragedy, the women of Willow Springs find that with friendship, there is hope, and with love, there is everything. (978-1-60282-877-3)

Desolation Point by Cari Hunter. When a storm strands Sarah Kent in the North Cascades, Alex Pascal is determined to find her. Neither imagines the dangers they will face when a ruthless criminal begins to hunt them down. (978-1-60282-865-0)

I Remember by Julie Cannon. What happens when you can never forget the first kiss, the first touch, the first taste of lips on skin? What happens when you know you will remember every single detail of a mysterious woman? (978-1-60282-866-7)

The Gemini Deception by Kim Baldwin and Xenia Alexiou. The truth, the whole truth, and nothing but lies. Book six in the Elite Operatives series. (978-1-60282-867-4)

Scarlet Revenge by Sheri Lewis Wohl. When faith alone isn't enough, will the love of one woman be strong enough to save a vampire from damnation? (978-1-60282-868-1)

Ghost Trio by Lillian Q. Irwin. When Lee Howe hears the voice of her dead lover singing to her, is it a hallucination, a ghost, or something more sinister? (978-1-60282-869-8)

The Princess Affair by Nell Stark. Rhodes Scholar Kerry Donovan arrives at Oxford ready to focus on her studies, but her life and her priorities are thrown into chaos when she catches the eye of Her Royal Highness Princess Sasha. (978-1-60282-858-2)

The Chase by Jesse J. Thoma. When Isabelle Rochat's life is threatened, she receives the unwelcome protection and attention of bounty hunter Holt Lasher who vows to keep Isabelle safe at all costs. (978-1-60282-859-9)

The Lone Hunt by L.L. Raand. In a world where humans and praeterns conspire for the ultimate power, violence is a way of life… and death. A Midnight Hunters novel. (978-1-60282-860-5)

The Supernatural Detective by Crin Claxton. Tony Carson sees dead people. With a drag queen for a spirit guide and a devastatingly attractive herbalist for a client, she's about to discover the spirit world can be a very dangerous world indeed. (978-1-60282-861-2)

Beloved Gomorrah by Justine Saracen. Undersea artists creating their own City on the Plain uncover the truth about Sodom and Gomorrah, whose "one righteous man" is a murderer, rapist, and conspirator in genocide. (978-1-60282-862-9)

Cut to the Chase by Lisa Girolami. Careful and methodical author Paige Cornish falls for brash and wild Hollywood actress Avalon Randolph, but can these opposites find a happy middle ground in a town that never lives in the middle? (978-1-60282-783-7)

More Than Friends by Erin Dutton. Evelyn Fisher thinks she has the perfect role model for a long-term relationship, until her best friends, Kendall and Melanie, split up and all three women must reevaluate their lives and their relationships. (978-1-60282-784-4)

Every Second Counts by D. Jackson Leigh. Every second counts in Bridgette LeRoy's desperate mission to protect her heart and stop Marc Ryder's suicidal return to riding rodeo bulls. (978-1-60282-785-1)

Dirty Money by Ashley Bartlett. Vivian Cooper and Reese DiGiovanni just found out that falling in love is hard. It's even harder when you're running for your life. (978-1-60282-786-8)

Sea Glass Inn by Karis Walsh. When Melinda Andrews commissions a series of mosaics by Pamela Whitford for her new inn, she doesn't expect to be more captivated by the artist than by the paintings. (978-1-60282-771-4)

The Awakening: A Sisters of Spirits novel by Yvonne Heidt. Sunny Skye has interacted with spirits her entire life, but when she runs into Officer Jordan Lawson during a ghost investigation, she discovers more than just facts in a missing girl's cold case file. (978-1-60282-772-1)

Murphy's Law by Yolanda Wallace. No matter how high you climb, you can't escape your past. (978-1-60282-773-8)

Blacker Than Blue by Rebekah Weatherspoon. Threatened with losing her first love to a powerful demon, vampire Cleo Jones is willing to break the ultimate law of the undead to rebuild the family she has lost. (978-1-60282-774-5)

Silver Collar by Gill McKnight. Werewolf Luc Garoul is outlawed and out of control, but can her family track her down before a sinister predator gets there first? Fourth in the Garoul series. (978-1-60282-764-6)

The Dragon Tree Legacy by Ali Vali. For Aubrey Tarver time hasn't dulled the pain of losing her first love Wiley Gremillion, but she has to set that aside when her choices put her life and her family's lives in real danger. (978-1-60282-765-3)

The Midnight Room by Ronica Black. After a chance encounter with the mysterious and brooding Lillian Gray in the "midnight room" of The Griffin, a local lesbian bar, confident and gorgeous Audrey McCarthy learns that her bad-girl behavior isn't bulletproof. (978-1-60282-766-0)

Dirty Sex by Ashley Bartlett. Vivian Cooper and twins Reese and Ryan DiGiovanni stole a lot of money and the guy they took it from wants it back. Like now. (978-1-60282-767-7)

The Storm by Shelley Thrasher. Rural East Texas. 1918. War-weary Jaq Bergeron and marriage-scarred musician Molly Russell try to salvage love from the devastation of the war abroad and natural disasters at home. (978-1-60282-780-6)

Crossroads by Radclyffe. Dr. Hollis Monroe specializes in short-term relationships but when she meets pregnant mother-to-be Annie Colfax, fate brings them together at a crossroads that will change their lives forever. (978-1-60282-756-1)